© Copyright 2005 David Harold Olsen.
All rights reserved. No part of this publication may be reproduced, stored in a retrieval system, or transmitted, in any form or by any means, electronic, mechanical, photocopying, recording, or otherwise, without the written prior permission of the author.

Note for Librarians: a cataloguing record for this book that includes Dewey Decimal Classification and US Library of Congress numbers is available from the Library and Archives of Canada. The complete cataloguing record can be obtained from their online database at: www.collectionscanada.ca/amicus/index-e.html
ISBN 1-4120-5411-7
Printed in Victoria, BC, Canada

Printed on paper with minimum 30% recycled fibre. Trafford's print shop runs on "green energy" from solar, wind and other environmentally-friendly power sources.

TRAFFORD

Offices in Canada, USA, Ireland and UK

This book was published *on-demand* in cooperation with Trafford Publishing. On-demand publishing is a unique process and service of making a book available for retail sale to the public taking advantage of on-demand manufacturing and Internet marketing. On-demand publishing includes promotions, retail sales, manufacturing, order fulfilment, accounting and collecting royalties on behalf of the author.

Book sales for North America and international:
Trafford Publishing, 6E–2333 Government St.,
Victoria, BC v8T 4P4 CANADA
phone 250 383 6864 (toll-free 1 888 232 4444)
fax 250 383 6804; email to orders@trafford.com

Book sales in Europe:
Trafford Publishing (UK) Ltd., Enterprise House, Wistaston Road Business Centre,
Wistaston Road, Crewe, Cheshire CW2 7RP UNITED KINGDOM
phone 01270 251 396 (local rate 0845 230 9601)
facsimile 01270 254 983; orders.uk@trafford.com

Order online at:
trafford.com/05-0307

10 9 8 7 6 5 4 3 2 1

Prologue

"Hey Tex, I got one for ya!"
"Okay Billy, shoot."
"Knock, knock,"
"Who's there?"
"Peking."
"Peking who?"
"Peking Tom, he's a real turkey."
"Gawd, Calsen! You're such a hambone."

1
*

Once upon a time and long ago before men walked on the moon, William Francis Carlsen flunked Grade 12 French. To paraphrase the immortal words of Chester A. Riley: this was a revolting development. It seemed inevitable that Billy would be banished to that seasonal Devil's Island known as summer school. There was, however, a glimmering ray of hope that lightened this dismal prospect.

It was 1961. John F. Kennedy was in the White House, John Diefenbacker was in Ottawa, Yuri Gagarin had circled the planet and Wayne Gretzky was born in Brantford Ontario. Master Will didn't give a fiddler's fart for these historical happenings. Of uppermost importance to his callow mind was he had landed a summer job up in the District of Muskoka.

As Bill said to his Mom, "I'm almost eighteen, and I've never been away from home."

His mother didn't want him to neglect his schooling, and go up north but he was adamant. Reluctantly she said, "Billy, I'll have to talk this over with your father. If he agrees, then it's okay with me."

"Gee thanks, Mom." Bill placed his arms around his mother and gave her a big hug.

His father got home from the midnight shift at Trans-Canada Airlines at eight o'clock the next morning. Bill was still in bed, but heard his parents talking in low voices in the kitchen. When the discussion ended his father came upstairs and shouted his usual morning wake-up call: "Roll over, rise and shine, daylight in the swamp."

Bill feigned sleepiness, but his heart was pounding with excitement. While he dressed in his jeans and sweatshirt, his father sat at the end of the bed, then cleared his throat. "Your mother and I have been talking and we think if you really want to go up to cottage country to work for the summer, then we won't stand in your way."

"That's great news Pop! I'll probably need two years to complete my Grade 13 anyway"

"Well Bill, if you put your mind to it and attend summer school, you could likely do it in one."

"Pop, I appreciate your confidence in me, but I really need this job just to see what the outside world is like."

Summer of '61

"Yeah, I understand son, and don't tell your mother this, but I felt the same way when I was your age. During the depression I didn't have a job and there was little hope of finding one in Vancouver. I rode the rails during the summer of '33 looking for any kind of employment. I never did find steady work, just the odd day here or there but, the people I met and the experiences I had were an education to last a lifetime."

"Gee Pop, I never knew that." Bill's eyes widened in astonishment

"You know, some of the kindest guys I ever met were in the hobo camps along the Canadian Pacific rail line," his father continued. "When you were hungry and needed a meal they would usually dish up a plate of stew, pour you some coffee into an old soup can and tell you where there may or may not be work. He paused and looked thoughtfully at his son. "I guess this is your summer to do the same type of thing.

"I won't disappoint you Dad I'll try to learn all I can."

His father smiled, "We'd better go down and tell your mother. She still thought that I might have been able to persuade you to stay here and get your French at summer school."

Bear hugging would have been out of character, but Bill's radiant smile stretched to both ears as he pumped his dad's hand.

Bill and his family lived in Georgetown, about thirty-five miles northwest of Toronto. This sleepy little backwater was close enough for his father to commute to Malton airport, where TCA had one of its major bases. His mother worked as a clerk for the Town. In those days, Ontario required that you have five years of high school, and at least one language other than English before you could go on to university. This was the main reason that Bill's parents were so upset that he was heading up north to cottage country to work at a restaurant. Without the summer school upgrade he would need an extra year to finish his secondary education. Fully equipped with the knowledge acquired by nearly eighteen years of strolling over a small portion of the planet, Bill's attitude was: "What the heck, a lot of guys I know spent a year doing Grade 14."

Over breakfast Bill and his parents discussed his summer plans. His mother agreed, if reluctantly, and Bill was so excited he could barely swallow his eggs and toast. Two months on his own and no Miss Marble. Life was great!

Their French teacher was a dyed-in-the-wool spinster. Bill's best friend, Dave Graham, said, "That's because she's so damned ugly."

Bill thought that was kind of cruel. "Maybe Miss Marble never met the right guy."

"Come on, Carlsen. She's just plain mean and vindictive. Look at all the formal detentions she's given us."

Formal detentions were served in a room adjacent to the school office. There students spent an hour adding up the sums of the cubes of a series of large numbers. The hook was if they got the right answer they could go early. No one ever did.

"I've been thinking of a great way to get even," Dave proclaimed one day, a sly look on his face.

Their French class was always the first period of the day, and Dave had noticed that Miss Marble visited the door marked "Women's Staff every morning before coming to class. His plan was simple. Bill would sneak into the Ladies washroom and place Saran Wrap over the top of the toilet bowl, then carefully lower the lid. "You're a lot smaller than me Billy," Dave reasoned," and you wouldn't draw as much attention." At 6' 2" and 210 pounds, Dave was as hard to hide as a moose in a candy store.

Bill accomplished his task one Tuesday morning just before class began. With his heart galloping and his mouth as dry as the Sahara Desert , Bill reported to Dave that the deed was done. The rest of the class never knew why they were suddenly told to go to the Library's study hall. Dave and Bill could not restrain their bouts of rib-bursting laughter. When the ego-driven lads confided in a select group of their buddies, all sworn to silence, about the dirty trick, someone ratted and Miss Marble exacted her revenge. Both received a mark of 48 in French, the passing grade was 50. Vinegar on an open cut would have stung less. Since Miss Marble was also their homeform teacher, she enjoyed the delicious satisfaction of smiling smugly as she handed out their final report cards. So much for secrets and so-called friends. But now Billy was escaping from them all: To Muskoka and freedom!

Bill's Grandmother McNair, who lived with them, had prepared a survival kit for him, which he packed carefully into his father's wartime duffel bag: Mecca ointment, a homemade mustard plaster, Vics Vapo Rub (complete with tea towel), cod liver oil, calamine lotion, castor oil, Alka Seltzer and a cake tin full of cookies.

Summer of '61

He was safe from everything except an outbreak of the Bubonic Plague.

It was now lunchtime on D-day and Bill was waiting for his grandmother to return from the liquor store. A bottle of Hudson's Bay whiskey would be safely stowed in her fish-net shopping bag when she got home. "A wee nip in the evening warms the blood," she was fond of saying. "Helps me rheumatiz and acts as a natural sleeping pill." She also firmly believed that if you touched a toad you would automatically get warts, and if you rubbed a stye under your eye with a well worn gold wedding ring, it would go away. "Don't knock it, he told Dave when he scoffed at the remedy. "I tried it and it worked." Maybe his grandmother was a medical genius.

As the old grandfather clock in the hallway struck twelve, Bill thought of the supper his father had cooked the night before. His dad opened a can of China Lily chop suey mix, a can of mushrooms, and finally a can of spam. All the ingredients for a gourmet meal. His father was a true artist with a can opener. Some brown bread slathered with white margarine, a glass of ice cold powdered milk and he concocted a meal fit for a Queen.

After lunch on that hot mid-June afternoon Bill and Granny McNair sat staring out the living room window awaiting Paul Evans. He was the owner of the Harbour Restaurant in Port Carter where Bill would work as a dishwasher. Bill had never met Paul. He had been hired on the recommendation of one of his mother's friends. Excited and impatient as a racehorse at the starting gate, he pushed away from the window and began to pace the well worn carpet, chomping at the bit to be on his way. Yet he knew too, as he gazed fondly at his grandmother that he would miss them all.

The minutes yawned like an eternity. Billy felt exhilarated, as if he were standing on a the brink of a high precipice. He was about to step out into space, into the unknown, and he would fly. Perhaps this was the arrogant optimism of youth. As his grandmother would say, "You seldom find grey heads on young shoulders."

At last, at one-thirty after Bill and his grandmother had just finished watching a snowy, black and white edition of *Search For Tomorrow,* Paul Evans pulled into the driveway. Billy raced to the door, flung it open, and ushered Paul into meet Granny McNair. Paul made polite conversation, but Bill and Granny McNair realized that a three-hour drive was necessary to get to Port Carter.

Paul hadn't said anything directly, but they could tell that he was in a hurry. His grandmother gave him a kiss on the cheek and said, "Take care of yourself Sonny, and remember: two teaspoons of cod liver oil everyday.

"Without fail Gram," Bill said, crossing his fingers behind his back. She would never know that he had poured the entire contents of the foul-tasting remedy down the sink.

When he got into Paul's well travelled, blue Volkswagen Van, Paul asked him if he had a driver's licence.

"Sure have," he said proudly, and reached into his wallet to show his recently upgraded commercial ticket.

"Bill I want you to drive. I didn't sleep very well last night, so I think, I'll crawl into that sleeping bag back there, and catch forty winks on the trip up to Port Carter." He had swung by Beeton southwest of Barrie the previous night to pick up several sacks of potatoes which were stacked neatly along each side of the van. He handed Billy a well-worn Ontario road map and quickly showed him how to get to their destination. No way would Bill admit he hadn't driven a car with a shift on the floor, let alone a Van. With a minimum of gear grinding and some vague memories of attempting to play-drive his dad's old '38 Chev, he managed to get them pointed in the right direction.

Paul slept the major part of the trip, awakening only when they were twenty miles from the end of their journey. When Bill asked Paul a little bit about himself, he said between yawns that this was his fourth summer of running his restaurant. Billy learned that he was twenty-eight years old and his wife's name was Sally.

The Muskoka Lake District is located one hundred and twenty-five miles north of Toronto. It is a very popular cottage area with several large tourist lodges gracing the shores of the bigger lakes. The country they were travelling through was typical of the Canadian Shield. Lots of rock cuts along the highway, surrounded by seemingly endless vistas of pine, oak, spruce and white birch. In the last fifteen miles they had driven by a dozen sparkling lakes of various sizes. Port Carter, where Bill was to spend the next two months, was built along the shores of the Chippewa River.

Summer of '61

    Just as they approached the bridge crossing the river, Paul told Bill to follow River Road which ran parallel to the Chippewa. He drove a short distance along this narrow, twisting street to the small parking lot in front of the Harbour Restaurant. The restaurant overlooked the river, and the view was spectacular. A set of concrete stairs at the side of the building led to the restaurant's private dock. The boating set would arrive at the Harbour's wharf in their highly polished launches, then enjoy a leisurely meal.
    Backing the Van up to the front entrance, Bill helped Paul carry the sacks of potatoes to a storage room next to the kitchen. After they finished stacking the spuds, Bill and Paul proceeded to the cash register at the end of the restaurant's counter.
    A knock-down gorgeous blonde wearing a tight-fitting waitress's uniform came up to Paul and gave him a sizzling kiss. Wow, Bill thought, the advantages of being a restaurant owner.
    "I'd like you to meet my wife Sally," Paul said, wrapping his arm around her slender waist. Bill's love-at-first-sight galloping heart slowed to a plod.
    "Very pleased to meet you," he managed, "is Paul ever a lucky guy to have such a beautiful wife." Bill beamed his best man-of-the-world smile.
    "Welcome aboard Bill," Sally grinned, then turned away to attend to a customer who'd just entered the restaurant. Paul then led Bill to a set of stairs on the south side of the building, and pointed upwards. He was to stow his gear and sleep in the room at the top right. Slinging his duffel bag over his shoulder he climbed a set of well worn squeaky steps.
    His quarters were small but clean and neat, with old army bunks painted battleship grey and covered by brindle-brown wool blankets. He could see by the rumpled blankets that the bottom bunk was already taken. He placed his duffel bag on the top tier and began to unpack. Hearing a slight noise, he turned to find a tall skinny kid wearing horned-rimmed glasses leaning against the door jamb.
    "My name's Bob Tucker," he grunted. "You must be my new roomie." he sounded about as friendly as a rooster finding another cock in the same pen.
    "Hey put her there,"Billy grinned unabashed. "I'm Bill Carlsen, the best pot scrubber in the north."

Bob's long beak sniffed. "I'm being trained to be a short-order cook." *So this turkey's a peck ahead of me.*

Bob sauntered over to the bunk beds and rested his back against the metal frame. "Bill there are few rules that Paul wants me to pass on to you," Bob raised a hand and ticked off the do's and don'ts on his fingers.

"No booze in the staff quarters, no girls in the boys rooms."

"Well that's not too bad," Bill lit up like an aurora. "At least we can be in the girl's rooms."

"Listen up Carlsen," he snapped. "I'm not finished yet."

Bill resisted the urge not to mock-salute. Bob sounded just like the drill instructor Billy had encountered the previous summer in the Lorne Scots Cadet Corps, but even he had more of a sense of humour.

"You can have anything on the menu—" he began, counting fingers again. "—except chicken, steak, pork chops, and rainbow trout. If you're late for work or violate any of the rules I've just mentioned, then it's a twenty-five dollar fine."

Bill stifled a groan. This was a hefty hit considering his dishwashing pay was only a hundred bucks a month.

"Okay that's it,' Bob glared then headed out the door and clambered noisily down the stairs.

Oh joy, Billy thought, raising his middle finger in the air. This guy's idea of fun would be sprinkling ant poison on my hamburgers. Maybe he'd be needing some of Gram's quick cure remedies after all....

2
*

    Bill's stomach began to grumble and growl. He was hungrier than a grizzly bear in the springtime. Bob who had just returned to the bunkhouse to pickup his jack-shirt was ready to eat as well. Acting like a snotty tour guide, he led the way to the back entrance of the kitchen, then introduced Billy to the Hungarian cook Leo and his wife Joan. Assuming the role of commander and chief, Bob decreed, "We can order here and Leo will have it sent out to us." Bill decided on a hamburger-works, a plate of fries smothered in gravy, and a cherry coke. Life wasn't really that bad, and who cared about chicken anyway.
    When they were comfortably seated at the end of the counter, Bob puffed himself up like a cock grouse in the mating season and simpered, "The staff aren't allowed to sit in the main dinning room." *Oh!oh!, more rules.*
    Their meals were brought to them by Virginia Hudson, one of the student waitresses. Bill thought she was a dead ringer for Ava Gardner and for the second time that day he was totally in lust. Virginia was a tough chick from the east side of Toronto.
    Bob did the introductions, but before Bill could open his mouth Virginia snarled, "Yeah you got the name right, so spare me the Virgin for short, but not for long crap."
    Billy was taken aback, but in all innocence he managed to sputter, "I-I was thinking, yes there is a Santa Claus."
    "A real smart ass," Miss Virgin rumbled menacingly. "If you want to wear this chocolate milk shake for a helmet then just keep it up." At this point Bill was convinced that she could chew up nickels and spit out nails.
    They attacked their food like a pair of hungry wolves, leaving behind only the shine on the plates. Bob's next task was to show Bill the Hilltop Café, a new restaurant that Paul had just purchased.
    Halfway up Bridge Street they passed the local propane dealer. Gas fridges and stoves were displayed in the front of the showroom window. Propane tanks were filled at the rear of the store. Bob stopped for a moment, then gently elbowed Billy in the ribs.
    "This place's kind of a tourist attraction."
Bill looked around totally confused, until Bob pointed out the sign above the entrance.

Fred Fartham: Propane Appliances & Tank Refills:
See Fartham For Gas

  Bob snorted loudly before saying, "This is the most photographed sign in the District."
  The Hilltop was much smaller than the Harbour Restaurant. Five chrome-legged tables covered with worn checkered tablecloths, and a long narrow Formica counter adjacent to the kitchen, provided seating for twenty-eight patrons.
A jukebox that looked more like a fridge made up to be a pinball machine decorated one of the sidewalls. Someone had placed a dime in the old Nickelodeon, and Patsy Cline's song "Crazy" was softening the air of Paul's new greasy spoon. Bob ushered Billy into the kitchen, and introduced him to the Chinese cook, Wong Hong Lo.
  "Wong makes the best pies you ever tasted, "Bob said, catching a whiff of cinnamon and brown sugar.
  "You boys want pie"? Wong asked, revealing several missing teeth when he smiled.
  "Sounds good to me," Bill said, trying hard not to drool.
  He devoured a large slice of pie and two scoops of ice cream. Bill figured that being deprived of steaks and pork chops for the summer would not be a problem.
  When they returned to the "Harb" as the locals called it, Bob and Bill went straight to their bunks. Barely able to turn out the lights, the two sleepy heads faded into a world of sweet dream filled slumber.
  The next day, Bill reported to the kitchen at eight in the morning. He was surprised to find that Bob wasn't there. His roomie had said just before they went to sleep, that he was on duty at seven. The mystery evaporated when Leo told Bill, in halting broken English.
  "That crazy Chinese cook at Hilltop, had big argument with Paul about monies. He swing meat clever around." Leo demonstrated by making erratic chopping motions with his hand.
  "What happened then?" Bill asked, amazed at what he was hearing.
  "Paul fire him. Bob do cooking up there for now."
  Bill's mouth became an open fly trap, as Leo informed him that he would begin training as the Hilltop's number one chef. Wow, he thought, that's a raise to one hundred and ten smackaroo's a month.

Summer of '61

We are in the money!

    The days of learning to be a cook went by quickly. Leo and Bill got along well together, and Billy was fascinated by the stories of Leo and Joan's escape from Hungary in 1956. It was the first time in his life that Bill realized how lucky he was to be born a Canadian.

    "Hilltop is simple, people in hurry. Here they like fancy meal and look at river," Leo wheezed trying to explain the difference between the restaurants. "They come to Harb in big boats for nice dinner, at Hilltop they want food fast."

    Billy was secretly glad to be going up to the Hilltop to do the cooking. The KISS philosophy of life suited him just fine. As his father would say, "Keep It Simple Son."

    William Francis learned to make french fries, several types of hot sandwiches, toasted westerns, pancakes, bacon and eggs, liver and onions, southern fried chicken, steak and mushrooms and a passable poutine. Four days later he was granted his degree in Greasysoonology.

    They were still working off season hours and open from 8 a.m. to 6 p.m. The summer help consisted of four waitresses, two cooks and two dishwashers. Bob and Bill were the cooks, and Paul had just hired Danny Foster and Joey Blanchard as plate purifiers. In addition to Virg, as Bill called her but never to her face, the other hash handlers were, Bonnie Baker, Donna Rogers and Jennifer Rossini. Sally worked as a full time waitress at the Harb and Paul was a trained cook. With Joan and Leo figured in, the staff was nearly set. Shortly after the boys had gathered together the discussion got around to the fairer sex.

    "Gosh does Paul ever know how to pick em! Bonnie reminds me of Marilyn Monroe, Donna could be Sandra Dee's sister and Jennifer must be Sophia Loren's cousin," Joey broadsided, wide-eyed as teenaged boy at a Burlesque House for the first time.

    "Yeah that Bonnie has to be at least six Hogan's!" Danny grinned wolfishly.

    "What's a Hogan?" Bill asked, totally mystified.

    "A Hogan is equal to one cubic mouthful of tit," Danny winked knowingly.

    The girls had all finished their senior year of high school, and were heading to various post-secondary institutions in the fall.

Much to Bill's dismay they looked at him as he were a baby brother. He wasn't discouraged, figuring that in time a younger man might appeal to these older women.

Danny Foster was from Ajax just east of Toronto, and owned a hot set of wheels. The car was a 1950 Ford, Flathead eight. It was decked out with fender skirts, a wheel spinner, and a pair of purple sex lights mounted on each side of the front seat. An air freshener card, displaying all the charms of a very pretty young lady, hung by a string tied to the rear view mirror. Dan was eighteen, had graduated from high school and was going to start on the line at General Motors in Oshawa next fall.

Bob still playing the unofficial leader of the pack whined in a disbelieving tone, "If you've got a job at the car plant, why did you hire on here as a dishwasher?"

Before answering, Danny absently scratched at the part in his duck's ass, then quickly smoothed his sideburns. He shot Bob a Kookie Byrnes-like smirk before saying, "One of my buddies worked up here last summer. It was party city and he had a real blast."

"Yeah, I know what you mean, Billy grinned, his mind alive with images of the La Dolce Vita. "We may not get rich on a hundred bucks a month, but the fringe benefits could be very interesting."

Joey Blanchard was sixteen. A nice kid from Niagara Falls who had a winning smile and a booming voice. Bill thought he looked a lot like Tab Hunter.

The large room above the Hilltop was to be the boys living quarters for the summer. A set of army surplus bunks had been placed along one wall, and another pair at right angles to them. In the middle of the room was a large window that overlooked Bridge Street. Four chairs and a table completed the furnishings.

The washroom and a small storage closet were located along the hallway near the entrance to the bedroom. At the end of the narrow passageway a wooden staircase led to an outside door adjacent to the kitchen. In order to keep the bees separated from the honey Paul had decided that the girls would live in the two bedrooms on the second floor of the Harb. By the next evening all four boys had moved into the penthouse above the Hilltop Hilton.

The following morning, Bill was in the kitchen shortly before eight, lighting up the gas grills.

Summer of '61

Jennifer Rossini was the waitress on duty, and Bill thought that this could be his big chance. Jen, as she liked to be called was from Brampton, not too far from Georgetown where Bill lived. She was the school's head cheerleader. A very erotic picture of Jen doing a cartwheel rocketed through Bill's mind.

"You know Bill you remind me of my younger brother who's fifteen."

"I-I'll be eighteen in August," Bill stammered, awakening abruptly from his fantasy.

"My boy friend's twenty, and just finished his first year at Western. He gave me his pin this spring," she said, in a gloating tone.

As Bill admired the eight Hogan pair that threatened to burst through the buttons on Jen's tight fitting uniform, he thought, well that's almost like being engaged to get engaged to be married. Strike three and you're out.

The Port Carter Community Hall was directly across from the Hilltop. It was the home of the Port Town Players. The summer stock company was the proving ground for many aspiring actors, set designers, stage managers and other theatre trades. Most of the Players ate their breakfast at the café.

Following the brief discussion with Jen, Bill cooked up a variety of menu favorites: pancakes, sausages, bacon, assorted styles of eggs, and Red River Cereal. When the breakfast rush was over Billy came out to the counter and took a break, just as a good looking, solidly built six footer from the stage crew came in with an order. He sat down beside Bill, then handed Jen a list of coffee break items. Billy swiveled around on his stool and introduced himself.

"My name's Bill Carlsen, I'm the resident nutritional engineer."

"Sounds pretty impressive to me, and I bet you can cook too," Ken McClean chuckled, as he clamped Bill's hand in a vice-like grip.

Holy shit! Just like Charles Atlas, but without anyone kicking sand in your face, Bill thought as he checked for broken fingers.

Ken, was from Barrie, fifty miles north of Toronto. He had just finished high school, and was apprenticing to become a stage manager. Jen quickly put things together, and several minutes later gave Ken a box full of drinks and sugar packed snacks.

Bill took an instant liking to the personable kid from Barrie and was pleased when Ken said, "Why don't you come over to the theatre this evening and have a look see."

"Jeez, I'd love to!" Bill whooped, a big Tony the Tiger smile lighting up his face.

At 6:30, Bill entered the open main door of the community center, and timidly approached the front of the hall. Ken and three others were grouped stage left, painting a large wall made of plywood and two-by- twos. Ken explained that this was part of a set that would eventually look like the store front area of a small town.

"I want you to meet Tim Black, our carpenter," Ken began." Barb Wallace who's helping out with props, and our set designer Martha Taylor."

"So you're the one who tries to poison us several times a day, " Martha smiled. She was a large jovial women who reminded Bill of Yogi the Bear.

"Guilty, but I'm hoping to have my arsenic soup recipe perfected by the end of the summer."

Barb, a striking strawberry blonde, whose emerald green eyes really got your attention said, " Well a least you have a sense of humor."

"Mate would you mind going stage right and pick up that piece of plywood," Tim said, in an obvious British accent.

Bill turned to face an imaginary audience, then proceeded in the correct direction to get the four-by-four sheet.

"The young lad has been around a theatre before," Tim declared, duly impressed.

"Yeah, I was in a couple of school plays," Bill grinned, assuming the posture of a preening bantam rooster.

"Well young Will," Martha chuckled, "We can always use another hand around here if you're interested."

"I'd be glad to, anytime I'm not busy trying to make you people wretch and and gag"

"Bloody marvelous!" Tim snorted.

"Why not now," Barb smiled, as she handed him a brush. Bill painted away for the rest of the evening, wondering what he had gotten himself into.

The next morning while cooking breakfast for the Port Town crowd , Jen came into the kitchen with an order from one of the actors in the company.

Summer of '61

"Billy, this guy wants his eggs soft boiled," Jen paused briefly, as she puffed up her beehive hairdo. "He's very insistent that they be two-and-a-half minute eggs."

Bill wasn't too concerned, and eyeballed the immature Kentucky fried's at three minutes.

Shortly after the order was sent out, Jen stuck her head through the kitchen door and said, "According to his know-it-all-ness these eggs were cooked for three-and-a-half minutes."

By Golly, Bill thought, this guy really knows his soft boiled's. He got out a timer, and set it for exactly two minutes-and-thirty-seconds. When the eggs were done, he asked Jen to deliver them to Mr. Perfect.

"No complaints this time," Jen sighed, stabbing a pencil into the side of her beehive. "Apparently this guys name's Aaron Gant, and he's one of your bona fide jerks."

Not bad for a chick who's pinned to some college dipstick from Western, Bill thought.

"I've noticed that his friends call him Ari," Jen continued, "Boy, is he ever stuck up."

Billy nodded to himself as it began to sink in. Ari Gant, now that's a good one.

*

When things slacked off, Bill had time to think about his girl friend Doris Marshall. She was sixteen, and a year behind him in school.They had been going steady now for six months and nine days, but heart break hotel loomed ominously on the horizon. Doris was working as a lifeguard at the Georgetown pool. Pete Rawlins her new heartthrob worked with Doris, and was one of Bill's teammates on the high school football club. Pete was the quarterback, student council president, looked a little bit like Rock Hudson's brother, and was an honour student.

Billy got the Dear John letter from Doris at the end of June. He was really ticked and couldn't figure out what Pete had to offer. He had a strange ache in his throat, but consoled himself with: if you're not near the one you love, you love the one you're near. Bill was an unfettered man, but he still wore his heart firmly attached to his sleeve.

The next evening Danny, Joey and Bill were sitting around the table in their quarters above the Hilltop. Danny stretched, then kneaded his forehead before saying, "That Leo's a pain in the ass the way he orders you around eh?"

"Yeah." Bill hesitated for a moment. "But he's okay once you get to know him."

"Bullshit!" Danny exploded. "He's nothing but a dirty DP."

"Hey wait a minute," Joey said, his collar steaming. "Just think about it for a minute. For instance, where did your grandpa Carlsen come from Bill?"

"Norway," he replied proudly.

"Where did your grandfather come from Danny?" Joey bored in relentlessly.

"One was from Ireland and the other came from Germany," Danny shot back."Well do you think they enjoyed being called a Displaced Person, let alone a dirty DP.?"

Danny thought this over for a moment, before saying, "Yeah, but that's different."

"Baloney!" Joey flared. "If you can't see the ocean for the water, then I guess that's your problem."

Holy smokers, Bill thought, this kid sure has his act together. Joey however, was soon to have his view of the universe tested in a way that no one would have ever predicted.

3

It was July 1st, Dominion Day, and Canada's 94th birthday. It was also the beginning of the "season" in the Muskokas. Paul had hired an additional short-order cook at the Hilltop to cover the extended hours of 7:00 a.m. to 11:00 p.m. The new cooks name was Harry Thompson. Harry looked like an overgrown version of Sam Snead, and true to his physical appearance he was a golf nut.

Bill once had a Junior Membership at the Georgetown Golf Club. During the summers of '58 and '59, he caddied at the course weekdays and packed groceries at the IGA every weekend. Whenever he wasn't working, he was on the links having a ball. From the start, Harry and Billy got along like two sandboys in the desert. The second day on the job chef Thompson conducted a trading session with cook Carlsen.

"Two or three times a week, I like to shoot a couple of rounds with my buddies." Harry said, as he made a practice swinging motion with his arms. "I may need you to cover a shift or two."

"No sweat Harry."

"Hey that's great! I'll pay you back in time, or if you want, I could loan you my car now and again."

Jeez, that's one sweet deal Bill thought, because Harry owned a '57 Chevy Bel Air convertible, and it was a great looking set of wheels. He had visions of cruising around the Port in the sure fired chick catcher, the top down, the radio playing: *Hello Mary-Lou, Good-bye Heart*—Ricky Nelson eat your heart out, Hot Machine Carlsen's in town! The reality of a sixteen hour shift to earn that privilege hadn't sunk in; but what the hell it would be worth it.

Bonnie Baker was the waitress on shift at the Hilltop for the first part of the week. She was a blonde bombshell, a flirt, a tease, and without a doubt one of the hottest babes that Billy had ever met. On the second morning he gathered up his courage and said to her cautiously, "I guess you have a steady boyfriend at home eh?"

"No I like to play the field." Wow! Bill thought, maybe there is a good fairy.

Bonnie smoothed the ends of her page boy before she continued, "That Brad King who works over at the boat works is so cute, and he's asked me to go to Dunn's Pavilion this weekend."

"Boy that's great," Bill sighed, totally deflated. "I hear that, Woody Herman and The Woodchoppers are playing Friday and Saturday."

Dunn's in Bala, was legendary in the Muskokas. Some of the great names in show business performed there, and several of the remaining big bands made the occasional appearance. They didn't have a liquor licence, so the drill was to sneak in a bottle, then buy ice and mix from the waitress who served your table.

"I guess Brad was born with the proverbial silver spoon in his mouth," Bill added judgmentally.

"Just because his daddy owns the King Boat Works, doesn't mean he's spoiled," Bonnie pouted.

Well it did smooth out a few speed bumps, he thought.

"His Corvair convertible's oh so groovy!" Bonnie gushed in state of near euphoria. "He has his own speedboat but it's used, so I don't know why you're so hard on him."

"May you both live happily ever after, and may your tribe increase," Bill spat out with a much sarcasm as he could muster.

"You know Billy Carlsen; you can be a real pill at times," Bonnie snapped back.

Bill's mother would call him by his full name when she was angry. He decided to back off. It was just as well that Bonnie didn't know that his middle name was Francis. He was really sick of those "talking mule" jokes.

It was a beautiful July day. The sky was dotted with puffy white clouds. Clouds that changed from elephants to airplanes, as you lay on your back and watched them drift lazily across the roof of the world. This was Bill's day off, and he was content to be a lazybones, enjoying the town beach on the Chippewa River, quietly letting the world roll by. It was just a short stretch of sand, smeared along the down river side of the municipal boat launch, but to Bill on this glorious day of indolence it was paradise.

He lay there quietly daydreaming, until he became aware of a shadow blocking the sun. When he looked up he saw Danny Foster puffing on a Players Navy Cut .

"You want to drive into Bala?" Dan asked spontaneously.

"I thought you had to work today," Bill grunted, squinting uncertainly at the large figure hovering over him.

Summer of '61

"I did, but I switched afternoons with Joey," Danny replied, dragging a comb through his greasy hair in a feeble attempt to imitate James Dean.

"Hey that's great," Bill yawned, getting up slowly and shaking his towel. "As Jackie Gleason would say, away we go."

They cruised the streets of Bala for twenty minutes, but saw nothing interesting. Looking to his left as they passed the Brewer's Retail, Billy spotted two prime examples of poetry in motion. Without warning the Ford came to a screeching halt.

Billy rolled down the window as the pair of lovelies nervously approached the vehicle.

"Hi there, my names Bill and this here's my friend Dan."

"I'm Stacy," The taller of the two said, with a giggle in her voice, "And this is Elaine."

"We're up here for the summer working at the Harb in Port Carter," Danny said, giving them his best Elvis profile.

"We've got jobs in the District too," Elaine smiled, as she discreetly adjusted the C cups in her halter top. "We're lifeguards at Toledo House."

Toledo House was the biggest lodge on Lake Muskoka. It catered to the rich crowd from New York State and the Toronto area.

"Well hop in and we'll go for a little spin," Danny grinned, a shy Fabian-like twinkle lighting up his coal black eyes.

They drove around town for awhile before Danny suggested that they drop by the Liquor Store and pick up a bottle of lemon gin. Bill was apprehensive, because to buy booze in Ontario you had to be twenty-one-years-old. Danny was a big kid and looked older than his eighteen years, but legal age was a bit of a stretch.

Dan parked the car in front of the LCBO and proceeded boldly through the door. He returned three minutes later with a two-six of Gilby's Lemon Gin. Amongst the males of the species, this particular brand of firewater was known as liquid panty remover.

"Feed em a couple of drinks of this stuff," Danny had proclaimed a few days earlier. "And it's St. Peter at the pearly gates.

Danny drove the car to a little used public beach not far from the town. Giggling like happy young children, the four teenagers frolicked along the water's edge until they reached a rocky point.

The playful couples sat on an old pine drift log, letting the clear, clean waters of the lake, gently wash over their bare feet. Bill put together four healthy drinks of lemon gin, mixed with Lime Ricky. They chatted, joked, necked and consumed a sizeable portion of the bottle.

The late afternoon gave way to early evening as they watched the diamond sparkles of the rippling waters turn to glowing rubies. The girls were dressed in halter tops and shorts, the boys were attired in clam diggers and T-shirts. As the sun began to sink, and flame the surface of the mirror like lake, the first cool of days end came upon them. Reluctantly they returned to Danny's car.

The four sunburned beach bums were beginning to feel the effects of the lemon gin. The bottle by now, was three quarters empty. Danny and Stacy suddenly became very quiet as they disappeared below view in the front seat. Elaine snuggled up close to Bill, in the couch like luxury of the back seat. She placed her lips to the base of his neck, and gave him a long sucking kiss. Wow! Bill thought, this lemon lightning really works.

"Billy," Elaine whispered softly. "You're so cute and cuddly! I can't help but think that I'm right next to an overgrown teddy bear."

Bill was five-ten, and his curly black hair resembled a shorn mop head. He had a well proportioned muscular build, and played halfback for Georgetown High. In some ways he looked like a life-sized version of Paddington, without his Mac.

Several minutes of open mouth kissing, led to an unrestrained session of ardent petting. Bill passed first base on the run, slid into second, stole third and was gunning for home plate when a very strange thing happened. The car seemed to assume a life of its own and began spinning around like a top. After frantically emerging into the cool night air, he spent several minutes in a one-way conversation with Earl, on an imaginary white telephone. It must have been the power of suggestion, because when Billy looked up between expulsions he saw Danny hanging over the hood of the Ford, working on the second of his dry heaves.

"You guys are real pussies," Elaine thundered disgustedly. "I think I should airmail the pair of you back to your mama's." There was absolutely no sympathy in femaleland.

Summer of '61

Stacy who had the constitution of a sailor got the ignition keys out of Danny's pocket, and with Elaine's help, they poured the two boys into the back seat. Stacy then drove the car to the bush side of the Toledo House staff parking lot.

"Let's let dufus and doorknob, sleep it off," Elaine said, as she opened the passenger's door. "Their heads will be as big as barrage balloons in the morning." The girls left the windows partially rolled down, and allowed the two reprobates to snore peacefully in the back seat.

Bill woke up with a strange buzzing sound in his ears. His mouth felt like dried cotton, and he wished that the big guy in the black suit would stop hitting him in the head with a sledge hammer. Still half-asleep, he shook Danny's shoulder, and managed to get him back to the land of the living.

"Holy shit, the car's full of mosquitoes," Billy shouted, swatting and scratching. "We've got to get the fuck out of here."

Danny fumbled around in the dark for a moment, but finally got the Ford started . He drove like Sterling Moss at the Grand Prix, trying to get away from the swarming insects. Two minutes later, with all four windows wide open, the bugs finally cleared out.

"You know," Bill said, when they were safely pointed in the direction of Port Carter. "I think we'd better read the instructions a little more carefully on the next bottle of panty remover we buy."

Lumpy, puffy, and beginning to itch like a terminal case of hemorrhoids, all Bill could think of was the bottle of Grandma's calamine lotion stored in his survival kit. His head felt like a big toe that had just been stepped on by a buffalo, prompting him to make a solemn vow, to stay off the hooch for good and forever, but that resolution was to be short lived.

4
*

At six-thirty, Billy managed to place both feet squarely on the cold floor, but he had to hold on to the bed to keep the room and his stomach from doing flip-flops. A six piece band complete with tuba, produced a thumping pain between his left and right ear. He reached into the duffel bag, and pulled out two alka seltzer tablets—plop, plop fizz, fizz was the start to his day. This was Bill's first experience with serious drinking. He had sneaked the odd beer from his dad's two-four on occasion, but now he knew first hand what the word hangover really meant. His father's voice echoed loudly in his ears, "If you want to dance son, then you have to pay the piper."

When Bill entered the kitchen, Bonnie looked at him suspiciously and giggled, "You must have had a great time last night Billy, because your eyes look just like two piss holes in the snow." She then returned triumphantly to the counter.

It was mid-morning before he began to recover. After that the day seemed to dissolve like honey in hot water. He got off work at three, then headed straight for his bunk. Dan was there playing solitaire at the kitchen table. It was still a complete mystery to Bill, how Danny had so easily purchased that two-six from the Liquor Control Board of Ontario. Unable to contain his curiosity Billy said, "I realize that you look a little older than you are, but twenty-one is a bit hard to swallow."

Danny extracted his wallet from a back pocket and removed a plastic card from the billfold; he then handed it over for closer examination. Bill was amazed to see that one Daniel Clarence Foster was born on May fifteenth 1940.

"Hey, that really does make you twenty-one."

"Yeah and the tooth fairy leaves you nickels under your pillow. Come on Carlsen this is a fake ID, if you know the right people where I come from, you can pick these up for twenty bucks."

Danny looked closely at Bill for a moment, then exclaimed, "Billy, what's that mark on your neck?"

"Mark, what mark?" Bill asked uneasily.

"Holy shit Billy it's a hickey! That Elaine's one hot tomato eh?"

Bill sawed it off for a couple of hours, then wandered down to the kitchen. He decided to help Harry with the flood of supper orders.

Summer of '61

When things had settled down, Billy made himself a hot beef sandwich. He sat at the counter and tucked into his meat, mashed potatoes, gravy and cold slaw. For desert he had a chocolate sundae topped with walnuts. He washed all this down with a strawberry milk shake. His stomach was definitely back to normal.

He had just finished the last spoonful of ice-cream, when Ken McClean charged through the door. With a note of panic in his voice, he blurted out, "I need a couple of Cokes real fast. The props manager completely forgot, and we have to have them for the second act." Ken placed the required coins into the Coke machine, and retrieved four cola's. Turning to Bill he said, "Come on backstage, and we'll watch the rest of the play from there."

The two boys ran across the street, then entered the theatre through the backdoor. The first act of the play, *Picnic* was coming to an end, so they were just in time. Ken handed the soft drinks to the prop-girl, who was thankful to finally have all her ducks in a row. Ken was the assistant stage manager, and worked feverishly for the rest of the play. Bill managed to stay out of everybody's way, and thoroughly enjoyed the frantic backstage activities.

Following the final curtain call the sky-high cast quickly disappeared to the cacophony of their dressing rooms. Ken carefully checked the set from the last scene. Satisfied that all was well, he said to Tim Black, "Let's put her to bed."

Bill helped out, and when they were finished Tim said, "Well done mates, there's a party in the basement common room, and I think it's time to hoist a pint or two."

As they entered the large room, Bill noticed that two galvanized wash tubs, swimming with ice and cold drinks, had been placed on a sturdy trestle table. One tub was jam-packed with Carling's Red Cap ale, and the other was crammed full of Hires Root Beer. Ken handed Bill an ale, then got one for himself before saying, "Tag along with me, and I'll introduce you to some of the actors."

Most of the people Bill met were polite, but none too friendly. Aaron Gant, true to form was down right rude.

Bill was feeling discouraged until he met Gordon Prescot an actor from Newfoundland, and the star of the play.

"I had a job as cook in St. John's after I got out of he Army," Gordon said, revealing a charming Newfie accent.

"Our best dishes were cod au gratin, Jiggs dinner, fish and brews, but my favorite was seal flipper pie."

"Wow! You must have been the chef at a pretty fancy restaurant," Bill smiled, feeling an immediate kinship with Gordon.

"Maggie's Diner was anything but high class there boy," Prescot chuckled. "Martha our wizard of the sets is having a party at her cottage on the river, so Ken, if you Tim and Bill want to come along; we'll see you later. "He shook Billy's hand, grabbed an ice cold Red Cap from one of the wash tubs, then went over to greet a group of local patrons.

The cottage was a short ten minute walk from the theatre. As they strolled along in the cool night air, Ken said, "We call her place Martha's Vineyard."

"That's because she likes that bleedin' French red wine," Tim grunted.

"I don't know anything about wine," Bill replied. "My dad calls it Bingo, and says that real men would rather drink beer."

As they approached the Vineyard their nostrils were tickled by the sweet smell of white birch logs burning on an open fire. The cottage was a solidly built clapboard structure, and the centerpiece of the spacious living room was a large field stone fireplace.

"This is a great camp!" Bill shouted, impressed by the size of the cottage.

"Is that some kind of colonial term?" Tim asked innocently.

"Hell no, our family has a small cabin west of North Bay, and they call them camps in that part of Ontario."

Martha greeted them at the door, and said, "There's food on the table, beer in the fridge, and of course, a bottle of red wine on the wash stand by the door."

"Thanks Martha." Ken blinked, trying to adjust to the harsh light of the hallway."This is a neat place."

Despite his father's opinions, Bill poured himself a glass of wine and took a sip. It had a tangy berry-like taste. Ken introduced Bill to Jim Finney, a playwright and author, his play, *The Red Bike* was to open the following week. Sitting beside Jim was the costume designer Laura Collins, a raven haired beauty who had her arm draped possessively around Jim's shoulder. Bill had never met an author before, and asked if any of his books were at the local library.

Summer of '61

"Not yet," Jim sighed. "I've written a few short stories that were published in the *Star Weekly,* but nothing in hard cover yet."

"He's going to be a bloody great author some day," Laura declared, slurring her words.

"I'm working on a novel about the First World War," Jim said, smiling at Laura. "My father was in the trenches and got gassed, so I wanted to write something about his generation."

"Yeah I can relate to that," Bill frowned. "My grandfather McNair was wounded at Vimy Ridge, so the Great War was an important part of our family too."

"The other reason for the book has to do with my own experiences," Jim said uneasily. "When I was eighteen, I joined the Royal Canadian Air Force, and wound up as a wireless operator on Lancasters. I tried to write about my time in the RCAF, but I couldn't."

"My Uncle Steve was at Ortona and the Scheldt Estuary, and he won't talk about what happened in the war either."

"My father's war and from what you tell me your grandfather's war, is where I'm at."

Laura felt neglected, and was in no mood to be ignored any longer. She slammed her beer mug on the coffee table and shouted, "If you two pansies want to keep talking all this military shit, then I'll have to go skinny-dipping alone."

"Hold on for a few seconds and I'll go with you," Jim smiled shyly, perking up like a plump Lab puppy about to be petted.

A good plan Bill thought, because as his mother used tell him, always swim with a buddy. He had polished off a second glass of wine, and was starting to acquire a taste for the fruit of the vine. In his minds eye he could see French peasants, working in the warm sun, crushing grapes with their bare feet. Purple feet while you brown was a pleasant pastoral image.

Gordon Prescot had arrived at the party, and it wasn't long before someone handed him a guitar. He sang a folk song by Pete Seeger and a ballad about Newfoundland that he had written himself.

When Gordon had finished; Ken flying high on his fourth beer, echoed like a droning fog horn, "Chef Carlsen here, can pick a tune or two." The guitar was quickly passed to Bill. Even though his face resembled Rudolph's nose, he did manage to choke out the folk tune:

Rye Whiskey, Rye Whiskey, Rye Whiskey, I cried, If I don't have Rye Whiskey, I surely will die. It was a hack job, but the crowd gathered in the living room were well enough oiled, that even Tiny Tim would have sounded good to them.

Tim the carpenter who had a lady by his side was handed the guitar next. Strumming it softly he said, "I'm from Liverpool, and I was at a church basement concert in me home town, when I heard this tune from a group called the Quarrymen."

He began to play a rock 'n' roll piece, that had something to do with someone else loving them, Ya! Ya! Ya!. This will never replace Folk Music Bill thought.

Just as Tim finished, Jim and Laura entered the living room, their hair still dripping wet. They had that Carnation Contented Cow look stenciled on their faces. Obviously skinny-dipping was good for your health.

"Boy, that water sure is pussy numbing cold," Laura gasped, her teeth chattering.

"Yeah I wouldn't want our cat Bozo to swim in that frigid water either, "Bill said, looking concerned. The crowd around the stone fireplace seemed to think that Bill's comment was completely hilarious, he smiled, and basked in the glow of Mr. Popular.

Billy began to relax, Harry wanted to golf in the afternoon, so he didn't have to work till three. Starting on his third tumbler of bingo he was in a reflective state of mind. He began to think about sex or the lack there of. He hoped that no one had noticed the large neon sign flashing over his head, telling the whole world that he was still a virgin. He and Doris had come close several times, but had not actually done it. As his uncle Olie would say, "Close only counts with horseshoes and tear gas."

*

Barb Wallace who shared the cottage with Martha entered the warmth of the living room, and stood with her backside to the fire. She noticed Billy standing by the washstand and on impulse came over to speak to him, "Would you mind getting me some wine, she whispered seductively. Ever the gentlemen, he reached for a fresh bottle of Burgundy, and hoping beyond hope that maybe she actually liked him, poured her a generous glass.

Summer of '61

His heart stood still as he gazed like a lost lamb into the soft glow of her angel-blessed emerald eyes.

"You know Billy you're awfully cute," Barb purred, placing her arm around his waist. "You kind of remind me of a young tiger."

"Well I don't want to be you're tiger, cuz tigers play too rough," Bill crooned. "Holy doodle! I think I'm trapped in an Elvis Presley movie."

Barb laughed politely at Bill's corny joke before saying, "Would you like to take a walk down to the dock?"

"Yeah, I need some fresh air," he replied, trying hard not to stare at the twin puppies that were snuggling contentedly under Barb's blouse.

They strolled slowly, arm-in-arm along a short path that led to the water. As they passed the boat house Barb casually let her hand brush the front of Bill's jeans, and said, "Let's look inside." He hoped that she meant inside his pants, but she was pointing at the building.

Moonlight passing through a small window lit the interior with an eerie glow, allowing them to see a sturdy wooden bench that was attached to the far wall. After they were seated, Barb put her arms around Bill, pressed her lips against his, then proceeded to give him detailed instructions on some of the finer points of major league petting. The wine had acted as a powerful aphrodisiac, and Barb was now afflicted with a condition that most physicians referred to as: Wet To The Knees Syndrome. A minute later she moaned, "I want you to make love to me, right here, right now."

Not wanting to disappoint a lady, he guided her onto the rough plank floor, and slowly began to unbutton her blouse. Without warning the door banged open, and Bill was able to make out Martha's ample silhouette framed in a silver light.

"I hate to break up a good thing, but if you two lovebirds don't mind, I need your help in the kitchen Barb," Martha chortled.

"I've got to fly Billy," Barb breathed softly. "After all she's my boss."

The balloon had definitely exploded into a million scattered pieces, and all that he could think of was: "Jeez, why me?"—but the sign still read—This Guy's Never Been Laid.

When Bill returned to the cottage, Laura was announcing that her world famous meatballs and kraut were ready.

The party crowd filed by three roasting pans full of peppered sauerkraut and spiced meatballs. There was fresh French bread, and a choice of ice cold beer or mellow red wine. That Jim's one lucky stiff Bill thought, or another way of looking at it—as long as Laura was around one part of Mr. Finney would always be fortunate and rigid.

Bill demolished two heaping plates and washed things down with several glasses of vin rouge—Miss Marble, take off eh! He started to stretch and yawn, so when Tim and Ken wanted to leave, he didn't argue.

"Boy that Bingo sure packs a wallop," Bill mumbled, as he tried without success to walk a straight line on the way home. So much for solemn vows.

5
*

When Bill awoke the next morning, his brain ached like a thumb that had just been clobbered by the blunt end of an axe. He belatedly remembered one of his grandmothers favorite expressions. "A hangover is the wrath of grapes." For the second morning in a row, he felt like death warmed over. Holy moly he thought, at this rate I'll be an alcoholic before August rolls around.

Billy arrived at the kitchen just as the breakfast hour was starting to taper. He replaced Harry at the grill and made himself a plate of bacon and eggs. While ignoring a very large elephant that insisted on doing a tap dance behind his eyelids, he choked down the greasy meal.

Bill was hunched over the counter listening to the Shirelles singing,"Will You Still Love Me Tomorrow" when Arron Gant came in and sat down beside him. Much like little Miss Muffet and the spider, was his first reaction. From what Joey had told him, Ari had an unhealthy appetite for young boys. He quickly gulped down the last piece of bacon, then scooted into the kitchen.

Due to the lure of the big top, or maybe it was the smell of grease paint and the roar of the crowd, most of the Hilltop staff were helping out at the theatre across the street. Joey had reluctantly confessed to his roommates the night before, that Arron Gant was a dick molester.

"It was two days ago," Joey said, in a taut voice. " We were sitting on a bench backstage when he suddenly reached over and started to massage my cock."

"The slime ball!" Danny exploded, pounding his fist on the table.

Bob was totally shocked, and stammered, "D-did you feed him a knuckle sandwich?"

"No, I was too scared. I jumped up, and got the hell out of there as fast as I could," Joey replied, obviously agitated. Arron Gant was definitely a scratch on everyone's Christmas card list.

Several days later, during the lunch rush , Bonnie Baker gave Bill an order for a hamburger, that was to be cooked for precisely three minutes on each side.

"His Ariship was very exact about the instructions."

"Don't worry Bonnie, I'll use the timer."

While he was cooking the burger a fly landed on the back window.

Bill smacked the insect with a rolled up piece of newspaper, then placed the squished bug directly in the center of the beef pattie. He put the meat on a bun, added the garnishes, then asked Bonnie to deliver the meal to Ari's table.

Billy entered the dinning area on the pretext of getting a glass of milk, and watched quietly while Mr. Pecker Grabber ate his lunch. Bill could hear his uncle Olie saying: " A turd in a sewer always travels down stream." He would never become a card carrying member of the Ari Fairy fan club.

Bill was finished at three, but stayed around to hear about Harry's morning eighteen.

"Someday if I ever get good enough, I'd like to be a golf pro," Harry sighed, stars flashing in his eyes as he pictured himself on the tour making one magnificent shot after another.

"That would be a great life," Bill smiled, a note of wonder in his voice.

"I like to follow amateur golf Billy, and I've been keeping track of a player who just turned pro, one of these days he'll be a great one."

"Who's that Harry?"

"Remember the name Jack Nicklaus."

"Jack who?" Bill asked, scratching his head.

It was mid-July, Chamber of Commerce weather, and the Town of Port Carter was hopping. Bill was working the three to eleven shift and was surprised to see Harry walk into the kitchen at seven o'clock.

"I've got a favour to ask you Billy. I want to play in a tournament at the Orillia club tomorrow, but I'll be gone all day, so I was wondering if you could cover for me?"

"Boy that'll a long haul, and we're awfully busy."

"If you'll fill in for me, I'll do half your shift the next day, and you can use my car in the afternoon."

Say the secret word and win a hundred dollars! It was a long sixteen hours, but he managed to get through in one piece. True to his word, Harry was on deck at eleven the day after Bill's marathon. He tossed the keys to Cook Carlsen before saying, "Handle the beast with kid gloves, she'll go like stink if you let her."

"Don't worry Harry, I'll be as careful as a seal at a polar bear's picnic."

Summer of '61

Donna Rogers was working at the Hilltop when Bill decided to drive the Chey into Bala. After discussing his plans with her, she squealed with delight, "I've got the afternoon off too, and it would be oh so groovy, if I could go with you."

Bill was a sucker for any girl who was the spitting image of Gidget. Trying to sound like James Cagney he rasped, "Listen doll, if you want to tag along, then that's okay, but keep your trap shut, or I'll have to slap you around."

"You're such a riot!" Donna giggled, placing her arms around Bill's neck, and planting a large wet kiss right on his lips. Hey it's true what they say he thought, a snazzy car really attracts the chicks. Master Carlsen did however, have a mission in mind. Using Danny's fake ID, he was planning to buy a two-four at the Beer Store.

Shortly after lunch they climbed into Harry's Chevy to begin the forty-five minute trip. It was like a wide awake dream. He had a gorgeous babe by his side, the top down in a flashy convertible, the wind blowing in his hair, and the radio playing. They sang along to Del Shannon's, "Hats Off to Larry", laughed, and chatted away like two little old ladies at a bingo parlor.

He deposited Donna in front of the IDA drugstore, and agreed to meet her later at the Captains Wheel restaurant. He swung by the White Rose gas station, put two bucks of regular into the tank, then proceeded to the Brewer's Retail. He sat outside for a minute thinking about what he would say. Billy just about chickened out, but what the he heck, they couldn't arrest you for trying to purchase a box of suds. Or could they?

He nervously approached the man at the counter, then blurted out in a dry squeaky voice, "I-I'd like to buy a case of beer."

"Let's see some identification there buddy," the store manager rumbled, while giving him the once-over

Bill felt that he was going to be refused for sure, but boldly reached into his wallet to retrieve Danny's phony birth certificate. Trying to keep his hand from shaking, all Billy could see was a black robed judge standing beside the gleaming metal rollers.

"When were you born?" the manager asked accusingly.

"In nineteen-forty, sir," Bill replied, a tremor of fear in his voice.

"You seem a little young, but I guess you're okay," The manager said, still looking doubtful. "How many do you want?"

Bill figured, might as well be hung for a moose as a deer, and replied, "Two cases of Old Vienna please."

He paid the suds slinger six dollars, then carried the two boxes of barley sandwiches out to Harry's car. Billy had it all worked out. He would sell most of the wobbly pops to his buddies for a quarter a bottle. If all forty-eight long-necks were snapped up, then he would double his money. He thought that entrepreneur had a nicer ring to it than bootlegger.

At two o'clock, when Bill entered the Captain's Wheel, he noticed that Donna wasn't there yet. After ordering a ginger ale, he flopped into an empty booth, placed a dime in the jukebox, and selected a song by Ricky Nelson. Ricky's "Travellin Man" was just about at Wikiki when Donna entered the restaurant. She spotted Bill immediately, and sat down beside him.

"I got the makeup I wanted, and I was able to buy a bathing cap at the Chainway," she bubbled, still excited from her shopping spree. "Did you get everything you needed Billy?"

"I just went to Canadian Tire, tooled around for awhile, then came back here," he said, grinning like a choirboy at his first rehearsal. Bill figured, what Donna didn't know wouldn't hurt her, and the two cases of O'keefe's in the trunk , definitely came under the heading of top secret.

After he finished the soda, they decided to take a drive to the public beach. Gidget and the rookie bootlegger, strolled hand in hand along the shore of the lake, and soon found a secluded rocky point.

"When's your birthday?" Donna asked, after they sat down.

"I'll be eighteen in August," Bill said, hoping to impress her.

"I turned nineteen in June, so I guess we're not that far apart in age," Donna said thoughtfully. "I broke up with my boyfriend just before I came up here, and you know, it still hurts."

"Yeah, I can understand what you're going through. My girlfriend Doris and I called it splitsville about two weeks ago, and I really miss her, though I try to let on that everything's cool."

They were sitting side by side on a curved sheet of rock that ran down to the waters edge. Donna put her head on Bill's shoulder, and he responded by placing his arm around her waist. They sat very still, watching the gentle waves softly caressing the granite shoreline.

Summer of '61

"You know Billy, I've always wanted to have a younger brother. You've been so kind to me, and I feel like you're part of my family."

Bill thought that this younger brother bit was a real drag. He remained silent however, and pursued his own version of the fantasy.

One hour later Bill wheeled into the parking lot of the Harb. Before Donna got out of the car she gave him a sister like peck on the cheek, then disappeared up the stairs that led to the girls quarters. He put the convertible into gear, then drove slowly to the Hilltop. He parked the car near the back set of steps, and carefully carried the beer up to the penthouse.

He placed the two squares of O.V. under his bunk, and covered them with a spare blanket. You would have to lie on your belly, then poke around under the bed to discover the stash.

Billy sold beer to Harry, his roommates, and various members of the Players. He only charged twenty-five cents a bottle, but was able to clear five dollars by the time the cases were empty. Bill couldn't help wondering if this was how Al Capone got started.

Little did he know that he would soon be playing the role of a guardian angel, much like Clarence in: *It's a Wonderful Life.*

6
*

Bill had talked to the milkman on several occasions . His name was Ian Livingstone, but everyone called him Doc, as you might presume. The Doc was in his mid-twenties and had lived in Port Carter all his life. It was the consensus of the Hilltop staff that the Doc could pass for Pat Boone's double. The waitresses all thought that Ian was a real dreamboat. Doc Livingstone lived with his mother in a two storey house on Bailer Street. His father had been killed in Holland near the end of the war.

Bill figured the Doc had the world by the tail. His milk route included the homes in town, and most of the cottages dotted along the shoreline of the nearby lakes. He started at six in the morning and was finished by one in the afternoon. The Doc spent the rest of the day water skiing. He had his own fourteen foot ski boat powered by a forty horsepower outboard.

It was a hot mid-July day when the Doc came into the Hilltop looking for Bill.

"We're not busy right now, so Bill went up to his room for a short break," Bonnie gushed, as she openly admired the handsome milkman.

The Doc climbed up the back stairs, and found Bill stretched out on his bunk.

"Hey, how's it goin' Doc?"

" No complaints Billy. If you've got em, I'd like four cold ones."

"Sure thing, and that's a buck you owe me." One picture of the Queen quickly changed hands.

"I'm going out in the boat this afternoon with my buddy Wayne , and you're welcome to come along if you want."

"Jeez I'd love to, but I'm not finished here till three," Bill grumbled.

The milkman pondered that for a moment before saying, " I'll tell you what, we'll swing by the town dock at three-thirty and if you're there, it'll be a go for a run up river."

Bill had finished his shift and was sitting on a park bench near the public launch when the ski boat came into view. After the speedy craft sloshed to a sliding halt, he hurried over to say hello.

"Do you know how to ski?" Wayne, a stocky-barrel-chested-pug face, asked genially.

Summer of '61

"I've done a little skiing at our camp," Bill replied, trying to sound confident.

They handed him a pair of skies and the tow rope. He carefully put his feet into the rubber footholds on the boards, and sat ready at the edge of the dock . Bill had a firm grip on the tow bar when Wayne gunned the motor. He flew off the dock, managed to keep his balance, and was really impressed by the speed he was able to achieve on the outside turns. Bill held his own until he misjudged the slack on a rapid in turn. He did an arse-over-tea-kettle bailout, and was quickly picked up.

The Doc jumped into the water and put on a slalom ski. When he was ready Wayne goosed the throttle, and had the boat at top speed in a flash. Doc Livingstone was completely at home on the single ski, and demonstrated a remarkable sense of balance. They skied hard for the rest of the afternoon, but had to call it quits when the gas gauge read empty.

After the boat was put away at Mitchell's Marina, they walked the short distance to the Doc's place. Mrs. Livingstone was at choir practice, so they had the house to themselves. Wayne grabbed three cold beers from the fridge, and handed them around at the kitchen table.

"One of these days I'm going to ski the entire length of the Mississippi River all the way to New Orleans," the Doc said, after a satisfying gulp of icy brew.

"Why do you want to do that?" Billy inquired, his curiosity aroused.

"It's just a dream, but without dreams life would never be special. Even if you don't see the dream through at least it was your dream."

"Hey Doc you're a great philosopher," Bill said admiringly.

"Naw, I'm just a simple milk jockey," the Doc grinned shyly.

"What's your dream Wayne?" Bill asked, continuing to ride the momentary crest.

Smiling wolfishly, Wayne replied, "I'd really like to marry a rich, American, nymphomaniac widow, who owns a liquor store in Florida."

Boys-oh-boys, that sure was a reality check.

In the evening, Bill wandered over to the theatre, and watched the last act of Jim Finney's, *Red Bike*. The play finished with a thundering round of applause, followed by several curtain calls.

Bill was scheduled for the morning shift the next day, but he was full of energy, and was in no particular hurry.

He went back stage where Ken and Tim were putting the finishing touches on a set in preparation for tomorrow's performance. Happy to see his friend, Ken shouted, "Hey Billy-boo what's happening?"

Ken had picked up this boo thing from Martha who called everyone in the stage crew by their first name, sometimes their last, followed by boo.

"I went water skiing with the Doc this afternoon Kenny-boo, and it was far out!" Bill said, imagining himself skimming over the placid surface of the river.

"Hey, that's really fab mate," Tim said, in his understated Liverpool way.

Ken raised his arms in a big stretch and said, " We're finished here, and boy am I ever beat. I've got a couple of letters from home that I want to read before I hit the pit, so it's time to blow this pop stand."

"Yeah, I could use a little extra sleep myself," Bill said drowsily. "I'll see you guys later."

Looking tired but determined, Tim yawned, "I'm going to stay here and do some work on the new sets we started today."

Bill was sound asleep, and having the most amazing dream about Doris when he felt someone shaking his shoulder. He came to slowly, and could see Ken standing there in the dim light of the bedroom.

"Billy I need to talk to you," Ken whispered, his voice taut.

Bill got up quickly and was dressed in one minute flat. He grabbed a couple of beers from under the bunk, then followed Ken down the backstairs.

"There's an old school bus parked in behind the theatre, the folding doors aren't locked, so we can talk there," Ken croaked, sounding really depressed.

It was a warm summers night, and they were quiet comfortable sitting on the large rear seat of the bus. Bill pulled a church key from his pocket, and snapped the caps on the two bottles of O.V. He handed one to Ken before asking, "What gives?"

Much to his surprise Ken broke into tears, and between sobs managed to say, "I just read a letter from my mom; she wrote to tell me that her and Dad are getting a divorce."

Summer of '61

Without warning Ken folded his arms across the seat in front of him, and let out the most heart wrenching cry that Billy had ever heard. He didn't know what to do so, he patted Ken gently on the back and kept on repeating," It'll be all right. It'll be all right."

Getting his emotions partially under control, Ken managed to choke out between sobs, "You know my mom didn't want me to come up here this summer, and maybe if I hadn't, I could have stopped it from happening. It's all my fault!"

"Ken, adults are responsible for their own actions and decisions; that's why they call them grown-ups. This was definitely not your fault," Bill stated flatly.

"But if only I'd been there," Ken moaned.

"If you keep on thinking that way it's going to drive you bananas, and you'll wind up no good to anyone, including yourself. Your mom will need your help more than ever now; it ain't pretty Mc-boo but that's the way it is."

Ken thought this over for a minute, then let out a shuddering sigh, "You're right Billy; it still hurts like hell, but I'll just to have to accept it."

He walked with Ken to the small tourist cottage on the river that he shared with Tim. Bill shook Ken's hand, but didn't know what else to say.

"You know I was seriously thinking of killing myself before we had our talk. You saved my life!" Ken rasped, a large lump in his throat, making speech difficult.

Totally thunderstruck, Bill managed to say good night, then headed back to the Hilltop. It had been a day of surprises, but another one was just around the corner.

7
*

Bill awoke the next morning still shook up from the events of the night before. He dressed quickly, then scampered down the back steps, in order to be at work by a quarter-to-seven. The grills needed warming before they could be used for cooking.
At seven-thirty Virgin for short came into the kitchen and said, " Your artsy craftsy buddy from across the street wants to talk to you."
"Virginia, I'm up to ass in alligators and scrambled eggs, so could you please tell Ken to come back here."
"And who was your servant this time last year?" Virginia growled, as she turned on her heel and marched back to the dining area. Ken came through the kitchen door sixty seconds later.
"Are you okay?" Bill asked, noticing the dark semicircles under Ken's eyes.
"I feel like old Sylvester who just got dragged through a knothole, but I'll survive. Things don't seem quite so bleak and gloomy this morning. Thanks for being there last night, Billy."
"All in a nights work for a roving short-order cook," Bill joked.
Ken then did something that Billy had only experienced in the euphoria of football, or hockey games. He crushed him with a mighty bear hug and said, "You know, you turkey, you really did save my life and I'll never forget it." Ken released his victory grip, then returned to the counter to order his usual breakfast of toast and Kellog's Sugar Frosted Flakes.
The morning went by quickly, and blended smoothly into the early afternoon. At one-thirty, Virginia came into the kitchen and said, "Bill there's someone out here who would like to see you."
Mc-boo again Bill thought, hoping that things were still all right. He hastily entered the dining area, only to be stopped dead in his tracks by the unexpected vision that appeared before him. He managed to recover from a temporary state of shock and sputtered, "M-Mom what are you doing here? Is there anything wrong?"
"Everything's fine dear," his mother smiled. "Aren't you going to say hello to Wilma?"
Bill was so shocked to see his mother, that he had failed to notice Wilma Lester sitting at a table by the window. Wilma worked with Bill's mom at the Georgetown Municipal Office, and was the one who had recommended him for the restaurant job.

Summer of '61

Wilma was a long time friend of Paul and Sally Evans.

Mrs. Carlsen took a seat opposite Wilma, looked affectionately at her son and said, " Your father's holidays have been changed. He now has the first three weeks in August, so we've decided to take a trip to Norway and visit some of your dad's family."

Hans Carlsen, Bill's Grandfather was from the Hvaler Islands south of Oslo. He had emigrated to Canada in nineteen ten, but had never been back home.Bill's father however, had always wanted to investigate his roots.

"We want you to come with us Billy, and your dad has already applied for the passes," his mother said, looking hopefully at her son.

Since Mr. Carlsen worked for TCA; he and his immediate family were eligible for airline passes to fly anywhere in the system on a stand by basis.

"Golly whiz, Mom I really appreciate you're coming up here to ask me to go to Europe and all, but I've got to stay and complete this job. When Paul hired me it was with the understanding that I'd be here for the whole summer. I've given him my word, and it would be wrong to go back on our handshake agreement ."

"Bill this could be the opportunity of a lifetime; your father and your sister will be very upset."

"Mom, Brenda will be tickled pink to have you and Dad all to herself for three weeks, and I think down deep, Pop would be disappointed if I didn't honor this commitment," Bill said forcefully.

"It sounds like you've got your mind made up Billy, and when I talked this over with your father; he said, that it had to be your decision."

Bill wrapped his arms around his mother,and said gratefully, "Thanks for treating me like an adult instead of a kid."

Mrs. Carlsen wiped away a tear, patted her son on the back, then managing to regain her composure said, "Well Billy, we haven't had lunch yet, so we'll eat here."

"Hey that's great Mom I'll get you and Mrs. Lester a couple of menus."

Since it wasn't busy, Bill stood by the table until his mother and Wilma decided on what to order.

"I think I'll have a grilled cheese on brown," his mother smiled.

"I'll have the same," Wilma said, folding her menu.

Bill returned to the kitchen to prepare the grilled cheese sandwiches. He was lost in thought, wondering if he had done the right thing. Yeah, he concluded, I have to see this thing through; besides it's kind of neat being on your own. When the meal was ready, he brought it to the table.

"Doesn't a dill pickle come with the grilled cheese?" Wilma asked, as she reached for a napkin.

"Gee you're right Mrs. Lester. In all the excitement I completely forgot. Just hold on a minute, and I'll get you and Mom a couple of pickles."

Bill returned as fast as he could carrying two whole dill pickles, one in each hand. His mother was horrified and scolded, " Billy Carlsen, where are your manners? You should have put those on a plate."

Wilma burst out laughing and said, "You know, your mother whispered to me just as you left to get those pickles , I hope he remembers to put them on a plate."

"Holy smoke! I'm sorry Mom, Mrs. Lester, I was in such a hurry, I just plain forgot."

Mothers will always be mothers Bill thought, and I guess I still have a lot to learn from Emily Post. Mrs. Carlsen and Wilma munched away happily, and had just finished their tea when Bill came back from the kitchen.

"Was it okay?" he asked expectantly.

"It was delightful dear, and the new pickles that you brought out on that nice clean plate were just delicious," his mother sighed contentedly.

Bill was taught by his father never to be wasteful, and had simply washed the pickles under the tap, placed them on a plate, then returned them to the table.

"Will you be in Port Carter for the rest of the afternoon?" Bill asked hopefully.

"No, Wilma and I have to be back for this evening, so we can't stay. I'll tell your father what you decided, and if things change , phone us right away," his mother said, as she got up to leave.

"All right Mom, but I've made up my mind. I'll be here for the summer."

Summer of '61

Billy kissed his mother good-bye and thanked Wilma for helping him to get the job. He accompanied them outside, and waited for the car to pull away. He waved until they were out of sight before going back into the café. He was surprised by the appearance of a mysterious tightness in his throat, and felt a lot like a little kid who had just stubbed his toe in the dark. Loneliness seemed to envelope him like a lake fog on a cool July night. These clinging mists of isolation however, would soon be blown away by the gentle breezes of a summer romance.

8
*

    Bill worked the morning shift again the next day. He was sitting at the counter, just after the breakfast frenzy had ended, when Scarlet O'Hara walked through the door. He could almost hear "Tara's Theme" playing in the background, as this quicksilver apparition of celluloid loveliness approached him, and said in a very earthly voice, " Could I have a 7 UP float please?"
    Bill was unable to speak at first, all he could think of was: I'm not Rhett Butler, and this sure as hell ain't *Gone With The Wind*, but it's a dynamite fantasy. He managed to recover and choked out, "Coming right up."
    He introduced himself, and Miss Scarlet followed suit by telling him that her name was Sandra King. She might have been Vivian Leigh's younger sister, but with a name like King Bill figured that it was highly unlikely.
    "Hey are you any relation to Brad King?" he asked, trying to get his pulse rate back to normal.
    "He's my brother," Sandra smiled, admiring Bill with her dark brown eyes.
    "Brad used to come in here for breakfast when Bonnie Baker was our waitress," Bill said, his voice still a little shaky. "Now that Bonnie's mostly down at the Harb, we haven't seen much of him."
    "Brad broke up with Bonnie and she's going with Dick Mitchell now," Sandra said lightly.
    " Does Dick's father own the marina?" Bill asked, catching a whiff of her spicy perfume.
    "That's the one," Sandra said, giving her ponytail a saucy flip.
    Just before he served the float Bill said, " Do you want a shot of cherry syrup with this? It's a nickel extra, but as my uncle Olie would say; we're only given a one way ticket in this life, so if you have a choice between steerage and "A" deck, then go for the bone china."
    "With a sales pitch like that, how could I refuse," Sandra said, batting her eyelashes ever so slightly.
    Bill put the finishing touches on the float, and placed it in front of her. She stirred the mixture slowly, put her luscious lips over the double straws, and began to draw the delicious liquid into her waiting mouth. He was totally enthralled.

Summer of '61

When Sandra was finished she asked Bill where he was from, how old he was, where he went to school, and what he wanted to do after graduation, all the usual getting to know the other person stuff. He found out that she was sixteen, went to high school in Bracebridge, and her boyfriend was working in Hamilton for the summer.

When Sandra got up to leave Billy started to panic, but managed to blurt out, "I-I'm finished work at three, so if you're not doing anything, would you like to take a walk down by the river?"

"That would be very nice. I'll meet you here at three-thirty," Sandra said, softly patting Bill's bare arm. She walked slowly out of the restaurant, pausing briefly at the door to take a quick look at Bill, as he disappeared into the kitchen.

The rest of the day went by slower than a July sunset on Baffin Island. When you're waiting for something that you really want to do, it's amazing how time becomes elongated. Bill figured that Einstein could probably explain that one.

Three o'clock finally arrived and Harry took over. Bill rushed upstairs, put on his best shirt, scrubbed a few grease spots off his jeans, and replaced his desert boots with a pair of thong sandals. He splashed Old Spice after shave on his face, then hurried to the front of the restaurant. He was just in time to see Sandra coming up the street. His heart skipped a beat as he watched her get closer.

They walked slowly towards the public beach, stopping occasionally to admire the lovely front yard gardens that lined Bailer Street. Just before reaching the Chippewa, they took a trail that ran along the river's edge to a place called picnic point.

It was late afternoon, and the area was completely deserted. The young couple sat side- by-side on a spruce log, and admired a loon that seemed to be drifting ghost-like on the glassy surface of the wide river.

"I've only been here once before," Bill said, pointing at a circle of stones that acted as a fire pit, "It was on a weekend and a young family were having a cook out, so I didn't stay very long."

"My parents used to bring us here when we were little kids. We'd roast hot dogs, toast marshmallows, and sing camp songs after it got dark," Sandra sighed, as she recalled pleasant images from the past. "Now we have a cottage on Lake Raddison, and our family spends most of its free time there."

Changing the subject abruptly, Bill asked, "So what's your boyfriend doing down in Hamilton?"

"His uncle got him a job at Stelco," Sandra replied, languidly as if emerging from a daydream. " He's working at one of the blast furnaces."

"Boy that must be a tough contract," Bill said, picturing flames erupting from the gigantic industrial dragon.

"Yes, it's hard, hot work, but they pay him a buck seventy-five an hour," Sandra said proudly. "He can put in fifty hours a week if he wants to, and by the end of the summer he'll have a fair bit tucked away for university."

Wow, Bill thought, that's an eighty-seven dollar pay cheque every Friday night. It'll take this guy less than three weeks to earn what I'll make all summer.

"What's his name?" Bill asked, trying not to sound jealous.

"Brian Miller, his dad's the manager of the Canadian Imperial Bank in Bracebridge," she said, then continued coyly. "Brian and I agreed that we'd put going steady on hold for the summer, so we could meet other people if we wanted to."

"Well you've just met another person," Bill whispered, reaching for her hand.

She reacted to his gesture by moving sideways on the log until their shoulders were touching. Bill turned her slowly towards him, then kissed her tenderly on the lips. Sandra responded by putting her arms around him and placing her cheek against his.

They sat there like that for a minute before Sandra broke the spell by saying, "I should be getting on home now. I promised my mother that I'd help her get the supper ready." Bill walked Sandra back to her house. It was a large two story structure folded into a side-hill at the top of Bridge street.

"I'm doing the day shift again tomorrow, but I have the evening free," Bill said, just before Sandra went in. "Would you like to go to the Odeon, and see the double feature?"

"I'd look forward to that," Sandra said, giving him a dazzling smile.

"I'll be here just after six," Bill grinned, pleased with her response.

On impulse, he kissed the back of Sandra's hand, then said good-bye.

Summer of '61

In a trance-like state he walked back to the Hilltop; his head only slightly above the puffy white clouds that drifted lazily across the deep blue sky.

After supper, Bill went across the street to see Ken. He stood at the rear of the theatre until the first act ended, then went back stage. He gave Tim and Ken a hand arranging the set for the second act, and watched the rest of the play from the wings. Arron Gant had a supporting role in the play, and Bill thought that he looked a little pale. Maybe the flies and other creepy crawlies that were being added to Ari's diet weren't agreeing with him. He hadn't come near any of the guys since the Joey incident. Feeling a twinge of guilt, Bill made a mental note to terminate any further protein supplements. He spent most of the next morning and afternoon daydreaming about the evening ahead.

The heat of the day was just starting to dissipate when he approached the King's grand residence. He knocked softly, expecting to see Sandra, but was startled when a woman about his mother's age opened the front door.

"M-Mrs. King?" Bill stammered.

"You must be William Carlsen," she said, smiling. " Sandra will be down in minute."

"Boy, I can sure see where Sandra gets her good looks from," Bill sparkled, trying to be suave and debonair. "You really look young enough to be her sister."

"Well aren't you the charmer," Mrs. King chuckled.

"Just the facts ma'am, nothing but the facts," Bill impersonated, in his best Joe Friday voice. Jack Webb would have been proud.

Sandra appeared behind her mother and said, "I'm ready to go if you are."

"Goodnight Mrs. King, and I'll have Sandra home by eleven."

"Have fun you two," Mrs. King waved, as she closed the door.

Sandra was wearing a pale blue sack dress; her hair pulled back in a ponytail, just like Betty on, "Father Knows Best". Bill had on a brown corduroy sports coat, spotless white shirt, narrow black tie, and charcoal grey slacks. This was his Sunday-go-to-meeting best.

After entering the lobby of the Odeon, Bill asked Sandra if she'd like anything to eat or drink before they went to into the theatre.

"A ginger ale would be very nice," she replied politely.

Billy was seduced by the smell of hot buttered popcorn, and asked the girl at the refreshment stand to add a medium tub to the soft drink order, while the brainwashing melody: *Lets all go to the lobby*, jingled through his mind.

They managed to get to their seats just as Woody the Woodpecker, let out his piercing call. The cartoon was followed by a leader proclaiming the wonders of the smash hit, *West Side Story*. Several seconds later like a Bomarc missile, *Splendor In The Grass* the first feature of the double bill, burst onto the screen in full Cinemascope and Technicolor.

The leading credits made a big deal about the screen debut of some guy named Warren Beatty. Bill figured this Beatty character would be a flash in the pan. Sandra however, thought that he was kind of cute. The second show was *The* Misfits.

"Clark Gable and Montgomery Clift are starting to look a little long in the tooth," Bill whispered. "But Marilyn Monroe is a great actress eh?."

"Only if you like blondes," Sandra said, trying hard not to meow.

"Yeah but brunettes are much prettier," Bill regrouped, in an attempt to play Prince Charming and save the day.

"Oh Billy, what a line," Sandra said laughing.

When the twin bill ended they left the picture show, and walked languidly up the hill towards Sandra's house.

"Would you like to stop at the Hilltop for a milk shake?" Bill asked.

"Oh that would be terrific," Sandra giggled, hooking her arm through his.

Jennifer Rossini was working the evening shift at the restaurant, so Bill did the introductions. They sat at a table by the window while Jen whipped up a couple of double chocolate specials.

"My mother wants you to come to supper at our place tomorrow night," Sandra said, swirling her straw around in the dark foamy liquid.

"Hey that would be wonderful. I haven't had a home cooked meal in a month," Bill grinned, his mouth beginning to water.

They finished their shakes and walked the short distance to the King's lofty castle. An old, squeaky, two-seated porch swing provided them with a place for intimacy.

Summer of "61

Bill slowly turned his head and kissed Sandra very lightly on the lips.

"God, you smell great!" he said, intoxicated by the alluring scent she was wearing.

"That's a new perfume I just bought called Evening in Paris," Sandra yawned sweetly.

"I wish this night would last forever, but I told your mother eleven," Bill said, as he inhaled her sweet fragrance. "I'll see you tomorrow at six." He gave Sandra a goodnight kiss, then reluctantly went down the steps.

Saturday at the Hilltop was a zoo. The tourists and cottagers, in town for the day, acted as if they hadn't eaten since Christmas. Billy didn't get a break until Harry arrived at three-thirty. He was a half-hour late, but the use of the Chevy from time to time, more than made up for any tardiness.

William Francis was feeling hot and grubby, so he quickly changed and made a beeline for the public beach to have a swim. The cool water felt refreshing on his clammy skin, and the clinging grime of the kitchen was gradually washed away by the slow moving current of the river.

He swam out to the raft anchored just inside the line of buoys, that carved out the safe swimming area. He lifted himself on to the flat surface of the small floating island, then stretched out to enjoy the sun. His eyes were shut tight, and he was peacefully drifting into a very pleasant reverie, when he felt the raft tip slightly. He quickly snapped back to reality when the image of a gorgeous redhead, wearing a brief two piece bathing suit, tweaked his optic nerve.

"Welcome to the good ship lollipop," he murmured, through a partial yawn.

"Are you a Shirley Temple fan or something?" the redhead asked amused.

"Not really but when I was a kid I used to like that song," Bill grinned, while openly admiring the goddess that had just emerged from the river.

"Well how about that so did I," his new shipmate chuckled.

Bill introduced himself, and found out that her name was Kitty Carson.

"I'm just up here for the summer," Billy said, trying to make conversation.

"Yeah me too," Kitty replied, as she turned her face to the sun.

"Are you working at one of the lodges?" he asked, taking in the magnificent swellings partially exposed by the stingy boulder-holder.

"No I'm a nurse at the Port Family Clinic," she said, smoothing her wet hair."I just graduated from the University of Toledo, and I'm staying at my parents cottage on the river. This summer nursing job came up, and I figured that it might be fun as well as good experience."

Boy, Billy thought, she sure is beautiful, but I'll bet that she's at least twenty-one.

"Well Kitty it's been nice meeting you, but I've got to go," he said, hanging his toes over the edge of the raft. "If you're ever at the Hilltop for a meal let me know, because I'm one of the short-order cooks there."

"When I go out to a restaurant in the Port it's usually at the Harb," she said, giving him a scrutinizing look. "You know Bill you sort of remind me of a teddy bear."

Oh no, not again Bill winced, as he dove into the crystal waters of the river, and swam for shore.

9

Bill arrived on Sandra's front doorstep at six. She led him into the living room, and introduced him to her father. She then excused herself, and went into the kitchen to help with dinner preparations. Mr. King was about Bill's height and maybe ten pounds heavier. He looked to be in very good shape. Bill told him where he was from, what his father and mother did , what sports he played, and what he was doing here for the summer.

"So your dad's with TCA; was he in the RCAF during the war?" Mr. King asked, trying to size up his daughters latest.

"No he was in the army," Bill said, feeling completely at ease with Sandra's father.

"Were you in the war Mr. King?"

"Yes, I was in the Air Force and flew Spitfires," Mr. King replied tentatively.

"Wow, a fighter pilot, I'll bet that was exciting," Billy said, picturing a twisting dogfight, and a sky filled with tracer rounds.

"Only in the movies Bill, most of the time I was scared to death," Mr. King frowned, a flicker of forgotten terror in his eyes. "I got shot down over France in forty-three, and spent the rest of the war in a German prison camp."

"Gee that must have been tough," Bill said , imagining the horror of the Stalag.

"What position do you play on the football team?" Mr. King asked abruptly, unwilling to talk anymore about the war.

"Well sir, I was a halfback on the offence, and a corner linebacker on the defence."

"A two-way player, you must be pretty good," Mr. King nodded approvingly.

"Not really sir, only twenty guys came out for our senior football team, so the coach was pretty desperate for starters."

Mrs. King came into the room and announced that dinner was ready. The circular dining room table had only four place settings, since Brad was in Gravenhurst visiting friends. After Bill and Mr. King sat down , Mrs. King and Sandra went to the kitchen, and brought out steaming plates of meat and vegetables. There was a platter of chicken—already carved—mashed potatoes, gravy, cranberry sauce, carrots, cauliflower and peas. Truly a meal fit for a King.

Bill noticed an unusual looking water glass in front of him, that contained a slice of lemon floating like a tiny yellow boat on a small placid pond. It was a warm day and he was very thirsty, so he picked up the glass to take a sip.

"What do you think of these fancy finger bowls that Sandra got her mother last Christmas?" Mr. King asked quickly, noticing what Bill was about to do.

"They're real nifty sir," Billy said, doing an instant midair recovery, and holding the bowl at arms length.

Mr. King winked, and Bill carefully placed the glass bowl on the table. In his books, Sandra's dad was a great guy

"Save your fork, there's lemon meringue pie for desert," Mrs. King declared, when they had finished the main course.

"Holy cow! That's my favorite, "Bill said, his eyes wide with anticipation. "Whenever we go to Vancouver for a visit, my grandma Carlsen always makes me a lemon meringue pie."

"So you're from BC." Mr. King said, sounding very interested.

"Yes sir, but we moved down to Ontario in 1950," Bill said, recalling the rough eighteen hour milk run in a rumbling DC-3.

"Why did your family move?" Sandra asked.

"My dad was working for TCA, but he got laid off," Bill said, bringing back things from the edges of his memory banks. " When business started to pick up again, they offered him a job at Malton Airport."

Mrs. King went into the kitchen and brought out the pie. Billy had two pieces, and a big glass of milk. After supper, Mr. and Mrs. King decided to go for a walk, so Bill offered to help Sandra with the dishes. He dried while she washed. *Real domestic eh? Just like Ozzie and Harriet.*

"Where was your home when you moved to Toronto ?" Sandra asked, her hands covered with soap suds.

"We lived on Fern Avenue near High Park," Bill smiled, opening the curtains on his childhood. "I remember the horse drawn milk wagons, and the smell of the streets was so different from Vancouver. Those horses left a lot of stuff behind, and in the summer it got pretty ripe."

"What was it like living in the city?" Sandra asked, as she handed him a plate to dry.

Summer of '61

"There were some amazing games, I had never seen before, "Bill reminisced, as his minds-eye slide projector fed him images from the old neighborhood. "The streets were lined with big chestnut trees, so we played a game called doany-whackers."

"I've never heard of that one before," Sandra said, a quizzical look crossing her face. "How's it played?"

"You put a hole in a chestnut with a nail," Bill said, remembering some of the intricacies of the game. "Next you take a shoelace with a large knot tied on one end, and thread the opposite end of the lace through the hole in the chestnut. One guy then places his chestnut into a small depression in the dirt, then the other guy swings his chestnut attached to the end of a shoelace in an attempt to smash the chestnut in the hole."

"That doesn't sound very exciting," Sandra said, handing him a pair of spoons. "What other games did you play?"

"Well there was flipsies, closest to the wall and alleys," Bill said, placing a cup on to a hook in the cupboard above him.

"I know about alleys, after all I have a big brother, but I've never heard of the other two," Sandra said lightly, enjoying Bill's stories.

"The big dairy in Toronto was Bordens and their milk bottle tops had a picture of Elsie the cow printed on them," Billy said, climbing back into his time machine, and punching the button for reverse. "You'd hold the bottle cap about waist high, give it a slight twist before you let it go, and it would flip end over end until it landed on the ground. If three pictures of Elsie came up , then the other guy would have to flip three bottle tops to try and match the three cow heads. If he couldn't, then you got his three caps."

"Why did you use milk bottle caps?" Sandra gestured palms up, before starting to rinse the sink.

"Strictly out of starvation," he grinned. "Nobody had enough money to buy hockey cards or anything else in that neighborhood, so we used what we had."

"How about closest to the wall?" Sandra asked, knowing that boys liked to talk about themselves.

"Oh, that was easy. A small group of guys , usually five or six, would get together and throw bottle caps at one of the walls of the school.The guy who was nearest the wall got all the other guys caps."

"Boys play some pretty weird games," Sandra sighed, hanging the dish rag over the tap.

"You know what was the really neat thing?" Billy said, the flashback of a happy memory making him smile. "My parents had rented a second story flat in a duplex, and the man who owned the house worked for Bordens Dairy, so I was able to get all the new bottle caps I wanted. For a while I was the most popular kid on the block."

Now that the dishes were sparkling clean, and put away in their proper hiding places, Sandra and Bill decided to get some fresh air on the screened-in porch. They sat down on an ancient overstuffed couch, and listened to the night sounds of crickets, tree frogs, and hungry mosquitoes.

"I'm sure glad we're in here," Sandra shuddered, snuggling up to Bill.

"Yeah, if we were out there it'd be Red Cross time," Bill shuddered, feeling safe from the blood sucking hoards, that were constantly bumping up against the fine copper mesh.

"You never told me if you'd a girlfriend back home," Sandra said, gently probing.

"Had is the right word," Bill groused, still feeling betrayed. "She dumped me for the captain of our football team two weeks after I got up here."

"Well my boyfriend's in Hamilton, so I guess we're both at loose ends," Sandra whispered seductively. Before things could progress further they heard the sound of the front door opening, and reluctantly went inside to greet Sandra's parents.

"That's a great night out there," Mr. King declared, as he entered the living room.

"We stopped in at the Hilltop for an ice cream cone," Mrs. King bubbled, the wonders of maple walnut still fresh on her taste buds. "The girl behind the counter sure looked a at lot like Ava Gardner."

"Oh, that's Virginia Hudson," Bill volunteered, thinking that he wasn't the only one to see the striking resemblance.

Mr. King arched his brows, "She seems like kind of a tough bird."

"Virginia's a little rough around the edges, but underneath she has a heart of gold," Billy said, as if he were a protective brother.

Summer of '61

"Well I think we'll turn in. You two kids have fun, but don't stay up too late," Mr. King said, covering his mouth to hide a mile wide yawn.

"Not to worry sir. I have to be up a six-thirty tomorrow morning," Bill reassured, shaking Mr.Kings hand. "Goodnight and thank you very much for the great supper Mrs.King, that lemon meringue pie was as good a my grandmother's"

"Well, I'll take that as quite a compliment," Sandra's mother smiled, sounding genuinely pleased.

When they heard the sound of the bedroom door closing, the young couple returned to the screened-in porch, and stood for a minute looking up at the heavens. There was no moon, but the ink black sky was dotted with thousands of tiny strobe-like stars.

"It's beautiful," Sandra sighed, placing her head on Bill's shoulder.

"Not half as beautiful as you," Bill said, meaning every word. They moved into each others arms, feeling the joy that comes with mystery and discovery.

"Before we sit down, could you please get me that blanket from the chair by the door," she asked casually.

Thirty seconds later they were hip to hip, arranging the blanket, so that it covered them below the waist. Sandra was a young lady who knew exactly what she wanted and where she was going. She was not the least bit shy when it came to discussing sex.

"I know you'll probably think that I'm quiet forward, but I like you very much and I want to get a few things straight," Sandra said, sounding quite determined. "The first time that I really do it will be on my honeymoon, but I don't want to deny myself certain pleasures in the meantime. I'll make you happy in a minute or two, but first I'm going to take off my panties."

Billy could hardly believe what he was hearing, but being a gentleman he figured whatever the lady wants the lady gets.

"I want you to touch me here," Sandra whispered, firmly guiding his hand.

"Now slowly move your finger up and down right there." She placed her head on the back of the couch and began to moan softly as he gently stroked her clitoris.

Several minutes later Sandra reached a shuddering climax, then her body relaxed as she drifted along in a state of lingering ecstasy.

"Do you have a handkerchief," Sandra asked, in a soft, sultry voice.

"Y-Yes I do," Billy croaked meekly, pulling a clean hankie from his pocket.

Sandra moved her hands under the blanket, and carefully opened the zipper on Bill's fly. She reached inside the slit of his jockey shorts, and slowly drew out his very erect penis. He suddenly realized why she wanted the handkerchief. Oh well, Bill thought, I've got to go to the coin laundry soon anyway.

"You see, it's possible to have a lot of fun without going all the way, and no worries about missing periods either," Sandra said, after they had rearranged their clothes.

Bill had never heard a girl talk so openly about sex, but then again, he had never met a young lady as unique as Sandra.

"Boy this has been a fantastic evening," he murmured, still high riding on an endorphyn rush. "Would you like to go for a walk, or something when I'm finished work tomorrow?"

"I'd love to, but my mother and I are going to the cottage for a few days, and we won't be back until midweek."

"Well, come over to the Hilltop when you get back to the Port, and we'll take a drive into Bala, "Bill sagged slightly, trying his best not to sound disappointed.

At the front door she gave him a chaste goodnight kiss; a rapid departure from passion on the porch. Bill didn't care, because he was too happy to be critical about kissing quality. He gave Sandra a brief wave when he reached the bottom of the front steps, then road a magic carpet back to the café.

When he entered the kitchen at six forty-five the next morning, Virginia was surprised by his cheerfulness and said, "What happened Billy-boy, did you get lucky last night?"

"Naw, it's just a great to be alive and tomorrow's my day off," he grinned, keeping the events of the previous evening close to his heart.

"You know Bill, when I first met you I thought you were a bit of a dork, but you've always treated me well," Virginia smiled, opening a locked door. "You'll help out at the counter if you're not busy back here, and even clean off the tables if you have time."

"Gee Virg, this could be the start of a beautiful relationship," Bill grinned, seeing himself as Bogie in a wet-shouldered trench coat.

"Are you into one of your movie fantasies again?" she asked, laughing.

Summer of '61

"Nope just foolin' around," he chuckled, coming back from his starring role. "You know Virg, I never thought we would get along either, but you're a real neat person, and you've got a world class sense of humor."

"Well before we become kissin' cousins, and start crying on each other shoulders, I need two orders of pancakes, sausages, scrambled eggs and brown toast," Virginia barked, before executing a rapid about-face, and marching back to the dinning room.

Just as Bill was putting the finishing touches on the order that Virginia had left him, Harry walked into the kitchen.

"Hi Billy, how's it goin'?" Harry shouted, in his usual cheerful manner.

"Not tea bag," Bill quipped, "I thought you weren't going to be here till three."

"Something's come up, and I've got a big favor to ask," Harry said expectantly.

"Shoot," Bill replied, as he loaded pancakes onto a plate.

"My sister's moving, and she needs me to help her this evening, so I'd appreciate it if you could work the afternoon shift," Harry said, pausing before delivering the clincher. "You can have my wheels tomorrow when I'm working three to eleven, and the gas is on the house."

"Nifty deal Harry," Bill replied happily. "That's my day off, and I can make good use of the Bel Air."

"Hey that's great Billy, you're a real pal," Harry grinned, as he bolted for the door.

Bill told Virginia about the change, but it really didn't concern her because she was off at three anyway. It was a long busy day, but the incentive of having a car at his disposal kept him going. When Bill finished at eleven, he was too tired to do anything but assume the horizontal till the next morning. He would need the sleep, because an unexpected adventure was about to come his way.

10
*

Billy awoke fully rested at eight on this bright sunny day of freedom. He hopped out of bed, dressed quickly, then made his way to the kitchen to get some breakfast. He said good morning to Paul, who was doing the early shift, then put together a meal of bacon and eggs. He added toast to his plate, then headed for the counter to eat. Virginia was standing by the coffee pot waiting to talk to him.

"I know you've got Harry's car this aft, and I've dreamed up a little scheme that might appeal to you," Virginia said, as she poured him a cup of coffee. "If you're interested, then come and see me at the Harb about four."

Bill was unable to get anymore information, but he did agree to meet with the beautiful Miss Hudson later on that day.

After finishing breakfast he went up to the penthouse, picked up his dirty laundry and left immediately for the coin wash. Placing his soiled hankie into the washer produced an erotic instant replay of sex on the sofa. *That Sandra sure is some piece of work!* When all his clothes were cleaned, he tucked them carefully into a pillow case, slung the white bag over his shoulder, and looking a lot like old St. Nick, he returned to the Hilltop.

It was a hot, hazy, humid afternoon, so Bill put on his bathing suit, grabbed a towel and sauntered down to the beach. He was pleasantly surprised to see Kitty Carson stretched out on a blanket by the waters edge.

"How's your belly for spots?" Bill asked, admiring the peaks and valleys below him.

"Well if it isn't Winnie the Pooh," Kitty chuckled, rolling over onto her stomach.

"Is this your day off?" Bill grunted, plopping himself down beside her.

"No, the clinic doesn't open till four on Mondays, and we close this evening at eight," Kitty said, putting on her sunglasses.

"How come your family travels all the way up here from Toledo?" Bill inquired, as he idly pitched a stone into the water.

"My Father came here after the war on a fishing trip and fell in love with the place. Two years later a cottage on the river came up for sale, and he bought it," Kitty said, before extracting a tube of suntan lotion from her beach bag and handing it to Bill.

Summer of '61

"Could you please rub some of this on the back of my legs."

"Glad to be of service there little missy," Billy mimicked, hoping that he sounded a little bit like the Duke.

He carefully applied the oily liquid to her silky smooth skin, and was mortified when he felt a large bulge forming inside his swimming trunks. To hide his embarrassment, he assumed the prone position, immediately after finishing his task, and waited for things to subside.

"How old are you Billy?" Kitty asked, noticing his flushed look.

"I'm seventeen, but I'll be eighteen in August," Bill rasped, trying to ignore his raging boner.

"How old do you think I am?" Kitty smiled, guessing at the reason for his discomfort.

"Oh, about sixteen," Bill squeaked, grateful for the shrinkage occurring south of his belly button.

"Boy, you sure have a smooth line for a kid," Kitty laughed.

A few minutes later he had managed to get things under control and said, "It's been nice talking to you Kitty, but I think I'll swim out to raft, then dry out in the sun."

"So long Teddy," she said, as he splashed his way into the water.

Well at least that's better than Poohie!

When Bill returned to the restaurant, he picked up the car keys from Harry and drove to the Harb. As he got out of the Chevy, he noticed Virginia standing down by the dock, and rapidly descended the cement steps to say hello.

"Hi Virg! What's the big deal," Bill asked, still intrigued.

"I was talking to a girlfriend of mine, and she put me on to a little plan that could get us a free dinner at a fancy dining room," Virginia burbled excitedly.

"You mean us, as in you and me Virg?" Bill said, taken aback.

"That's right Sherlock, you got it right the first time," she chuckled.

"Well please explain away," he said bemused.

"My friend Elaine is a life guard at Toledo house, I think you might have met her," Virginia said, grinning broadly.

"Well I guess you've got most of the details, so yeah I've met Elaine."

"That must have been quiet a night Billy," Virginia teased.

"Since then just the thought of lemon gin makes my stomach queazy," Bill groaned, recalling his conversation with Earl.

"You didn't fall for that panty remover myth, did you?" Virginia chortled, giving him a confidential wink.

"Okay Virg, let's skip the history lesson, just spill the beans eh?"

"All right Billy, here goes. One of Elaine's best buddies at the lodge works in housekeeping, and she knows for a fact that a very rich couple from Toronto have gone to stay overnight with friends in Huntsville," Virginia said, pausing to get the details straight. "The scheme is simple, we arrive at the dining room and say that we're the son and daughter of Mr. and Mrs. Stanley who are guests staying in cabin seven. If we don't get a hassle, then we dig into the best buffet dinner in the Muskokas. Since the Stanleys are there on a package deal, the meal is already paid for."

"Sounds like a swell idea to me," Bill agreed, thinking with his stomach and bypassing his brain.

In the early hours of an elongated evening, just as the heat of the day began to abate, they left the Chevy in the guest parking lot, and easily found the elegant dining room of the Toledo House. Elaine had instructed Virginia to sit at table twenty-five. The table was resplendent with a white linen cloth, real silverware, crystal wine glasses, fresh cut roses, and a scented candle.

"Here comes the waiter," Billy gulped, when they were safely seated. "R-Remember that you're Carol Stanley and I'm your brother Ron."

"I'm sorry, you must be at the wrong table, this one is reserved for Mr. and Mrs. Stanley," the waiter sniffed, full of puffed up importance.

"They're our parents Bill said confidently, as his stage fright evaporated. "We just got here from the city , but when we checked at their cabin they weren't there. One of the cleaning staff said they were away for the night, but would be back tomorrow. We were told to come here, and sit at this table in order to get something to eat."

"No problem sir, and when you're ready, please help yourself to the buffet," the waiter said, dropping his superior attitude. "Would you care for anything from the bar?"

"Can we charge it to cabin seven?" Bill asked, seeing the possibilities.

"But of course sir," the waiter said, his tone now obsequious.

"I'll have a martini," Bill smiled, beginning to enjoy his role.

Summer of '61

He didn't know exactly what a martini was, but they drank an awful lot of them in the movies, so what the heck.

"I'll have one too," Virginia piped up, not to be out done.

When their drinks were finished, they visited the overflowing buffet table, and helped themselves to: Caesar salad, fresh rolls, clam chowder soup, shrimp cocktail, snow crab legs, lobster tails, prime rib of beef, roast pork, honey glazed ham, fresh garden vegetables and finally black forest cake for desert.

"Boy this sure beats the shit out of hot hamburg sandwiches," Virginia sighed loudly, smacking her lips.

"Perhaps a cognac to go with your coffee," the waiter offered, returning to their table just as they started desert.

"No thanks," Billy replied, thinking about the drive back, and his promise to take good care of the Bel Air.

As soon as the waiter left a busboy appeared on the scene, and surprised Bill by handing him a note. It was from Elaine telling them to leave immediately, because the Stanley's had arrived back unexpectedly.

"Let's make tracks," Bill whispered, as he handed Virginia the note. The frightened teenagers timidly pushed back from the table, and a little shaky kneed, got to their feet.

Even though the waiter was eyeing them suspiciously, they continued to walk towards the dining room entrance. A couple old enough to be their parents just about bumped into them at the doorway.

"Excuse me, are you Mr. and Mrs. Stanley?" Bill sputtered, figuring that the waiter was still giving them the eagle eye.

"Yes we are," Mr. Stanley replied, wondering who this young man might be.

"I-I met you once in Toronto about a year ago sir," Bill said, as he enthusiastically pumped Mr. Stanley's hand and smiled warmly at Mrs. Stanley. "It's really nice to see you again."

"I'm Carol Jones and Ron's my boyfriend," Virginia said, straight-faced.

"Well it's been great running into you Mr. Stanley, and wonderful to meet you Mrs. Stanley," Bill said, trying to stay calm. "I hope you have a good holiday."

They walked nonchalantly to the front door of the lodge, then sprinted across the parking lot to Harry's car.

"Such a lovely young couple," Mrs. Stanley burbled, as she and her husband walked towards table twenty-five.

"I don't remember seeing Ron in the city, but I meet so many people in a year that it's hard to remember them all," Mr. Stanley shrugged, as they sat down.

"I'm glad you were able to talk to your son and daughter on the way into the dining room," the waiter simpered, testing the waters.

"That young man was just an acquaintance from Toronto, and the young lady was his girlfriend," Mrs. Stanley smiled, as she carefully placed a cloth napkin over her lap.

The waiter realizing his mistake, decided that discretion rather than valour should carry the day.

"Boy that was a close call Virg," Bill whistled softly, once they had reached the highway.

"You can sure think on your feet," Virginia said admiringly. "That was quite a line about Toronto and all."

"Well Virg, I saw that waiter looking at us, and I thought he might be catching on," Bill puffed, still full of nervous energy. "I figured that the folks at the door were probably the Stanley's, so I improvised."

"You should join the Port Town Players Billy, because you're quite an actor," Virginia said, starting to giggle. "Even if it was a play, I kind of enjoyed being your sister and girlfriend all in the same evening."

They both lost it at the same time, and within seconds, tears of hysterical laughter were flowing down their cheeks.

It was only nine-thirty when they arrived in Port Carter. Still feeling pumped from the Toledo House adventure, Bill and Virginia decided to go for a stroll along the sidewalk that ran parallel to the river. This was a popular promenade on a warm summers evening, and they passed several other couples doing the same thing. There was a lookout at the end of the walkway, and they stopped there to sit on a park bench.

"You were real slick back at the lodge," Virginia grinned, a sudden tidal wave flooding her brain. "Hey, I'm going to call you Slick Carlsen from now on."

Bill figured that was a lot better than some of the names that Virgin for short had used in the past.

Summer of '61

"Come on Slick, time to head for the barn," she murmured, in a dry, drowsy voice. He escorted her to the girl's quarters at the Harb, then said good night.

It was ten to eleven when Bill entered the kitchen to give Harry his keys.

"Hi Harry, was it a busy night?" Bill asked, fighting a case of the big fatigues.

"No, kind of slow but I'm ready for a good nights sleep," Harry stretched, while suppressing a major league yawn. "My buddy Al has got us an eight o'clock tee off at the Bracebridge club, so if you could work the morning shift, I'd owe you another big one."

"No sweat Harry, glad to help out, but right now my ass is really dragging. We'll see ya later constipator," Bill joked, as he headed up to his bed of rest.

The next day was overcast and it looked like it could rain. Bill was busier than a killer whale at a penguin party for most of the morning, but at ten-thirty the restaurant emptied as if Typhoid Mary had walked right in and sat right down. Fifteen minutes later he was able to come out to the counter for a glass of milk and a doughnut. Bonnie Baker was working hard to clear the tables when Doc Livingstone strolled in.

"What's up Doc?" Bill said, in his best Bugs Bunny voice.

The Doc gave a chuckle type snort before saying, "Wayne and I are thinking of going fishing at four this afternoon. If you'd like to come along, then meet us at Mitchell's."

"Holy holly, I'd love that!" Bill grinned, having an instant vision of a trophy bass tugging at the end of his line.

"If you could stick a six pack in your kit bag, then we'd be all set," the Doc said, adding two lumps to the coffee that Bonnie had placed in front of him.

"Sure thing Doc, and it's on the house," Bill said, honored to be included.

"Hey that's great, I should start calling you Billy the Kid," the Doc smiled, drifting along with the tumbling tumbleweeds.

Oh boy Bill thought, four years of High School with no nicknames, and I've already got two or three this summer.

"Well Doc we could really get into this fantasy, I'll be Wyatt Earp, and you could pretend to be Buffalo Bill."

"You know I used to like westerns when I was a kid," the Doc said, sliding into a Bob Steele Saturday afternoon serial at the Roxy.

"Yeah me too," Slick, Teddy, Billy the Kid Carlsen smiled whimsically.

"Do you remember Hopalong Cassidy and his horse Topper, Roy Rogers and his horse trigger, and the Cisco Kid and his horse Diablo? the Doc asked, time tripping back to his childhood, Red Ryder, the pony man and cap guns.

"Sure do, and my dad used to tell me about Tom Mix and his horse Tony," Bill added, filling in the generation gap.

"Where are those horse and cowboy heros today?" the Doc cried mournfully.

"I like to watch "Gunsmoke" on TV," Bill said, visualizing the opening showdown scene where Matt Dillon out draws the bad guy.

"Now that's the problem; Adult Westerns with phonies like James Arness and Dennis Weaver," the Doc exclaimed, helplessly immersed in his dreamworld. "I ask you, where can the children play?"

"Hey Doc lighten up it's still before lunch," Bill chortled.

"Well partner, there are still bottles of homogenized to be delivered to that pretty little school marm. Happy trails to you Billy the Kid, until we meet again," the Doc crooned, as he got up to leave.

"See you this aft," Bill grinned, giving the milkman a mock salute.

The Doc swaggered out the door, unhitched his milk truck, then road off into the sunset. A pretty good trick considering that it was quarter-past-eleven in the morning.

11

Bill arrived at the Marina just before the appointed hour, and experienced a rush of anticipation when Wayne's Edsel pulled into Mitchell's parking lot at four. The Doc carried three fishing rods and a tackle box, while Wayne followed with a large packsack. Bill had six bottles of beer in a paper shopping bag, and handed these to the Doc. When all their gear was safely stowed aboard, they took off up river.

"Looks like it could rain," Bill said, nervously eyeing the thunder clouds overhead.

"Yeah, but we've got a canopy for the cockpit," Wayne yelled, in order to be heard over the noise of the engine.

"Aren't you worried about the storm?" Bill persisted.

"Naw, the fish always bite better just before the thunder boomers hit," Wayne pontificated, giving Bill a taste of local folklore.

The Doc had reached a stretch of the Chippewa that was free of cottages for at least a mile. He slowed the boat down, then cut the motor at the edge of a large weed bed. Distant rolls of thunder could be heard, and the periodic flash of far off lightning gave ample evidence of the approaching storm.

"Should be just about perfect in ten minutes," the Doc predicted, as he watched the untamed sky.

"Yep. I'd better get things setup," Wayne grunted, as he reached into his packsack.

"Did you bring any worms?" Billy asked, trying to figure which of the fishing poles he would be using.

"Nope, just this," Wayne said, as he pulled a stick of dynamite and a two foot board from his pack.

"What the hell is that?" Bill asked, his eyes as wide as dinner plates.

"We call it a CIL plug," Wayne snorted, as he tied the dynamite to the board with a short piece of rope. Canadian Industries Limited was the largest manufacturer of explosives in the Province.

"Are we ready Wayne?" the Doc asked reaching into his pocket for a Zippo lighter.

"Fire away Doc," Wayne bellowed, as he handed over the board.

The Doc lit the fuse and carefully placed the short plank onto a small patch of lily pads.

Wayne had the motor idling waiting for the signal. He opened up the throttle when the Doc pumped his arm, then roared down river. He cut the engine thirty seconds later and all was silent for a moment. Suddenly there was deafening blast followed by the eruption of a gigantic geyser of water. If you were a cottager several miles away, it would have sounded like a loud clap of thunder. The Doc took over the controls, and returned quickly to the site of the explosion.

"Get out the boat paddles," the Doc instructed. "I'll net em, if you get me close enough.

"Jeepers creepers, there must be a dozen bass floating around in there," Billy marvelled, pointing in the direction of a gaping hole in the weed bed,

"See, I told you, they always bite best before a storm," Wayne snickered, as he began to paddle.

They picked up eighteen good sized bass, and started back to Port Carter just as the rain let drive. On the return trip, Wayne carefully attached each fish to a hook firmly secured to the links of a brand new chrome plated stringer.

After the boat was safely tied up at Mitchell's, they put the fish and all their equipment into the trunk of Wayne's Edsel. Wayne shifted the big Ford into gear, then drove directly to the Doc's place. They took the fish into the garage, and laid them out on a wooden work bench. The Doc and Wayne proceeded to filet the bass while Bill threw the guts and skins into a garbage can. When all the fish were done, and the filets placed into a plastic bag, the Doc led them into the house to clean up.

"Where's your mother?" Wayne asked, as he reached into the shopping bag to get three beers.

"She's in Bracebridge visiting Aunt Bertha," the Doc replied, grabbing an ale.

Wayne snapped a cap before saying, "We'll go over to the home real soon eh?"

"What in hell are you guys talking about?" Bill asked, totally bewildered.

"Oh, we're taking these filets over to Port Manor," the Doc said casually.

Summer of '61

"Yeah, that's the old folks home, and once a summer they have a fish fry," Wayne beamed, as he wiped foam from his upper lip.

"And you guys supply the bass," Billy groaned, filling in the blanks. "Aren't you afraid that someone might catch you at this dynamite poaching scheme?"

"Not to worry Billy, a friend of mine's the game warden, and his grandmother's in the home," the Doc said, reaching down to pat a black cat that had just entered the kitchen.

"What's the cats name?" Bill asked, smiling inwardly at the way Wayne and the Doc operated.

"I know it's not very original, but we call him Panther," the Doc grinned.

"Cat's are okay but I like dogs better," Bill sighed, as he pictured Brownie the families cocker spaniel.

"Yeah, I like dogs too," the Doc said wistfully. "But my mom won't keep one, because they're too hard on a house."

"What's your favorite animal Wayne?" Bill asked, seeing the far away look in Wayne's eyes.

"Roast chicken!" Wayne belched, as he licked his lips, before taking a strong pull on the long necked green bottle.

It was nine-thirty when Bill left the Doc's place, and walked slowly up Bailer street. The tree frogs were in fine voice, and the air was still hot and humid. He was in a reflective mood, and the thought crossed his mind that six months from now if you were in the same spot , you'd be up to his arse in snow and brass monkeys. Ontario sure was a Province of contrasts.

He stopped by the kitchen to see how Harry was doing, and to find out if there were any changes in the schedule. It was just as well that he did, because Harry had been invited to a money game at the Toledo House golf course.

"These rich Americans I met at the Bracebridge club want me to join their foursome tomorrow afternoon," Harry said, dollars signs rolling around behind his eyeballs." If you could work three to eleven for me Billy, I'd be able to make it."

"No problem Harry. What are you shooting for?" Bill asked, covering a yawn.

"Ten bucks a hole," Harry boasted, already counting his cash.

"Good luck buddy," Bill said, as he left the kitchen.

He climbed the stairs to the penthouse, and was surprised to see Danny sitting at the kitchen table.

"How are they hangin' Billy?" Danny asked, as he lit a Players Navy Cut.

"Things are just tickety-boo, or is it bipity-bopity-boo," Bill coughed, getting a snoot full of the acrid tobacco smoke.

"Gee that reminds me of the *Cinderella* movie that I saw when I was in grade one," Danny said, trying to blow a smoke ring. "You know in that whole movie I liked Gus the mouse the best."

"I was seven when my grandma Carlsen took me to see *The Wizard of Oz* at the Kingsway theatre in Vancouver, and I was scared shitless," Bill grimaced, remembering the green faced Wicked Witch of the North.

"That movie got to me too when I was a kid," Danny said, a twinkle of good humor appearing in his eyes." You know, I watched The *Blob* a couple of years ago, and it didn't scare me at all. I must be getting tougher, eh Slick?"

The nickname that Virginia had pinned on Bill was now very popular with the staff at both restaurants. He didn't mind it all that much, because Slick to his way of thinking, conjured up the image of a suave gambler type like Bret Maverick or Bat Masterson. The teenage ego is very adaptable.

Bill knew that Danny had been dating Bonnie Baker. This was all well and good, but Dick Mitchell was also going out with her royal highness. Two fish on the string suited the blonde bombshell just fine. She was a true prima donna, and enjoyed the attention immensely. Trouble however, was brewing between the two rival big horny sheep.

"Tell me Danderoo, are you and Bonnie going to Dunn's on Friday night?" Bill asked, interested in finding out how the soap opera was unfolding.

"Nope, that asshole Dick Mitchell got to her first. It must be nice to be rich and be the son of a big marina operator," Danny glowered.

"Well maybe she'll go with you the next time," Bill smiled, trying to be encouraging. "I hear that the Tommy Dorsey Band will be there the last week in July."

Summer of '61

"I think the big bands are a pain in the rear end," Danny grimaced, looking like he'd just swallowed a spoonful of laundry detergent. "I'd rather listen to rock 'n' roll any day, but going to Dunn's seems to be such a big deal, so I guess I'm stuck."

"Hey don't knock the Dorseys, remember that Elvis made his debut on their TV show," Bill reminisced, seeing a snowy image of the King on the families old ten inch Admiral. "When Elvis first came on, me and my sister Brenda thought he was great, but I can still hear my dad saying; he's nothing but a hood."

"Yeah, Elvis is the best," Danny said, rubbing his eyes. "Jeez I'm whacked, I guess it's time to hit the sack."

"Me too," Bill whispered, in a soft sleepy voice.

Slick and the Danderoo climbed into their bunks, and within minutes were experiencing the sleep of the just. Billy's mildly erotic dreams that night would pale in comparison to the real thing, that was just around the corner.

12
*

The next morning Bill slowly got his act together, then wandered down to the kitchen to grab some breakfast . Trying to wipe the sleepy grubs from his eyes, he said hello to Harry and Bonnie, then made himself an order of pancakes and bacon. He was half-awake, and sitting at the counter when Sandra walked into the Hilltop.
 "How were things at the cottage? Bill asked, instantly returning to the land of the living.
 "We did some painting and gave the place a good cleaning, but we had lots of extra time to swim and go canoeing," Sandra bubbled, sounding like she was pleased to see him. " What have you been up to Billy?"
 "Mostly trying to make a living, but I did get out for a boat ride with the Doc yesterday afternoon," Bill grinned innocently, deciding that the Toledo House caper, and innovative fishing techniques were secrets to be kept.
 "I've got my mother's car, and I was wondering if you'd like to go for a drive and a picnic?" Sandra asked, before placing her hand on Bill's knee.
 "Hey that would be great. I-I don't have to work till three," Bill stammered, aroused by the physical contact.
 He quickly finished his meal, then followed Sandra outside. Her mother's car, a red Volkswagen Beetle was parked in front of the café. "You drive," Sandra said, as she tossed him the keys.
 "Fantastic!" Bill shouted, his face lighting up like a Coleman lantern. "I've never been behind the wheel of a bug before."
 Following Sandra's instructions, Bill drove the bright red puddle jumper along a twisting secondary highway. Ten miles from Port Carter she told him to make a right turn on to a gravel road.
 "Where are we going?" Bill asked, as they chattered over a washboard surface.
 "My dad and three other men are partners in a hunt camp that they only use in the fall, so I thought it might be fun to go there for our lunch," Sandra said, giving him an enticing smile.
 Five minutes later they came to a locked gate. A sign above the gate read: Danger Logging Equipment: Keep Out.
 "Don't worry Billy, they're not logging right now, and I've got a key," Sandra smiled, getting out of the car to unlock the gate.

Summer of '61

"As a matter of fact one of the partners in the camp owns the lumber company."

Three miles of dodging cut stumps and boulders brought them to a small pristine lake. They then followed a well marked trail that led to a log cabin, located on a rocky point. Bill carried the hefty, red, all metal Coke cooler that contained their lunch. The cabin was backed by several tall red pines, and two stately white oaks. It was a scene right out of a picture postcard.

Bill and Sandra climbed the front steps, then walked across the narrow screened-in porch to the cabin door. She extracted a brass key from her tight fitting jeans , and used it to free the padlock that secured the building. The door noisily creaked open as they entered the sturdy pine log structure.

"Boy this place's great!" Bill whooped, admiring the view of the lake from the kitchen window. "Do your mom and dad come here often?"

"No, it's mostly used by my father and his three partners," Sandra said, standing close enough to Bill that their hips were touching. "In the fall they hunt deer and moose."

"Do your parents mind us being here today?" Billy asked, placing his arm around her.

"Well actually, I didn't tell them," Sandra whispered confidentially.

This made Bill a little nervous, but he figured the chances of Mr. King charging up the trail were pretty slim. They returned to the porch, and removed a tarp from an old couch that was up against a rough hewn wall. A beaver swam silently by the front of the cabin. It must have sensed them, because it slapped it's tail on the surface of the water, and with a loud whap disappeared from sight. It was suddenly very quiet and peaceful. The only sound was the soft hiss of the wind, as it passed through the tops of the old growth pines. They sat close together on the couch enjoying the tranquility of the beautiful lake.

"Are you hungry?" Sandra asked, as she ran her fingers through his black curly hair.

"Yeah, the pancakes and bacon I had for breakfast didn't stick, so I could eat anytime," he said, his stomach doing a deep rumble at the mention of food.

That Russian shrink Pavlov could have trained me real easy, Bill thought.

He got the cooler from inside the cabin, and placed it before them. Sandra lifted up the heavy, tight fitting lid, then handed him a ham sandwich. She took out a plastic pitcher filled with lime Freshie, and poured a glass for Bill and one for herself. There were also muffins and bananas for desert. Boy, it doesn't get any better than this Billy thought. *It was about to get much better!*

After they had eaten, Bill put things back into the cooler, and placed it by the screen door. When he returned to the couch Sandra snuggled in next to him, and rested her head on his shoulder. He placed his arm around her, and they sat like that for several minutes.

"You know the other night when I told you I didn't want to go all the way?" Sandra murmured, breaking the silence.

"Yeah," Billy gulped, thinking this might be his lucky day.

"Well, I still want to save it for my husband, but I was reading this marriage manual that I found in my parents bedside table," Sandra soothed, as she slowly stroked his upper thigh.

"Uh, huh," Bill gasped.

"There was a chapter on oral sex, and I thought that maybe you and I could do a little experimenting," Sandra purred seductively.

He was sure glad when she explained things, because he wasn't sure at first what she meant by oral sex. It wasn't just talking about it, which was his first assumption. Sandra described in detail what she wanted him to do to her.

Bill thought what the heck. As his uncle Olie would say, "If you're ever at Chinese buffet you should try to eat a little bit of each dish."

Sandra had a monumental seismic event that would likely be recorded as a number seven on the Richter Scale. By the time she finished, Bill was as excited as a two peckered goat.

"Now it's your turn," Sandra cooed, as she pulled off Bill's jeans followed by his jockey shorts.

Bill could not believe the sensations he was experiencing. He didn't say anything to Sandra while she was busy giving him pleasure, because he had always been taught, that it's impolite for anyone to talk to you when their mouth is full.

They locked up the cabin and walked slowly down the trail to where the Beetle was parked. Bill had to drive very carefully over the rough roads, and it took them fifty minutes to reach the Port.

Summer of '61

He gave Sandra a long, passionate, farewell kiss just before he got out of the car.

"Good-bye Billy," Sandra whispered innocently. "You have the nicest tongue I've ever come across."

"Holy doodle, that's the best compliment a guy could ever get," Bill blushed, feeling excited and embarrassed all at the same time. "I-I'll see you tomorrow."

He was just in time for work.

13
*

"I knew you'd be here," Harry grinned, as Bill entered the kitchen.
"Yeah I kind of lost track," he replied apologetically.
"Bonnie's already gone down the hill, but Virginia should be here anytime now," Harry said, as he placed his grease spattered apron on a coat hook. "I'm off to the Toledo links to skin a few rich Yanks. Have a great day off Billy!"
"Thanks Harry and good luck," Bill smiled, as he stirred the gum-like brown gravy heating in a large tin can on the back of the grill. Virginia arrived at the café ten minutes late.
"Sorry to be a bit tardy Slick," Virginia puffed, as she picked up a yellow order pad. "Danny and Dick Mitchell were having a set-to outside the Harb, but I was able to persuade the Danderoo to get the hell out of there and return to work."
"Yeah he's pissed off because tricky Dick is taking Bonnie to Dunn's tomorrow night," Billy sighed, shaking his head.
"Well I hope that's the end of it," Virginia said dubiously.
Danny wandered into the restaurant at six-thirty, and sat at the counter. Bill was busy in the kitchen with supper orders, but was able to fit in Danny's request for a hot pork sandwich. At seven o'clock, Bill emerged from the grease pit hoping to talk to the Danderoo, but he was nowhere in sight. He went to the front window of the dinning room, and looked outside. His first reaction to the frightening tableau spread out before was, "Holy shit!"
Dick Mitchell was backed up against the rear door of his Olds 88 convertible, and Danny was coming at him, brandishing a claw hammer. Bill was out the door in a heart beat. Before exploding into the cool evening air he had noticed a man with a cast on his leg, sitting on his front porch one door down from where Dick's car was parked. The man was now on a pair of crutches madly hopping along to get himself between the two combatants. He got there just in time to deflect a blow from Danny's hammer with one of his walking-sticks. Bill managed to place himself between Danny and the man. He could see the uncontrolled madness in his friends eyes. He was really scared because he didn't know what the Danderoo would do next. Bill had to act quickly.
"What's the best fucking engine in the whole world?" Bill demanded, shouting out the words.

Summer of '61

Danny moved menacingly towards him with the hammer raised, then a look of recognition appeared on his face. "The Ford Flathead-eight," Danny said, without even thinking. Bill knew he had broken the spell.

"Danny this guy isn't worth going to jail for," Bill reasoned, as he carefully reached out and took hold of the hammer. "Now if you're my friend, I want you to back off slowly, go into the Hilltop, and we'll have a cup of coffee together."

Danny hesitated for a moment, then turned around and made his way into the restaurant.

"I wouldn't say anything if I were you," Bill growled at a smirking Dick Mitchell, who was about to go motor-mouth.

"If you set him off again , I sure as hell won't be able to stop him."

Without uttering a word, Dick got into his Old's and drove away.

Bill entered the café, went behind the counter, picked up the coffee pot and poured out two cups. He added cream and sugar, then sat down beside the Danderoo. Danny's hands were shaking so badly he could hardly hold the cup.

"Hey, you know what my grandpa Carlsen used to do when the coffee was too hot?" Bill asked, trying to ease the tension. "He'd pour it into a saucer, put in a little cream, then blow over it before he drank it."

"You know Slick, my old man does that too," Danny grinned, starting to calm down.

They both poured coffee into their saucers, blew to their hearts content, and started to laugh. They laughed so hard that they nearly fell off their stools.

Danny left the restaurant at eight-thirty. He said that he was going out to Judd House to visit a friend who worked there as a waiter. Bill had his fingers crossed that Danny wouldn't run into Dick Mitchell again in the next twenty-four hours.

Billy was dead tired at the end of his shift and went straight to bed, but what the heck, tomorrow was his day off. He was having a very interesting dream involving Sandra changing her mind about being a wedding virgin, and things were getting to the critical stage when someone in the dream started to tap him on the shoulder. He woke with a start to see Harry bending over him.

"Slick, I've got a big one to ask you," Harry whispered, sounding a little desperate.

"This had better be good Harry, I was having the most incredible dream," Bill yawned, his eyes still puffy with sleep.

"It's real important Billy, or I wouldn't be here this early."

"What time is it anyway?"

"About six."

"So what's the big deal Harry?"

"Well, after I got home from the golf game at Toledo House, I got a call from the Pro at the Bracebridge course," Harry paused, trying to control his excitement. "Their representative to the Ontario Amateur Tournament broke his arm, and they want me to fill in for him."

"Gee that's great," Bill grunted, knowing what was coming next. "I guess you want me to work for you this morning huh?"

"Yeah if you could, I'd be really beholden to you," Harry said, pleading his case. "I'll cover for you real soon, so you can have the whole day and the car."

"Okay buddy, and good luck," Bill croaked, still half-asleep.

Harry mumbled a quick thanks, then sprinted for his Chevy.

Bill by now was bright-eyed and bushy-tailed, so he decided to wash up, have a quick shave, then go down to the kitchen to get ready for the breakfast onslaught.

"Slick what are you doing here?" Jennifer asked, when she arrived for work.

"Filling in for Slamin Sammy , " Bill said, as he absentmindedly turned over a strip of bacon with his cooking tongs.

At ten o'clock when things had settled down, Jen came into the kitchen, and sat on a chair by the door. This gave her a full view of the dining room.

"What's your boyfriend taking at Western?" Bill asked, remembering that the fetching Miss Rossini was pinned to some BMOC from London.

"He's in premed's and hopes to be a doctor someday, but you need super high marks to get into the medical faculty there," Jennifer sighed, picturing herself as a Mrs. MD.

"Tell me about it," Bill grumbled, thinking about Miss Marble. "I'll be lucky if ever I get out of high school."

Summer of '61

"What happened to Harry?" Paul inquired, as he reached for a clean apron.

Bill filled him in, chatted for a few minutes, then went up to the penthouse to crash. When he woke up, he noticed Joey sitting at the table reading a book.

"Hey Joey, what's happening?" Bill stretched, trying to chase away the hazy mists of slumber that stuck like cotton candy to his still drooping eyelids.

"Just reading a book," Joey said, intent on finishing the page in front of him.

"Yeah I can see that Joey-boo," Billy yawned. "The question I'm trying to get my half-sleepy head around is; what fucking book?"

"It's by Ernest Hemingway," Joey grinned.

"Oh I see, this is "The Sixty-four-Thousand Dollar Question", and you're Hal March," Bill said, recalling a shadowy image of the isolation booth.

"No, I'll keep it simple, I'm reading; *For Whom The Bell Tolls*."

"Hey I saw the movie, and Gary Cooper was great."

"Did you know that Hemingway died earlier this month?" Joey asked.

"No foolin', I don't read the papers very often, so this is news to me. How did he manage to kick the bucket?"

"According to the account I read in the *Toronto Telegram*, he accidently shot himself while cleaning a shotgun. The article went on to say that accidental was in doubt, and maybe it was suicide."

"I guess it doesn't matter a whole hell of a lot; the result is still the same," Billy shuddered, as he pictured a twelve gauge blowing someone's grey matter apart.. "We read Hemingway's, *The Old Man And The Sea* last year, but the teacher wouldn't let us enjoy the story, because we had to search for the hidden meaning and all."

"I know what you mean Slick. I really wonder if all that crap they dig up, was ever intended by the author," Joey snorted contemptuously.

"Spot-on Joey-boo," Bill sympathized, as he dusted off his internal library. "I had to read, *A Farewell To Arms* for a book report , and I really liked it. I'm sure glad we didn't have to study that one to death."

"Did you ever read *The Sun Also Rises?*" Joey asked, still in a bookish mood.

"No, but I saw that flick too," Bill nodded, drifting towards the silver screen. "Boy was Ava Gardner ever beautiful, and Tyrone Power was okay for a guy who got his dick shot off."

"If it wasn't for the movies your education would be sorely lacking," Joey chortled loudly.

The two literary pundits decided that they were starving, and headed for the kitchen. Bill offered to take over as chief cook while he made supper for himself and Joey. Paul readily agreed, because he needed to go down the hill, and attend to a business matter.

"Where did Paul get to?" Donna Rogers asked, when she entered the kitchen.

"He went down to the Harb for a minute," Bill said. "How are things with you?"

"Just fine Slick. I'm going to Dunn's Friday night with Danny," she glowed warmly, like a light in the forest.

"Hey that's fantastic," Bill grinned. "Has he gotten over that thing with Dick Mitchell?"

"Yes he has. We had a long talk last night, and Danny said that he was glad you helped to break up the fight."

"Yeah, he'd sure freaked out, and I was really afraid that he might kill young Richard," Bill gritted his teeth, recalling how tense things had been.

"Well he's on the beam now, and I'm looking forward to our date," Donna smiled. "Virginia and Bob are going along with us. Isn't that too cool?"

"That's swell, and may you all live happily ever after," Bill moaned, suddenly feeling left out.

The universe expanded, the earth wobbled, and Billy's private pity party would soon be erased by a memorable day with Doc Livingstone.

14
*

It was seven-thirty. Bill and Joey were sitting at the counter finishing their cheeseburgers when Sandra entered the restaurant. She had been to Gravenhurst with her mother, on an all day shopping trip.

"Hi Sandi," Bill grinned, tickled three shades of purple to see the stunning Miss King. "Would you like to join us for some blueberry pie? It's on the house!"

"There are some definite advantages of knowing a famous chef," Sandra said, transmitting a dazzling smile. "I'd love to, but a girl has to watch her figure."

"I'm heading down to the river to get some fresh air, so I'll see you two lovebirds later," Joey said, suddenly feeling like a fifth leg. "Don't do anything I wouldn't do Slick, and if you do, name it after me."

"He's a real card," Sandra giggled, as she watched Joey walk out the front door. "What's this Slick thing?"

"Oh just a nickname that someone branded me with," Bill said, giving her his best wings and harp look. "One of the waitresses thought I was real slick around the grill."

Before Sandra could ask anymore questions, Donna entered the dinning room carrying two orders of rainbow trout that Paul had prepared. She served the butter fried, lemon drenched fish, to a young couple who were enjoying a late evening supper.

Bill wandered over to the jukebox, put in a dime, made a selection, then returned to his seat.

As the soft strains of Henry Mancini's *"Moon River"* filled the café, the man pointed with his fork and said, "That's our favorite song, and tonight's our first anniversary."

"Did you see *Breakfast At Tiffany's*?" Sandra asked breathlessly.

"We sure did," the woman sighed.

"I'd like to be just like Audrey Hepburn," Sandra said, in a dreamy voice.

"You're twice as beautiful as that skinny babe," Bill protested, his heart missing a beat.

"You do know how to charm a lady sir," Sandra drawled.

The almost newlyweds, got up and started to dance. Bill rising to the occasion looked at Sandra and said, "Shall we?"

"But of course kind sir." Sandra smiled, imaging the grandeur of a Confederate ballroom.

The loving couples moved slowly to the gentle music, and spontaneously applauded at the end of the song.

"That was oh so romantic," the young woman said to her husband, as they sat down to finish their dinner.

When the anniversary sweethearts got up to leave, Bill and Sandra said good-bye, and wished them many years of future happiness. Several minutes later they left the restaurant and walked at a turtles pace towards the King's fine home. They stood on the front porch talking softly and slowly in order to prolong the evening.

"Do you want to go to the theatre Friday night?" Bill asked, getting ready to leave. "*The Death of a Salesman* is playing , and I know that Ken can get us a pair of tickets."

"I'd love to but we're going to be at the cottage this weekend," Sandra said, a sincere note of regret in her voice. "My grandparents, my cousins, my aunts and uncles will all be there. It's a King family reunion, and I can't weasel out of it."

"Yeah I understand," Bill said, trying hard to sound upbeat. Before leaving he kissed Sandra good night, then walked head-down back to the restaurant.

At eight-thirty the next morning, Billy entered the kitchen and saw Harry happily flipping flapjacks.

"What happened at the tournament?" Bill asked, still not quite awake.

"You won't believe this but I had the best game of my life and finished second. I may have a look in for another match in August ," Harry crowed.

"Hey way to go. This Jack Nicklaus guy you talked about had better watch out eh?"

Bill was mopping up the last of his fried egg yokes with a piece of hot buttered toast when Ken McClean walked in.

"How are things in the artsy fartsy world?" Bill asked, talking with his mouth full.

"A hell of a lot better than they are in the grease pit you work in," Ken countered cheerfully. "I hear you've got a brand new snuggy."

Snuggy was the current buzz word from the stage crowd for girlfriend.

Summer of '61

"Naw, Sandra and I are good buddies, strictly platonic."

"Don't quit your day job Billy-boo, because you'd starve to death if you ever tried to become an actor."

"Well I'll tell you one thing Mc-boo, it sure is rifles over tomahawks ahead of setting up pins in a bowling alley."

"Did you ever work as a Pin Boy?" Ken asked, displaying a great deal of interest.

"Yep! When I was in grade eleven that was the only job I could get during the winter. I set up two evenings a week. Both were school nights, so my parents weren't overly impressed."

"Hey, I did the same thing in Barrie," Ken said, munching on a crisp piece of bacon that Bill had offered him. "The money was good, but you had to work your ass off to earn it."

"Yeah I know what you mean," Bill sighed, rubbing his back as if it were sore. "I made five bucks a night for five hours work, but I had to handle two alleys, and set up for thirty two bowlers over the evening. I hate to admit it, but short-order cooking is a breeze in comparison."

"Speaking of cooking," Ken said, as Virginia approached them. "Could I please have a bowl of sugar frosted flakes, and two slices of brown toast.

"Honestly Ken, Virginia exclaimed arms akimbo. "If you ordered anything different I swear to God, I'd be sure to check that water still flowed downhill." She then disappeared into the kitchen to work the pop-up.

"I'm really not that hungry, so you might as well finish these sausages," Bill said, when Ken's breakfast arrived.

Ken was living on a shoestring, and Bill tried to steer the odd free-be his way, without being too obvious.

"Thanks Billy, I'd sure hate to see good food go to waste," he grinned, before popping one of the sausages into his mouth.

After breakfast they walked across the street to the theatre. "Are you coming to see the play tonight?" Ken asked. "I can still get those tickets I promised."

"I'd love to, but Sandra is off to her parents cottage for the weekend so, I'll take a rain check on that offer."

"See you later," Ken waved, as he headed backstage.

"After awhile crocodile," Bill joked.

He decided to take a walk to the public beach, and was half way there when the Doc pulled up in his milk truck.

"You want to come along with me on the milk run this morning?"

"Sure thing Doc, lets get them bottles of skim out to that school marm," Bill smiled, starting into his Billy the Kid role.

The Doc had finished the in town deliveries, so they headed out to the various cottages that were part of his route. The morning seemed to evaporate like pure alcohol on a platter, and before Bill could get used to the idea of being an assistant milkman, the Doc announced that they were at the home of his final customer.

"Come on in with me Billy, I want you to meet a couple of real nice dollies," the Doc chuckled, looking like a kid about to get a birthday present.

The Doc picked up a metal milk rack with two quarts of homogenized nestled in the circular slots, then climbed up the front steps of the cottage. Bill was standing right next to him when he knocked on the screened-door. An eye-catching blonde who was almost wearing a bikini appeared behind the copper mesh.

"Hi Gloria. How's tricks?" the Doc asked, tipping his hat.

"Very funny Doc," the curvacious blonde pouted. "Who's your cute friend ?"

"This here's Billy, and be nice to him, he's a real good kid."

Just as Bill was about to say hello to Gloria another vision of virginal loveliness emerged from one of the bedrooms. He thought she looked a lot like Brigette Bardot.

"My God Debbie, you're a real babe," the Doc shouted, as he placed his arm around a real live Barbie doll.

"I'm pleased to meet the both of you," Bill said politely, shaking Gloria's hand and then Debbie's.

"Such nice manners," Gloria gushed, chewing noisily on a piece of spearmint gum.

"Yeah a regular Prince Charming," Debbie echoed, in a thick syrupy voice.

Gloria invited Bill to sit on the couch that faced the picture window. He noticed that the Doc and Debbie had disappeared into one of the bedrooms.

"Boy, you get a great view of the lake here," Bill exclaimed, trying not to stare at Gloria's bulging bikini top.

Summer of '61

"We sure do honey," Gloria said, as she sat down very close to him. *She's probably in her early thirties, and very well preserved for an older woman. Built like a brick shirthouse was another thought that river-danced across Billy's mind.*

"So you're a friend of the Doc's," Gloria cooed, moving even closer.

"Yeah, we've known each other for awhile," he said, slightly intoxicated by her musky perfume.

"Well kid, since you're the Doc's pal, I've got a special for you," she purred, placing her hand on his knee. "As you've likely guessed, or perhaps the Doc already told you, I'm a working girl."

"That's okay," Billy squeaked, trying to stay calm. "My mom works too; she's a clerk at the Municipal Offices in Georgetown."

Gloria did a bit of a double take, but persisted in her presentation. "I'll get to the point kid. If you want to do me, then how does ten bucks sound?"

Flash bulbs started to go off in his head. Thoughts came a mile a minute. Holy smokes, she's a lady of the evening or early afternoon, given it was almost twelve thirty. She's a street walker even though she's just sitting on this couch. She's Charlotte the Harlot the cow punchers whore.

"So what do you say Billy?"

Gloria was now snuggled up very close, stroking the inside of his thigh. Stalling for time he said the first thing that came into his steaming brain, "I'd really love to because you're so beautiful and all, but I've got a steady girlfriend, and I've taken a vow of chastity."

In the back corner of his mind he could hear an approving King Arthur applauding this unselfish act of purity and virtue.

"Oh that's so sweet. You really are a good kid," Gloria smiled.

Boy that was a close one. Bill thought, because in reality he was thinking of his grade twelve health class. He could picture the jumpy, sixteen millimeter, washy-colored film, and see in his minds eye, good old Joe Buggins who had been with a fallen woman. Poor old Joe was now wandering around skid row crazier than a hoot owl. This was followed by the image of a horrified Biff Brindle who had a sore developing in a most awkward spot. Biff would never be able to go to the senior prom.

When the Doc and Debbie emerged from the bedroom, they were surprised to see Bill and Gloria still siting on the couch.

"Guess we'd better make tracks back to the Port," the Doc yawned, sounding a little worn out.

"Yeah, I've got to be at work by three," Bill said, wanting to bolt for the door.

They said good-bye to the ladies, then began their drive back to town.

"So you and Gloria didn't hit it off eh?" the Doc opened, when they reached the highway.

"Oh we got along okay, but I just couldn't afford the ten smackeroo's" Bill replied, keeping the real reason a secret.

"I can see your point Kid, but if you're ever there again, I'll set it up so that it's gratis."

"Weren't you a little nervous about picking up a permanent reminder of what you and Debbie were doing back there?" Billy quizzed, still remembering crazy Joe Buggins.

"No way, Debbie has a drawer full of rubbers, and always makes me wear one. It's kind of like taking a bath with your socks on, but it sure beats the hell out of the old wrist rocket."

"How much do they charge you?" Bill asked, wondering if the Doc had been offered the saw buck special.

"Zilch! Billy the Kid. They get free milk for the summer and I get free honey," the Doc beamed, looking like a bear who had just discovered a thick blueberry patch.

Bill was dropped off at two-thirty, leaving him just enough time to clean up before the afternoon shift. When he entered the kitchen Harry was getting ready for a fast exit.

"I'm heading out to Toledo House to shoot a practice round, but I may be able to pick a money game with some of the guys I know out there," Harry said, his hand on the door knob.

"Have a good one Sammy, we'll see you tomorrow at three."

"Yeah, and be kind to your web-footed friends," Harry winked.

Jennifer Rossini was working with Bill that evening. It was a bit slack at first, then the Player's crowd followed by the hoards of starving theatre goers, kept them hopping all evening. Things finally settled down at ten-thirty. Beginning to unwind, Billy went out to the dinning area, dropped a coin in the jukebox and selected "The Peppermint Twist". Jen came out of the washroom and started to clap her hands. She then beckoned to him, to get up and dance.

Summer of '61

The restaurant was completely deserted, so he got to his feet. Tired as they were from the madhouse night , Bill and Jen twisted away as if they'd reached the finals of a big dance contest.

When the music faded Jennifer burbled, "I'll bet that Bonnie and Donna aren't having as much fun listening to Tommy Dorsey as we are right now."

"Yeah, but I hope that Danny and Dick didn't get into it again," Bill shook his head slowly, recalling the wildness in Danny's eyes.

"Not to worry, Virginia was here earlier this evening, and she told me, that when Dick came to pick up Bonnie everything was cool. Apparently Danny arrived shortly after Dick got there, he walked over to Rapid Richard's car, they shook hands and that's all there was to it."

"Wow!" Billy marvelled. "I'm going outside right now to see if any bright stars are shinning in the east."

They closed up the Hilltop at eleven, and Bill walked Jen down to the Harb. Before going up the stairs, she gave him a quick brush on the lips and whispered, "Sweet dreams Slick."

"And you as well, fair Lady Jennifer," he said, before mounting his imaginary steed and riding off to Camelot.

15

The next morning Bill was standing by the grill turning an egg once over lightly, and beginning to think that things were getting a little boring, when his best friend Dave Graham walked into the kitchen. He knew that Dave was working at Bigwin Inn for the summer, but never thought he'd lay eyes on him again till the fall. The two friends were so happy to see each other that they wound up in a victory-like bear hug.

"Boy, what a surprise Tex. You look great!" Bill shouted, releasing Dave from the friendly wrestling hold.

Dave had picked up the nickname Tex, because his favorite football player was the Ottawa Roughriders quarterback Tex Gray.

"I scored a day off, and decided to hitch down here, but I've got to be at work Sunday midnight," Dave sighed, resting his back against the kitchen wall. "We run a graveyard shift at the Inn."

Bigwin was located on a large island in the Lake of Bays, seventy-five miles northeast of Port Carter.

"Well if you're hungry, then you've come to the right place," Bill said, noticing that it was just about lunchtime. "How does a toasted western grab you?"

"I've died and gone to heaven," Dave grinned, realizing how hungry he really was.

Billy put Dave's meal together, but was unable to spend any time with him until the early afternoon trade began to dwindle. Shortly after one he took Dave up to the penthouse, and pulled a single bed mattress out of the storage room. Dave had a bedroll tucked into his rucksack, so sleeping arrangements weren't a problem.

"How long did it take you to hitchhike to the Port?" Bill asked, as he flopped onto his bunk.

"About four hours," Dave said, placing his pack on the floor. "The last guy I got a ride with was only going as far as Bracebridge, but at the last moment he decided to come here and visit an old buddy of his, someone by the name of Doc Livingstone."

"Yeah, I know the Doc. I saw him yesterday as a matter of fact," Bill hesitated, still pondering the amazing events of the Gloria and Debbie show. "You settle in here Tex, and I'll finish out the rest of my day."

"That suits me fine Billy, I wouldn't mind an hour of sack time," Dave mumbled sleepily, while eyeing the soft mattress.

Summer of '61

Later on that afternoon after turning the reins over to Harry, Bill went up to see how Dave was making out. The sound of someone sawing logs with a chain saw greeted him as he walked into the bedroom. Tex awoke with a start wondering where he was.
"Welcome back to the land of the upright and uptight," Bill smiled. "Hey! How about we head down to the beach for a swim before supper?"
"Wow, that would be out of sight Willy C., but I didn't bring a suit with me."
"No problem Tex, I've got an extra one in my duffel bag. It'll be a little snug, but it's better than swimming buck-naked in a public place."
After changing into their swimming gear, Bill decided to drop by the kitchen to see how Harry was doing.
"Things are just fine Billy," Harry said, as he rescued a wire basket full of fries from the superheated cooking oil.
Bill introduced Dave, and was about to leave when Virginia came in with an order.
"Hi Slick, who's your friend?" Virginia asked, treating Dave to a sultry come-hither smile.
Bill went through the "pleased to meet you" routine again and said, "We're on our way to the beach Virg, so we'll catch you later."
"Don't keep your handsome buddy all to yourself," Virginia grinned, a distinct look of interest in her eyes. Dave really was good looking guy if you liked the Troy Donahue type.
"What's with this Slick bit?" Dave wanted to know, when they got outside.
"Oh for some reason Virginia thinks I'm some type of smooth operator, so this nickname Slick has kind of stuck," Bill said, thinking back to the Toledo house caper.
It was getting close to suppertime, and the swimming area was practically deserted. They stretched out on their beach towels, attempting to catch the last rays of the late afternoon. Bill was half-asleep, and drifting off into a peaceful daydream when he heard Kitty Carson say, "Hi Teddy, who's your friend?"
Bill was used to Dave bringing them in like flies to the honey pail, so he wasn't surprised when he looked up to see Kitty's admiring gaze.

"Kitty, I'd like you to meet my pal Dave Graham."

Dave was three months older than Bill, and had turned eighteen in May; with his size he could easily pass for twenty.

"Hi there David Graham," Kitty purred, as she sat down beside them.

Oh, Oh! Billy thought, she wants to make him a gift he won't be able to refuse.

"Did I hear you correctly? You called old Bill here Teddy."

"Yep, the first time I saw him, I thought he looked like one of the Teddy Bears I used to have when I was a little girl."

"So now you're Slick-Teddy."

"Tex, for a short July it's been a long summer."

"I think it's time for a swim, come on Kitty I'll race you to the raft," Dave offered, extending his hand and helping Kitty to her feet.

They ran into the water splashing and giggling like two children. The world turned in it's endless orbit, the sun moved slowly about the galaxy, and for that moment in time and space they were indeed children. Contentedly tired from their swim and horseplay, Kitty and Dave emerged from the water, and walked slowly hand in hand to where Bill lay counting his sheep.

"Hey Slick up and at em!" Dave bellowed. "Kitty says there's a big dance at Johnnies Surf Club tonight, and it sounds like a real riot. What do you say Carlsen, are we in, or what?"

"Yeah Tex, we'll swing by Johnnies later this evening," Bill yawned, trying to come fully awake.

"Gosh, it's getting late, so I'll see you two at the dance," Kitty smiled, as she Bunny-dipped to pick up her towel.

She slowly walked away into the fading light, like an ephemeral beam on it's journey into the murky past of the quantum experience.

"Heavy duty eh?" Bill said, marvelling at the wonders of the physical universe.

*

Several minutes later they returned to the Hilltop, and went upstairs to change. Danny was there reading a hotrod magazine. After shaking hands, Dave found out that Danny owned a souped up jalopy, and they became instant pals.

"Yeah, she'll do zero to sixty in a flash," Danny boasted.

"Dave whistled, "That's one mean muscle machine."

Summer of '61

"Well for sure, before you go back up to Bigwin, we'll have to take her for a little drag," Danny grinned.

"Solid man!" Dave's eyes popped like a Roman candle, as he looked forward to the ride.

"Hey you guys; sorry to be a party-pooper, but it's time to put on the feed bag," Billy interjected, finally getting the attention of the two car nuts.

He asked them what they wanted for supper, then told them to sit at the counter while he helped Harry in the kitchen. Bill took extra care in preparing the fish and chips that they had all agreed upon. He was particularity pleased after joining his friends, to see how much they were enjoying their meal.

"When are we heading over to Johnnies?" Dave asked, as he added ketchup to his chips.

"Well it's eight o'clock now, and the first show starts at eight-thirty, so I'd say anytime after we finish with the chow call, "Bill half-grunted between mouthfuls. "'Rompin Ronnie Hawkins and the Hawk's are there tonight, and the joint should be jumpin'."

"Are you coming with us Danny?" Dave asked.

"I'd really like to but, me and my girlfriend Donna are driving over to Judd House this evening for a late night snack."

"Yeah, the family that eats together stays together," Bill shrugged, with a sly wink in Dave's direction. They said their good-byes to the Danderoo, then headed for Johnnies.

16
*

The Surf club was an old renovated warehouse that had been built on the south side of the Port Carter bridge. It was butted up against the King Boat Works. The building's interior had been converted into a nightclub by erecting a stage, and constructing a raised seating area around an open space that served as a dance floor.

Dave and Bill approached the entrance to Johnnies, and asked the girl at the door how much.

"Five bucks each," she sniffed, while popping some very pink Dubble Bubble.

"Hey that's highway robbery," Dave erupted, looking around for the ghostly galleon.

"Like it or lump it," the bubble gum queen hissed defiantly, blowing a rosy protective sphere over Johnnies impregnable kingdom.

"Forfuckinggetit!" Dave and Bill replied in unison, as they retreated down the steps of the dance hall.

"Billy, this bunch of Shylocks ain't going to beat the good guys."

"Yeah Tex, lets case the joint, and find a way to sneak in."

Their first cerebral lightning bolt, was to try getting up onto the roof. They found a decaying maintenance ladder on the wall between King's and the club. To their amazement and delight, they also discovered an open men's room window just below the level of the overhang. There was a narrow gap between the wall separating Johnnies and the boat builders.

"I'm going to wedge myself between those two walls, and by applying reverse pressure, I'll work my way down to the open window," Dave said, studying his route.

Bill looked into the abyss, and got a bird's-eye view of the pilings supporting the boat works. They resembled the naked shell-topped trees of a desolate battleground. It appeared that the two buildings were constructed over the river itself.

"As soon as you're through the window Tex, I'll follow you," Bill declared, oozing false confidence.

Dave started his descent, but had miscalculated one small thing. The metal walls coated with condensation were as slippery as a well oiled mud wrestler."Oh shit," Dave cried, as he slid rapidly down the nearly frictionless surface.

Summer of '61

Billy heard a loud splash as his best friend made a crash landing in the oily waters.

"You all right Tex?" Bill asked, fearing the worst.

"Yeah, just a little bruised," a shaky voice answered from the depths of the swamp." I'll try to find a way out of here, and meet you around the front."

It was just about dark when Billy reached the entrance to Johnnies. Ten minutes later he was relieved to see a half-soaked Tex Graham walking towards him.

"Still in one piece?" Bill asked, suppressing the urge to laugh out loud.

"Nothing broken," Dave shivered, as he smoothed down the legs of his wet blue jeans. "It's pretty dark back there, but before I got to the street, I discovered a rear window just to the left of the stage."

"Was it locked?" Bill squeaked, trying to curb his excitement.

"I tested the sucker and it cracked open," Dave crowed triumphantly.

"Sensational!" Bill whooped, seeing a rose covered passageway to the land of milk and honey.

They crept stealthily along the side street bordering the surf club, and when no one was watching, deeked into the poorly lit alleyway. After carefully prying open the small, grimy window, they scurried through the narrow chasm, and stood as still as mannequins in the darkened area adjacent to the stage.

"Were in like Flynn," Dave puffed, starting to breathe again.

"Who's Flynn?" an ominous voice reverberated, from depths of the blackness.

They turned around ever so slowly, and saw a huge, hulking figure, materialize from the shadows.

"You're the sixth and seventh tonight ," Goliath snorted, smelling the blood of an Englishman.

"Well you won't believe this sir," Bill croaked.

"You're fucking right I won't," the Colossus bellowed. "If you two punks know what's good for you, then you'll climb back out that window, and disappear into thin air."

"T-That sounds pretty sensible to me sir," Billy stammered, getting ready to make like Harry Houdini.

The bouncer had made his point, so dragging their tails behind them, they executed a perfect about face, back into the cool night air.

"Well here we are in front of Johnnies, no further ahead, and still without the ten bucks to get in," Dave grumbled.

They were about to leave when Bill saw George Raven approach them. Bill had met George at the Doc's two weeks ago. He was from Port Carter, but spent his summers in Brampton playing lacrosse for the Excelsiors. George was one of the best Junior lacrosse players in Canada, and a member of the local Chippewa band.

"Hey George, how's it goin'?"

"Just fine Billy the Kid," George replied cordially.

"This damp around the edges character is Dave Graham," Bill grinned, pointing towards his soggy cohort. "You just home for the weekend?"

"I go back to Brampton tomorrow," George said, reaching into his pocket. "Do you guys know Kitty Carson?"

"Sure do," Bill replied, wondering where all this was leading.

"She's inside, and sent me out here to give you this."

He handed Bill a piece of paper with a ten dollar note folded inside. On the paper was a brief message: *I saw you talking to Boyd the bouncer, and he told me what happened. See you inside. Kitty.*

"Jeez, thanks George. Are you going back in there?" Bill asked, tucking the ten spot into his jean's pocket.

"No, I want to go fishing with my dad tomorrow morning, so I'm heading home." George shook hands with Dave and Bill, then disappeared into the night.

After paying at the door, and getting their hands stamped, they looked around to find Kitty. They froze instantly when they heard a booming voice behind them. "I see that you's guys are legit now, so relax and enjoy," Boyd boomed, full of smiles and chuckles.

Bill breathed a sigh of relief when the rippling bouncer returned to his small, dark corner, to wait for eight and nine. They soon spotted Kitty, sitting at a table near the stage.

"Gosh, thanks, that was really nice of you," Bill grinned, taking a seat across form her.

"I thought you two must have wanted to get in here pretty bad, so I decided to oil the waters," Kitty smiled, looking directly at Dave.

"That's mighty kind of you ma'am," Dave drawled.

Summer of '61

"Well then, sit right down stranger, and we'll have a drink," she charmed, acting like the owner of the Longbranch Saloon.
  Bill noticed a large bottle of ginger ale on the table, and a bowl of ice cubes. Kitty extracted a mickey of rye whiskey from her purse, then poured healthy shots into the clean glasses that were sitting on the table. When Ronnie Hawkins came on stage for his second show of the evening, they stopped talking, and listened to some good old rock 'n' roll music, any old way you choose it. As soon as Rompin Ronnie started to play his hit song, "*Mary-Lou*", Dave asked Kitty if she'd like to dance.
  "Love to you sweet talking cowboy," Kitty bubbled, a giggle in her voice.
  They had a great time on the dance floor, while Billy was quite content to sit and sip his rye and ginger. Just before they returned to the table, Kitty spotted a girlfriend of hers across the floor, and went over to say hello.
  "I think she really digs you Tex."
  "Well, we sure had fun dancing."
  Before Dave could utter another word, Kitty returned with her friend Audrey in tow.
  "This is Tex, and the cute cuddly one is Teddy," Kitty said, happy as a Prom Queen.
  Oh great Bill thought, she's forgotten my real name. The two couples danced like they were regulars on "American Bandstand", and guzzled a tanker load. As Rompin Ronnie was announcing the last tango, Kitty invited them back to her place.
  When they arrived at the Carson's little shack on the river, Kitty put on the coffee pot, while Dave touched a match to the wood that had been laid out in the open field stone fireplace. With white birch logs burning quietly in the hearth, they sat on cushions in front of the comforting warmth, and drank their coffee. "It's awful late, and I'd better be getting home," Audrey murmured, starting to yawn.
  "I'll walk you to your cottage," Bill volunteered, rising to his feet.
  "That's real nice of you Billy," Audrey smiled gratefully.
  They offered their farewells before leaving Dave and Kitty to the magic of the glowing fire. Bill escorted Audrey to her front door, said good night, then headed back to the Hilltop. It had been quite a day, and he was as tired as a sailor in whorehouse on two for one Fridays.

17
*

Bill went straight to bed, and was asleep before he could count to ten. The next morning he noticed that Dave was on the floor curled up in his bedroll. It was eight-thirty but, no problemo, he wasn't on deck till three. Bill turned over, and decided to get a little more sleep. Thirty minutes later he awoke with a start, and was amazed to see Dave rapidly stuffing things into his packsack.

"Hey what's the big hurry Tex?"

"Got to make tracks Billy, the last boat for the island leaves at seven this evening."

"Okay but let me get you some breakfast before you make like Superman and fly away." When Dave was finished his packing, they scooted down to the kitchen.

"Bacon and eggs all right Tex?" Bill asked, as he replaced Harry at the grill.

"Yeah, I'm hungry enough to eat a road-killed whistle pig," Dave joked.

Bill began his interrogation as soon as they were seated at the counter. "So what happened last night?"

"Well Slick, gentlemen never discuss their adventures with the fairer sex in detail, but, here goes," Dave half mumbled, as he munched on a piece of bacon. "That Kitty's one talented chick. There's a piano at the cottage as you probably noticed, and she played, "*The Theme From a Summer Place*", by Percy Faith and some tunes from *Westside Story* by Bernstein. Boy, can she ever tickle the ivory."

"Yeah, but I bet she really wanted to play the upright organ by Graham," Bill quipped, testing Dave's sense of humor.

Dave laughed before saying, "That's all she wrote Billy. I fell asleep on the couch, and when I finally opened my eyes, the sun was just starting to rise. Kitty was already up, and asked me if I wouldn't mind leaving before it became full daylight."

"Sounds like a fairy tale to me Tex," Bill scoffed.

"Boy Scout's Honour," Dave replied, a sly smile on his face.

Bill wouldn't know for sure, though he was well aware that Dave had never been a card carrying member of Lord Baden-Powell's exalted troopers.

Summer of '61

"Can you make it down again this summer?" Bill asked, as they stood by the side of the highway near the edge of town.
"To tell you the truth William Francis, I wasn't really here this time. You see the management at Bigwin doesn't allow the summer staff to leave the island except in the case of emergencies."
"So how did you mange to pull this one off?"
"Well lets just say that Granny Graham was sick on her death bed, but she made a miraculous recovery."
"Tex you could sell salt water in Halifax," Bill chuckled. "Well partner if I can get Harry's car sometime and a day off, I'll try to get up to the Lake of Bays to see you."
"That would be terrific Billy!" The two boyhood pals shook hands, then reluctantly said good-bye.
It was Sunday, and the sidewalks were rolled up in Port Carter. At eleven o'clock bells started to ring from the lofty pinnacles of the four places of worship in the small town. Bill walked into the United Church, and took a seat in a back pew. He was totally amazed when Kitty Carson entered the building, and sat down beside him. She said nothing, but as the congregation stood to sing the first hymn, she reached for Bill's hand. He couldn't help but notice a tear trickling down her cheek. When the service was over he walked Kitty back to the cottage.
"You know that friend of yours is quite a guy," she said, a far away look in her eyes.
"Yeah, Tex is a keeper."
"So Teddy, how would you like to cook me a late breakfast?" Kitty smiled, changing her mood completely.
When you're not near the one you love.....What the hell, Bill thought.
He found pancake batter, eggs, maple syrup and a package of sausages in the refrigerator. He rolled up the sleeves of his crisp, white open-collared shirt, and twenty minutes later presented her with scrambled eggs, flapjacks, fried sausages, two slices of toast and perked coffee.
"Teddy if I wouldn't be accused of robbing the cradle , I'd take you straight home to Toledo with me. This is a great meal."
"Golly whiz, I'm only three months younger than Tex."
"So you are my sexy little man," Kitty purred.

"D-Dave says you play the piano," Bill stammered, his face turning cherry red.

"I just fool around a little on the black and whites," she said teasingly.

"Well, when we're finished eating maybe you could play something for me."

"Okay Teddy you're on."

After clearing away the dishes, she sat down at the upright piano, and asked Bill what he'd like to hear.

"Do you know anything from *Finian's Rainbow*?"

Bill was flabbergasted when she rattled off, "Old Devil Moon."

"Wow, you're terrific! That was our school production, and I played the leprechaun."

"So you're a thespian as well," Kitty grinned mischievously.

"Hell no!" Bill replied. "I only like girls."

She saw that he had a worried look on his face, and decided to just let it pass.

"Turn about is fair play," Kitty said. "I hear that you plunk away at the guitar."

She then disappeared into one of the bedrooms, and returned with a twelve string Martin.

"I-I can only chord, and I can't sing very well, but here goes," Bill sputtered nervously.

He played, "This Land Is Your Land". The music was by Woody Gutherie, but a Canadian group the Travellers had added some definitely Canuck verses. Kitty sang along with Billy and their voices blended very well.

"You're pretty good Teddy," Kitty smiled reassuringly.

Bill knew that she was just being nice, but he was pleasantly stroked by her kindness.

"Have you heard this new folk artist, Joan Baez?" Kitty asked.

"Wow! Yeah! She's far out!" Bill replied.

"I've got a couple of her forty-fives at home," Kitty said, a hint of melancholy in her voice." I sure wish I had them with me."

Bill looked at his watch and was startled to see that it was two-thirty. "I've got to make like Gordie Howe and get the puck out of here," he blurted without thinking. "Oh sorry Kitty. I forgot my manners."

Summer of '61

"You're a real character Billy Carlsen," Kitty grinned, as she stepped towards him. She kissed Bill on the forehead, then ushered him out the door. At least she knows my real name he thought.

Bill was just in time to get cleaned up, and made it to the kitchen by three.

"So where's the golf game this afternoon Harry?" Billy asked, as he picked up an apron

"No such luck Slick, I've got to go to my parents place for Sunday dinner. I guess you know where I'd rather be." Harry waved halfheartedly at Billy, then wandered out to his car.

He wasn't busy at first, but the supper hour kept him over employed until things cooled off in the early evening. Shortly after eight Sandra walked through the back door of the kitchen. Bill was aware that his heart did a sudden flip. He was really starting to like Miss King, a lot.

"How was the reunion?" Bill inquired, momentarily overwhelmed by the captivating spell of her presence.

"It was okay, but after awhile I got bored with: what do you want to do after school, it's a nice summer, and isn't this the best potato salad you've ever tasted," Sandra lamented. "So how were things in town while I was away?"

"Slower than a dry fart on a calm day, as my uncle Olie would say. Hold the phone Sandi," Bill simpered apologetically. "Sometimes old uncle Olie could get carried away."

Sandra projected a regal, we are not amused look, but said nothing. This was a bit of a smoke screen on Billy's part, because he had wisely decided that the milk run with the Doc, and the events of the weekend were best kept in the land of mum.

"Yesterday I talked to my parents, and they said it would be okay if you and I went out to the cottage tomorrow," Sandra smiled primly. "It might be fun to take a boat ride, and do a little fishing."

"Hey, that sounds great. I've got the morning and early afternoon to play with, so we're all set," Bill grinned, looking forward to being alone with her.

"I'll pick you up in the Beetle at eight-thirty," she said, moving closer. Sandra gave him a lingering open-mouthed kiss, then quickly returned home.

The next morning while putting his breakfast together, Bill inquired about Harry's Sunday night supper.

"It was terrific. My mom makes the best pot roast in the District," Harry bragged.

"Yeah, that's one of my top ten as well," Bill declared, suddenly realizing how much he missed his own mother's cooking.

Slick Carlsen wolfed down his breakfast, and was out front waiting for Sandra at eight-twenty. Two minutes later the Doc pulled up in his milk truck.

"Hey, what's happenin' Kid?"

"Just waiting for Sandra, we're going out to her camp to do some fishing."

"Sure you don't want to come along with me, and deliver a little milk to Debbie and Gloria?" the Doc inquired archly.

"I'll have to take a rain check on that one Doc," Bill gulped, as he remembered Gloria and her micro-bikini.

"Catch you later Billy the Kid, and don't forget, they always bite better before a storm."

Chuckling to himself, the Doc climbed into the truck and continued on his route. Sandra arrived ten minutes later.

"Sorry I'm late, but I had to help my mother with the breakfast dishes."

"No big deal Sandi, the Doc came by and we chewed the rag for awhile. One beauty day eh?"

With Sandra behind the wheel it took them thirty-five minutes to get to the King's cottage on Lake Raddison. The building was more like a home. It was a large frame bungalow highlighted by cove siding on the outside walls. Inside was a spacious kitchen, gigantic living room, enormous dining room, four bedrooms and a huge three piece bathroom.

"Wow! Hydro, and no shack out back. This is some neat place," Bill said, mentally comparing things to his families cabin near North Bay.

After a brief tour of the King's summer palace they made their way to the boat house. Inside was a King day cruiser. Sandra grabbed two spinning outfits that were standing in the corner, and placed them, along with a tackle box into the storage space behind the cockpit of the highly polished teak and cedar speedboat. Bill put the cooler containing their lunch beside the landing net.

Summer of '61

The engine was a V eight in-board and it made the craft move along like a sleek wild stallion.They raced up the lake for ten minutes, then anchored off a rocky point. Sandra cast into shore with a Williams Wabler, and latched into a two pound small mouth.

"You're pretty handy with that spinning rod," Bill shouted excitedly, after netting the fish.

"My Dad taught me how to fish before I could read," Sandra responded whimsically.

Bill boated a three pounder five minutes later, so they decided to call if quits. Two good sized bass were more than enough for dinner that evening.They retrieved the anchor, and travelled a short distance up the lake until they came to an old logging dock sticking out from the shore of a large deserted island. Bill secured the boat to a rusty but serviceable cleat, and together they lugged the heavy cooler to a secluded sand beach. Sitting side by side on an ancient spruce drift log they ate their egg salad sandwiches.

"I've been thinking about things ever since I talked to my cousin Sarah this weekend," Sandra said, when she had finished her lunch. "Sarah has been doing it with her boyfriend for the last two months, and says there's no problem as long as you use protection." Sandra's biggest fear wasn't the inevitable lose of her virginity; it was the concern about getting pregnant.

"Billy if you could only get us some protection, then I'd really like to make love to you."

Willam Francis was a little confused, so he relied on the—no dumb questions—philosophy that his father had taught him.

"What exactly do you mean by protection?" he asked hesitantly.

"A cock safe," she stated bluntly.

"Oh!" Bill murmured, as if the most important secret of the universe had just been revealed to him, and perhaps it had. "I can get those at a drugstore."

"Well then you get them, and the next time we get an opportunity we'll do it."

There was something cold and calculating about the whole thing, but Billy was so desperate to experience real sex that he was willing to go along with most anything.It was getting late, so they made their way back to the boat and returned to the cottage.

Sandra pulled up in front of the Hilltop at two-fifty, but before Bill got out of the car she informed him that her mother wanted to spend tomorrow shopping in the city.

"We're heading down to Toronto, and we'll be staying with my spinster aunt, Beatrice Bennet King," Sandra bubbled.

"Hey, that's B.B. King, I wonder if she plays the guitar," Bill mused silently.

"Eaton's is first on our list and then Simpson's, so watch out Yonge Street, here we come," Sandra warbled, happier than a child going to the fall fair for the first time.

"When will you be back?" he asked, already starting to miss her.

"Probably not till Friday, and maybe by then you'll have those things we talked about."

"I'll get them for sure," Bill promised, sounding determined. "Hey what does your aunt do anyway?"

"She's a French teacher at Humber Collegiate."

"That figures," Bill said, smiling broadly.

"What do you mean by that?" Sandra asked testily.

"It's a long story, and some day I'll tell you. Have a great trip, and hi to your mom and dad." He gave Sandra a long passionate don't be away too long kiss, then tumbled out of the car.

"You might as well take off now, and I'll see you tomorrow afternoon Harry," Bill shouted, as he entered the kitchen.

"Thanks Slick, I've got to get the car in for an oil change, and if I'm lucky maybe I can shoot nine holes before dark." Harry then vanished like a puff of white smoke before Bill could turn around.

For the rest of the afternoon and evening, Bill was busier than a beauty queen working at a Nevada cat ranch. It seemed that everyone in town wanted an early supper, an after theatre snack, or just about anything edible. When Billy was finished he wearily climbed the back stairs, flopped on his bunk, and instantly went lights out. He was one tired little teddy bear.

18
*

Bill was standing behind the counter when Ken came in for breakfast. He deposited himself onto one of the swivel stools before saying, "Tim and I are having a little barbecue after the performance tonight, so if you'd like to join us, drop by at ten-thirty. If you can't make it, could I get eight Dow Ale from you later on today?"

"I'll be there tonight with the suds," Bill said, looking forward to a late night cook out.

The rest of the day zoomed on by, and at three o'clock Harry arrived ready for work. After getting the greasy feeling of the kitchen off his skin, and changing into something that didn't smell like french fries, Billy headed across the bridge to Dingleburys Drugstore.

He nervously approached the prescription counter, and waited to be served. One minute later a man wearing a white smock asked him what he wanted.

"I'd like to buy some rubbers," Bill blurted out, starting to perspire.

"Sorry son we don't have those here, maybe you can get a pair at the sporting goods store down the street."

Bill was too scared to notice the look of pure mischief in the Pharmacist's eyes, so he plodded on.

"What I mean sir is; I want to purchase a safe."

"Don't have those either sonny, maybe you should go across the street to the bank of Nova Scotia."

Bill was becoming frustrated, and tried another approach. "Let me put it another way Mr. Dinglebury, I want to buy some protection. "

"I can surely understand that young man, in these days when murderers and armed robbers are running wild, don't we all."

Bill was really at a loss, and was considering Sandra's blunt words when Druggist Dinglebury decided to end his game of cat-and-mouse. "I think what you're trying to tell me is that you wish to purchase some condoms."

Bill figured this was the medical term, so trusting his instincts he managed to sputter, "Y-Yes sir, I'd like to get one condom from you."

"They only come in small boxes of three," the druggist rumbled authoritatively.

This threw Bill for a bit of a loop, because he'd only planned on one time. Seeing the wisdom of possible future encounters, he replied, "A box of three would be just fine."

Mr. Dinglebury leaned over the counter to get a closer look at Billy and said, "Aren't you that young fella who works for Paul Evans at one of his restaurants?"

Absolutely mortified, he was able to choke out, "Yes sir I'm a cook at the Hilltop."

Mr. Dinglebury was relentless, and pointed a finger accusingly, "You're the one that's been seeing Al King's daughter."

"Yes sir, Sandra and I are friends."

"May I then ask, what you want these condoms for?"

Bill knew the jig was up and had to think fast. Inspiration grabbed him, and he went forth where angels feared to tread.

"It's for a practical joke, Mr. Dinglebury," Bill improvised, steadily gaining momentum. "You fill the condom with water, and when you see your buddy coming down the street, you lobe it at him before saying catch. One wet buddy eh?"

Mr. Digglebury assumed his you layman, me professional posture and said, "Under the laws of this great Dominion, I'm only allowed to sell these—he held up a box of three lubricated Sheiks—for the prevention of disease."

"I guess that means that water bombs are out," Bill rasped meekly.

"Precisely," Druggist Dinglebury replied triumphantly.

Billy thanked the Pharmacist for his time, even though he wished that he could vanish instantly like the invisible man. He was determined however, that the next time he visited Bala a three pack would be on his shopping list.

Bill did not pass go, luckily he didn't have to go straight to jail, nor did he stop till he was in the safety of his digs above the café. He finally got things into perspective, and thought that a visit to the Port Town Players might calm him down before supper.

When he arrived at the theatre, he was surprised to see Laura Collins alone on the stage mending a costume.

"Where's everybody?" Bill asked.

"The entire crew went down to the beach for a swim," Laura said, working her wizardry with thimble, needle and thread.

"How's Jim Finney anyway?" he inquired in a friendly tone.

Laura suddenly bent over double and started to cry.

Summer of '61

Boy the fatal Carlsen charm is working overtime, Bill thought, wondering what he had said wrong.

"That little dickhead dumped me for some dumb blonde who lives in Hamilton," Laura cried out, with a note of anguish that would shatter the heart of Nikita Khrushchev.

Wanting to make her feel better, he said forcefully, "The dumb one is Jim; if he left you for another girl, then he should have his head read."

She didn't know Bill very well, he was only the young kid who cooked at the Hilltop, but needing comfort she jumped up from the chair, and launched herself into his arms.

"There, there," Billy soothed, as he hugged her like an older sister.

Laura was completely wrung out, and finally released her death grip. "You know, in time, I might get that yo-yo out of my system."

"Gee that's swell Laura," Bill smiled.

She had a fit of the giggles, but managed to say, "Thanks for the shoulder young Will."

He was relieved to see Ken and Tim walk into the theatre. Their hair was still wet, and they seemed to be in a jovial, towel slapping mood.

"Time to make like Sergeant Preston of the Mounties, because I reckon this case is closed," Bill said, gently squeezing Laura's hand. "We'll see you after the performance Mc-boo."

Totally transcended to another world, he left the hall with his loyal dog King in tow, and returned to headquarters. The threesome on the stage could almost feel the chill of the Yukon, caressing them like the morning mists on Dawson Creek.

19
*

When Bill got back to the café, he met Bob Tucker at the top of the stairs. Bob was on his way down the hill to finish the evening shift.

"Hey Slick, just the guy I was looking for," Bob said cheerfully.

Since he worked exclusively at the Harbour Restaurant, Bill didn't see much of Old Bob. Danny had tagged him with the nickname, claiming that Bob reminded him of an old woman.

"Yes your Oldness," Bill replied unctuously.

"Your mom called and she wants you to phone home," Bob grimaced, disliking intensely the name that Danny had christened him with.

Without further explanation , he walked out the door and headed for the Harb. Bill took the stairs two at a time on his way to Ma Bell's one armed bandit. He dialed operator, gave his home number, deposited seventy-five cents, and was just starting to bite his finger nails when his mother picked up the telephone.

"Is everything okay? Bill quavered, near panic in his voice.

"Oh hello dear, everything's fine, I just wanted to tell you that your father's holidays have been moved ahead, and we're leaving tomorrow," his mother said, reassuringly. "We fly to Montreal first, and then on to Duseldorf."

"That's terrific Mom," Bill sighed, his heart-rate returning to normal.

He could hear his mother clear her throat before continuing. "Yes, we're all packed, and your dad has been studying *Europe On Five Dollars a* Day."

"I hope that you have a fantastic trip," Bill said, suddenly finding it difficult to speak.

"Now you take care Billy and remember if there are any problems, phone Grandma."

He bit his lower lip till it almost bled, and managed to choke out, "I love you Mom!"

"Your three minutes are up sir," the operator said, in a sweet mechanical voice; a faint click echoed in his ear, and the connection was broken.

Bill ate a light supper, before going up to his bunk to catch some sack time. He assumed the vertical at ten o'clock, counted out nine bottles of Dow Ale from the case under his bunk, placed them in a paper bag, then left for Ken and Tim's rental cottage on the river.

Summer of '61

When he arrived at Williamson's Muskoka Camp, he heard muffled voices coming from behind a small cabin, and headed in that direction.

"Billy-boo right on time," Ken shouted, recognizing the outline of his friend in the dim light of two citronella candles.

Bill gave Ken the bag full of wobbly pops, and sat down on a lawn chair. Tim handed Bill two dollars, then pulled out a church key.

"What kind of barbecue is that?" Bill asked, as Tim passed him a beer.

"Mrs. Williamson, our landlady, bought this at the Pro Hardware in Gravenhurst," Ken said, stirring several flaming briquettes with a poker. "She says it's called a Hibachi or something like that."

"It sure uses a lot less charcoal than a regular colonial stick-burner," Tim joked.

Bill had managed to liberate three hamburg patties, three buns and several large dill pickles. He placed his bag of booty beside Ken's chair.

"Hey, along with the roll of Polish sausage and cheddar cheese that Tim picked up, we've the makings for a fine feast," Ken said, arranging things in front of him.

"How's your snuggy doing there mate?" Tim asked, after he took a swig of beer.

"Sandra's okay," Bill replied, smiling fondly. "She's gone to the big smoke with her mother to do some shopping."

Ken noticing that the charcoal had a nice even red glow, asked Bill if he'd do the cooking.

"A busmans' holiday eh?" Billy grinned happily.

He listened with a trained ear to the patties and sausage coins sizzling on the two small gratings. When he judged that they were almost done, he moved the meat on to one grill and used the other to toast the buns. Bill then served the hamburgers and sausage while Ken placed slices of pickle and cheese onto paper plates. They sat quietly, contemplating the empyrean canopy above them, and greedily devoured the overflow from their very own cornucopia.

"That was bloody marvelous," Tim belched contentedly, when he had finished.

"Are you going back home after the summer?" Bill asked, munching on the last of his dill pickle.

"This theatre stuff has gotten into me veins, and Martha thinks she can get me on as a carpenter at Stratford this fall," Tim declared proudly.

"Hey that's fantastic Tim," Bill said, pulling a tooth pick out of his shirt pocket. "So what's happening in the world Kenny-boo?"

Bill knew that Ken was a news freak and, read the *Toronto Telegram* everyday.

"There's a story on the sports page that caught my attention. Ty Cobb died. You know he was probably the greatest all-round baseball player who ever lived."

"Hell no, the Bambino was the best," Bill protested. "Didn't you guys see *The Babe Ruth Story* with William Bendix."

Ken simply snorted and decided to leave Bill's world of fantasy alone.

"Speaking of William Bendix," Tim said. "We used to get a Yank show on ITV at home called, "The Life of Riley". Did you blokes ever watch that one?"

"Holy smoke that was one of my favorites," Bill exclaimed, his eyes brightening like a pair of dancing fireflies.

"Two different countries and a big pond in between, and we're watching the same things on the Teley. Bloody amazing!" Tim marveled, slowly shaking his head.

"Have either of you ever smoked grass?" Ken asked, leaving the question dangle like a yo-yo in a sleeper mode.

Bill had no idea what Ken was talking about, and thought it was bad enough that cows ate the stuff, let alone people smoking it.

"I tried it once down by the docks in Liverpool," Tim admitted.

For a moment Bill looked at the grinning carpenter, as if he had stepped off a spaceship.

"Well, an actor who just left for the city gave me these." Acting like a magician Ken pulled three skinny cigarettes out of his jack-shirt pocket.

Billy finally caught on, marijuana, Mary Jane, reefers. Holy fuck!

"This is all new territory for me, but I'm willing to give it a try," Bill said gamely.

"Okay, take it way down into your lungs, and hold the smoke there as long as possible," Ken instructed, before lighting up one of the joints, and inhaling deeply.

Summer of '61

He passed the roll-your-own to Tim who repeated Ken's performance. Bill was next but not being a smoker, he coughed up a steaming white cloud, and wound up doubled over gasping for breath as tears formed in his eyes.

"Have a sip of beer Billy, and try it again," Ken smiled encouragingly.

The next time Bill was able to hold the smoke down for thirty seconds. He couldn't help but think that the stuff smelled just like smoldering mosquito coils. Ken lit a second joint, and dutifully passed it around the circle.

"This grass isn't doing a thing for me," Billy said, after his third hit.

Ken and Tim had become very quiet, and were happily sitting in their chairs staring at the white ash glow of the charcoal fire. Bill looked upwards, and saw the bright full moon hanging like a Christmas ornament in the sky above his head. He could make out faces, cites, highways, purple oceans and rice pudding. The moon increased in size, and he reached out to touch it, but it sped away leaving behind bright tracers of red and orange. With what seemed like a crashing about his ears he was suddenly aware of simply sitting on a hard chair gazing at his two friends.

"You were gone for fifteen minutes," Ken grinned, as Billy's eyes started to focus.

"Holy cow! I've never felt anything like that before," Bill whispered, checking his watch.

"That's really fab weed," Tim echoed, in a dream-like voice.

"Would you guys like sausage or cheese?" Ken asked. "There's lots left over."

Bill had never tasted anything so good. He took a mouthful of beer, and it was like ambrosia from the heights of Mount Olympus. He could have eaten all the sausage in Poland; it was that tasty. Time seemed to be suspended again as he ate and drank. Tim's voice came out of nowhere like the light at the end of a very dark tunnel. Bill snapped back to reality at the speed of thought, and all appeared to be completely normal.

"So what flicks have you seen lately?" Tim asked, knowing that Bill was a rabid film fan.

Billy started to talk about the Clarke Gable, Montgomery Clift movie that he and Sandra had taken in at the Odeon.

"Marilyn Monroe was pretty good in the Misfits. I read somewhere that her husband wrote the screen play," Ken said, when Bill had finished his account of the picture.

"Gee, I didn't know that Joe DiMaggio could write too." Bill bowed his head, in total awe of the great talent of the man.

"She's married to Arthur Miller now you turkey," Ken laughed, while rolling his eyes.

"Well she should have stuck with Joe," Bill stated emphatically. "I'll bet this Dusty Miller guy never hit fifty-six in a row."

This struck them as the most hilarious thing that they had ever heard. They laughed, howled, guffawed, and snorted like prime Yorkshire pigs, until they could hardly see for the wetness in their eyes. They were close to hysterics before settling down.

"My God Billy-boo, if the Russians could use you as their secret weapon this new wall they're building in Berlin would be a joke," Ken said, starting to laugh again. "The rest of the world would be so enchanted by your sense of humor that all would be forgiven."

"Hey Billy lad it's almost two in the bloomin' morning," Tim yawned, his voice beginning to thicken with fatigue.

"Holy smokers, I'd better get back," Bill said, adjusting to reality. "I've got to be up for the dawn patrol tomorrow."

"Yeah, ta! ta! for now mate," Tim sighed wearily.

"Billy it's been a sensational time," Ken grinned, still on a cannabis after-buzz. "You have a good nights rest and I'll see you soon."

"Thanks Mc-boo this sure was a first for me but, in a way it's becoming a summer of firsts," Bill said, thinking that his words of wisdom were good for the ages. "I knew in my heart when I came up here that things would be different, and so far no disappointments."

Bill shook Ken's hand and set course for the Hilltop. He was a little concerned because the "Drug Education" pamphlets that he had been given at school, all said that one puff of pot and you were hooked for life. He had visions of rummaging around in garbage cans with Joe Buggins by his side, but he let that image go in a hurry figuring that it was all schoolboy scare tactics. Maybe it was just a bunch of literature that had been translated from the French by Miss Marble. What the hell she could be wrong. Bill was tripping again, but it felt fine.

Summer of '61

Just about straight, he climbed the stairs to the penthouse, and quietly opened the bedroom door. He was greeted by the resonating sounds of soft snores and half-mumbles. It wasn't exactly the Royal York, but it was home. He was securely in the land of all things possible before his pillow was warm.

20

*

It seemed to Bill that he had just closed his eyes when six-thirty arrived at the speed of light, much like a flash message on Dick Tracy's wristwatch radio. Although he was still spaced from the puffing's at the pot party, he made a quick dash to the kitchen, and was surprised to see Bonnie standing by the door filing her nails.

"How's life with Raunchy Richard?" Bill asked, after the good mornings had been exchanged.

"I wouldn't know, I'm going out with Doc Livingstone now," Bonnie said imperiously.

That sly old milkman, Bill thought. He figured that Bonnie probably changed boyfriends more often than she changed her panties.

When Ken and Tim came in for breakfast he was able to pause for a brief chat.

"That was a great feast last night mate," Tim groaned, his head drooped over.

"Yeah, but I'm still floating on a silver-thin cloud," Bill replied, trying to stay focused.

"You'll be okay by this afternoon," Ken assured him, as he bit into a piece of toast.

"Two breakfast specials," Bonnie snapped impatiently, when she steamed by the counter.

"See you later guys," Bill yelled over his shoulder, as he rushed into the kitchen.

The Doc strolled in at ten and ordered a cup of coffee. Bonnie was all charm and giggles. It wasn't too busy, so Bill came out to join them.

"How's that six gun hangin' Kid?"

"It's well oiled Doc, but not getting much action," Bill replied straight-faced.

Bonnie was staring at the Doc all google-eyed when Wayne suddenly appeared.

Ever since they had gone water skiing, Bill was convinced that Wayne Saunders, the local breadman, was a dead ringer for Rocky Marciano—five-ten, one-ninety and tougher than a chew-eared Terrier.

"Nice day eh?" Wayne said, as he straddled one of the counter stools. "So are we still going golfing this aft or what?"

Summer of '61

"The Doc and I are driving up to Huntsville," Bonnie stated firmly, taking charge.

It was obvious that she had the Doc wrapped around several of her well manicured fingers.

"Well, I guess I'll see you later then," Wayne muttered dejectedly.

"Have a good one Wiener," the Doc waved, as Wayne left the restaurant looking like a little puppy that had lost it's way in a storm.

Bill returned to the kitchen marvelling at the effect that Bonnie had on the male of the species. Maybe it was true, blondes have more fun, or was it that gentlemen prefer blondes. Bill then began his preparations for the lunch crowd by boiling several eggs that would be used to make egg salad sandwiches.

The rest of the day went by quickly, and he was ready for a break when Harry arrived at three. Billy went up to his bunk to bag out for an hour, thankful that he was no longer feeling the effects of the wondrous weed.

When he finally emerged from the land of the comatose, he heard Danny and Joey having a heated discussion. Bill got up and went into the bathroom for the pause that refreshes, then returned to the bunkhouse to join in on the spirited exchange.

"Have you ever met a colored person?" Joey asked, sounding exasperated.

"Well not exactly, but my dad says they're all stupid and lazy."

"I thought that you said, Jim Brown was the best running back ever!" Bill fired away, opening up with both barrels.

"Yeah but..."

"I remember that you said, Harry Belafonte was one of the top entertainers in the world."

"Yeah but..."

"Didn't you tell me that Sidney Potier was great in the *Defiant* Ones, and should have won the Oscar."

"Yeah but..."

"But what?" Joey thundered, hard on the heels of Bill's three points. "You're just not thinking for yourself. Now don't get me wrong, you've got to respect your father and all, but he may not be right all the time."

You could see in Danny's eyes, that a spark of understanding was slowly emerging.

"Okay you guys give me a break. I know my old man's prejudiced, but he's the only old man I've got."

"Now you're thinking for yourself," Joey smiled, a tone of deep delight in his voice.

"Two summers ago," Bill began. "Just after school ended, my dad and I went down to Florida. He had a one week posting to Tampa airport as the Radioman on duty."

"Your father works for the big silver bird company, and he fixes their radios," Danny muttered.

"Give the man a cigar," Joey exclaimed.

"We travelled down there on a DC-4," Bill continued, remembering the pleasure of having his father all to himself. " It was a five hour trip, and we were picked up at the airport by the owner of a motel in Clearwater."

"So what's the point of all this ancient history?" Danny demanded, feeling antsy.

"Well this was the first time I'd seen segregation. You drive along the causeway to this motel, and there's a beach that has a sign—For Colored's Only. We went to a railway station one day to pick up a box of vacuum tubes, and there were two drinking fountains—Whites Only—Colored's Only. There were even separate waiting rooms and eating areas."

"You've got to be kidding," Danny blinked, his mental blinders showing cracks in the leather.

"No I'm not, and to top it all off, the man who ran the motel where we stayed told us how proud he was that the County was building a brand new high school just for the niggers."

"How can they take it?" Joey cried. "There's bound to be blood in the streets down there someday soon."

"So what are the babes like in Florida anyway?" Danny asked, bringing the serious talk to an abrupt halt.

*

The next day was a Thursday, the last day in July. Bill had been in Port Carter now for five weeks, and it was beginning to feel like home. He loved this small Muskoka town, and thoughts of someday having a cottage in the area danced like sugar plumb fairies across the fluid stage of his mind.

Summer of '61

He was hard at work in the kitchen still dreaming of his mansion on Lake Raddison, when Donna Rogers handed him an order for a club sandwich.

"Hey Slick, come back from the land of Oz, and get with it."

"Sorry Donna, I was flying with the wild geese, as my grandmother would say."

"That's okay Billy, but Danny would like to know if you still want to go up for that floatplane ride on Saturday?" Donna asked, as she watched him put the new order together.

"Yeah I'd love to. It's fifteen bucks a pop for a flip in the Beaver, so that's five each eh?"

"Boy, and I thought you were slow in math," Donna joked. "So when's Sandra coming home?"

"I hope tomorrow, but she said they may not be back till Saturday if the Friday night traffic looked like it was going to be bad."

"Well Billy my money would be on Saturday, because the highways will be jammed solid, since it's the Bank Holiday weekend," Donna said, exiting the kitchen with a triple-decked sandwich resting on a clean plate.

Perhaps it was a delayed after-buzz, but Bill started to transport himself to Europe with his parents and sister. He was just about at the Eiffel Tower when things snapped back to the present. What the flying fuck Bill thought, next summer will be my turn: Paris, London, Rome, whatever.

21
*

The afternoon dragged on, and he was glad when Harry arrived at three-fifteen.

"Sorry I'm a little late Billy, but we had a bit of a celebration at the nineteenth today."

"Not a hole in one," Bill gasped.

"Yep, on the par three third, and did it ever feel good," Harry whooped, happier than a constipated man in a rhubarb patch. He wasn't feeling any pain either. The ace and several whiskies had left their mark on Sammy Thompson.

"Mind if I borrow your car for a couple of hours? I want to make a quick run into Bala," Bill said, taking advantage of Harry's euphoria.

"Your stock running low again?"

"Yeah, and I want to get something at Canada Tire," Bill fibbed.

"Try some of that Carlings Black Label. I think you might like it."

"Hey Mabel Black Label," Bill sang out, imaging the buxom barmaid in the plaid blouse.

"By George I think he's got it," Harry laughed, as he handed Billy the keys to the Bel Air.

He drove very carefully, not exceeding the speed limit, and pulled into the parking lot of the Brewers Retail forty-five minutes later. The man on the counter knew him from a previous visit, and it wasn't necessary to produce Danny's fake ID. He placed the two-four of Mabel's finest into the trunk of the Chevy, then tootled on over to the Rexall Drugstore.

He had learned from his past experience, and boldly asked the Pharmacist for three condoms. The elderly druggist took a small box of lubricated Trojans from a top shelf, and placed the package into a brown paper bag. Looking at Billy suspiciously he said, "That will be seventy-five cents young man."

Bill handed him three moose heads, and quickly left the store. He was back in Port Carter just after six.

He checked to see if the coast was clear, then carried the case of suds up to his room. Since all the summer staff bought beer from him, he was only concerned about Paul and Sally. Bill found Danny's knapsack on the floor, and put the birth certificate into one of the side pockets. Now that all the ribbons had been tightly tied, he hurried down to the kitchen for his evening meal.

Summer of '61

"How's the beast running?" Harry asked, as Bill tossed him the keys.

"Like a top," Bill replied, grabbing some sliced meat from the fridge.

"I thought it was idling a little rough the other day. I think I'll put a new set of plugs in her, and adjust the timing tomorrow," Harry wrinkled his brow, as he used an ice cream scoop to deposit a mound of mashed potatoes on to a plate. "Can you work the evening shift for me on Friday?"

"No problem Harry," Bill nodded, looking around for a fresh loaf of bread.

"Jeez, I'd really appreciate that Billy," Harry grinned, still riding a high from his shot on the third.

Billy took his hot pork sandwich out to the counter, made himself a vanilla milk shake, then attacked the steaming mountain of fat and protein. After mopping up the last drop of the gravy, he decided to take a walk up town. The air was starting to cool, and you could feel a hint of August in the air. July was always the best month of summer, but quite often things started to change come the first days of the eighth month.

Westside Story was playing at the Odeon. On an impulse, Billy pulled a quarter from his pocket and bought a ticket. He was totally enthralled by the music and dancing. At the end of the movie he was head over heels in love with Natalie Wood, and the song "Maria" kept playing over and over again in his mind.

As he emerged into the fresh night air, he heard a voice behind him say, "Hello Teddy."

He turned around quickly and said, "By golly Kitty, we'll have to stop meeting like this eh?"

She raised one eyebrow in mock concern and laughed. "Yeah, what would the neighbours think."

Bill smiled at that one, because he had heard his mother parrot the same thing a million times.

"Any word from Tex?" Kitty asked, looking a little flushed.

"Nope, I probably won't see Dave till the fall, but there's an outside chance that I'll be able to visit him before the end of the summer." Bill said, suddenly very aware of her captivating beauty.

"If I get up to Bigwin I'll be sure to say hello from Kitty, and in the meantime ma'am, may I have the honour of escorting you home?"

"Oh Teddy, you're a real sweetheart."

"Now don't go all mushy on me," Bill said, shooting her a mischievous grin.

Content in their growing friendship they walked arm-in-arm down the hill towards the bridge. Bill stayed at Kitty's long enough for a cup of coffee, then made his way back to the Hilltop.

The first of August was a chamber of commerce day, and Bill wasn't on shift till three. He reveled in the enjoyment of the moment. As his uncle Olie would say, "Friday might have been like sheep shit, and Sunday may turn into a cow plop, but don't let that spoil Hockey Night in Canada eh?"

He had a quick breakfast, then went across the street to see if Ken was working on a set. When he entered the theatre, he noticed Tim up on the stage nailing several two-by-fours together.

" Have you seen Ken?" Bill asked, looking into the wings.

"Well mate the last time I laid eyes on im, he was out back unloading some props."

Bill scooted for the back door of the Hall, and saw Ken and Barb carrying an old table into the properties storage area.

"Hey Billy-boo! How are things goin'?"

"Just fine Ken, and how are you today Barb?"

"No complaints Billy, but if you two will excuse me, I've got to find Martha," Barb said, before scampering away like an old tomcat that had just been peppered with rock salt.

"So what do you think of this new sales tax that's coming in today?" Ken asked, collapsing into one of the prop easy chairs.

"Yeah, I heard about that, but it's just a luxury tax eh?"

"If you can call gasoline and clothes a luxury, then I guess so."

"Well, it's only three percent," Bill shrugged.

"That's true but the next time you pick up a case of beer it will cost you, three dollars and ten cents."

Bill could see his profit margin dropping, but he was already ahead by twenty bucks, so he could absorb the hit.

"Gas will be thirty-five cents a gallon, and I don't know where it'll stop," Ken sighed, scratching his head.

Summer of '61

"You can be sure of one thing, if Canadians have to pay more than fifty cents a gallon there will be riots in Ottawa," Bill proclaimed, with absolute conviction.
In typical Ontario humour this new tax was called "Frost Bite" in honour of Premier Leslie Frost, who had instituted the unpopular cash garb.
"I don't mean to be rude Billy, but I've got to get some things done like yesterday, for tonights show, so I'll see you later," Ken declared, jumping up from the over stuffed chair.
Bill said a quick farewell, then ambled across the street to the restaurant. He came in the front entrance, and was startled to see Sandra sitting at the counter.
"You're home early!" he shouted, in a voice overflowing with happiness.
"Yes, my mother thought that it was better to return yesterday, but we didn't get back here till midnight," she replied, uneasily.
"Would you like to take a walk down to the beach?" Bill asked, hesitantly.
"I suppose that would be all right," Sandra murmured.
Halfway to the beach she stopped in midstep and in a sobbing voice confessed, "I got a call from Brian when I was in Toronto, he's been laid off at Stelco, and will be coming home tonight. He still loves me, and I guess the long and short of it is; I'll be wearing his school ring around my neck again."
Bill was shocked, but deep down in his vitals he had been expecting this, because he knew it was just a summer romance. Partially regaining his composure he sputtered , "I-I understand Sandi, but I'll always think of the great times we had together."
"Oh Billy, you're the best," she quavered, grabbing his hand.
"Remember to name your first kid after me," Bill grinned gamely, in an attempt to make light of the situation.
"What if it's a girl?" Sandra asked, wiping a tear from her eye.
"Yeah, I can see your point , William Miller would be kind of a weird name for a chick," he smiled thinly.
His drugstore adventures seemed rather futile now, but Billy figured that he could always keep one of the condoms in his wallet. This was a popular thing to do at his high school.

The height of coolness was to have the rubber ring in your billfold long enough, so it formed a circular imprint on the leather. This was the sign of a true swordsman. What the hell, he'd be just like the Boy Scouts, "Always Prepared!"

Sandra gave him a chaste kiss on the cheek, then reluctantly said good-bye. He decided to continue on to the beach, and was deep in thought as he walked down Bailer Street. He felt hollow inside, because it was beginning to dawn on him, that he may not be God's gift to the fairer sex. Dumped by Doris and sacked by Sandra all in six weeks. This was not an impressive record, but slitting his wrists wasn't an option. He therefore took great comfort in the fact that he was only seventeen, mind you almost eighteen, and with any luck, fickle old Mr. Cupid might strike again.

"Fuckin' A!" Billy concluded gamely, as he watched a log in the middle of the wide river drift slowly towards Lake Raddison.

If Teddy Carlsen had been able to look into the future, it would have eased his mind, because an incredible series of amorous adventures were to come his way, before the summer played itself out.

22
*

Bill kicked around the beach for awhile, then returned to the Hilltop seeking the security of his bunk. He went into a deep, dreamless sleep, but woke up with a start at two-thirty. He cleaned up quickly, then hurried down to the kitchen to begin his shift. Harry did his patented rapid exit, wanting to get in eighteen holes before sunset.

Since it was the start of the big holiday weekend, the restaurant was very busy. Donna reminded Billy to be on the Marina dock at nine-thirty the next morning, so they could be first in line for a ride in the Beaver. Bill didn't get much of chance at conversation for the rest of the evening, but was able to close up shortly after eleven. He was emotionally wrung out, and beginning to experience a deep sense of grief over his break up with Sandra. He slept fitfully, and his dreams were from the land of darkness.

Saturday morning was cool, but exceptionally clear, a perfect day for flying. Billy had a hurry up breakfast, and arrived at Mitchel's dock just as the town clock rang out nine bells. He was relieved to see Donna and Danny appear on the scene five minutes later.

"There she is," Danny shouted, pointing towards the skyline.

Bill looked around quickly to see who Danny was talking about, then spotted the Beaver approaching from the south. The single-engined DeHavalind splashed down like a loon making a perfect transition from air to water. The aircraft approached the dock with the engine barely idling. The pilot cut the motor fifty feet from the end of the rugged wharf, and sailed slowly forward. He emerged from the cockpit, and waited for the left float to make contact with an old rubber tire, that was nailed to the side of a sturdy plank.

He descended onto the pontoon, grabbed a rope, and tied it off to a cleat.

"Hi there," the intrepid birdman said, from behind a pair of the coolest sunglasses that Bill had ever seen. "Picked up a good tail wind on my way up from Lake St. John, so I'm a little early. Do you folks want to be first?"

"That would be terrific," Danny responded fearlessly.

Donna and Danny wanted to be together, so they made themselves comfortable on the rear bench seat. Bill sat in the copilots seat, and of course was fully prepared to take over in case of an emergency.

He had seen a CBC play on TV, where the crew of a Northstar was incapacitated by food poisoning. One of the passengers was given instructions over the radio on how to land the aircraft. A wise old airline Captain on the other end of the microphone talked him through to a perfect touchdown. Bill immediately looked around to locate the radio.

The pilot untied the pontoon rope, then climbed into the left hand seat. He primed the engine, set the throttle, mixture, and prop pitch, then hit the starter. The four-hundred and fifty horse radial engine barked into life. He adjusted the flaps and trim for take off, and checked all instruments, he then advanced the throttle for maximum power. The plane accelerated rapidly over the water, and suddenly became a flying object, instead of a speedboat. After they were safely airborne the pilot reduced power slightly, and began a climbing turn towards the town. When the aircraft was straight and level he shouted to Bill over the noise of the engine, "Would you like to try flying her?"

"Gangbusters!" Billy boomed, unable to contain his excitement.

The pilot demonstrated briefly what the control yoke and rudder pedals would accomplish, then he let Bill have the airplane. He was very nervous at first and kept on over-controlling. When he finally began to relax, he was able to keep the wings level and the nose on the horizon. In his mind Bill was already imagining himself to be Billy Bishop flying a Nieuport 17 in search of the Red Baron, or Buzz Beurling in an RAF Spitfire, on the lookout for Me-109's in the skies over Malta. Donna and Danny were too busy sightseeing out the side windows to notice that Billy was flying the plane.

Ten minutes later the pilot indicated that he had control again, and started to turn back to Lake Raddison. He set up his approach with a minimum of effort, and Bill was completely astounded when he realized they were back on the water. There was no bump or splash, the plane just seemed to settle gently onto the floats.

As soon as the Beaver was securely fastened to the dock, Bill paid the pilot, thanked him for the flying lesson and shook his hand. This was a day he would remember as long as he lived. Danny was working a split shift, so they made a beeline for the Harb. Bill said good-bye, then walked quickly back to the Hilltop. Before heading upstairs, he checked in at the kitchen to talk to Harry, and was astonished to see Paul there.

Summer of '61

Paul managed a strained smile before saying, "Just the guy I'm looking for."

Oh,oh! Billy panicked, he's found the stash under my bed.

"My sister was in a car accident, and she's still in the Hospital," Paul said ruefully. "I want to go to the city tomorrow to visit her, then pick up a load of potatoes on the way back."

"Gee Paul, I'm sorry to hear about your sister."

"I need you to come with me to do most of the driving," Paul continued, trying to hide his feelings. "You can stay at your parents place, and we'll be back here by Monday evening. Bob will cover for you while were gone."

"What time do want to leave?" Bill asked, his head spinning with the news.

"I'd like to get away first thing, so let's make it seven tomorrow morning," Paul said decisively. "Well, I'm off to the Harb to tie up a few loose ends. See you bright and early."

"Sounds like quite a trip Billy," Harry whistled softly, as Paul walked out the door.

"Yeah, my parents have gone to Europe, but my grandmother will be there."

Bill didn't say anything, but he was hoping to meet up with Doris. After all she did say in her Dear John letter that she still wanted them to be friends. Bill told Harry that he'd see him at three, then headed down the hill towards the bridge. He passed the Port Carter elementary school, and admired the Union Jack luffing in the mid-morning breeze. Below it, flying proudly, was the Canadian Ensign. It was hard to believe that sixteen years after the great global conflict, Canada didn't have its own flag, but as his father said," It'll be the Ensign some day soon. A lot of guys died while carrying that standard in the war, and the Legion will make sure that it becomes this countries banner." The Great White North was starting to sprout its nationalistic wings. "O'Canada" as the official anthem to replace "God Save the Queen", and a truly Canadian flag were just beyond the blue horizon.

On the other side of the Chippewa, Bill bumped into Gilford Gibbons, Virginia's current flame. When they were first introduced Bill thought that Gibby looked a lot like Anthony Perkins on a bad Brylcreem hair day.

"Hey Slick what do you know?" Gilford huffed, removing a spit-soaked pipe from his grinning mouth.

"Not a hell of lot Gibby," Bill coughed, getting a strong whiff of the cheap tobacco smoke, that hung like a heavy grey cloud around Gil's hay-burner.

"Did you see the poster at the store?" Gilford blinked, his eyes watering slightly from the miniature forest fire burning three inches from his nose. Gil was working for the summer at, The Great Atlantic and Pacific Tea Company.

"What's on the poster?" Bill asked, risking the cat's demise.

"Glenn Miller!" Gibby smirked, as if Bill were depriving some village of an idiot.

"Gee I thought he died in a plane crash during the war," Billy grinned, leading Gibby on. "I saw the *Glenn Miller* Story with June Alyson and Jimmy Stewart, so you can't fool me."

"No you smart ass, the Glenn Miller Band is coming to Dunn's on August the fifth," Gibby shot back, totally exasperated. "Ray McKinnley is running things now."

"Hey that's really great Gil," Bill smiled, oiling the waters. "Maybe I can get Harry's car for the night, and we could double date."

Gilford smoked a pipe because he thought that it made him look more mature, and gave him the image of a university man. Trying to play Joe Cambridge he sniffed, "That would be most enjoyable, William old chap."

Bill rolled his eyes, completely ignoring Gibby's attempt at sophistication, and said, "Ride you later elevator."

Further up Bridge Street he spotted Bongo Charlie. Every town has its characters and Charlie certainly qualified. He was the last of the beatniks.

"Hey man what's happening?" Charlie gasped, his eyes partially closed, while his pulsating hands kept time to some internal rhythm.

"Just hangin' around Charlie, how are things with you?"

"Groovy man, cool like a cat, far out, if you know what I mean."

"You had lunch yet?" Bill asked, knowing that Bongo was a little down on his luck.

"I'm on a diet man, too much protein can warp your mind."

"If you'd like to join me Charlie, I'm going up to the Hilltop to grab a cheeseburg and some fries."

Summer of '61

"We use low protein, full fat hamburg up there, so no sweat."
"That's like off the scale man."
Bill took this as a yes to his invitation, and started to walk towards the bridge.
"You know what really flies?" Charlie muttered, when they were halfway to the restaurant.
"I'm almost afraid to ask," Bill replied cautiously.
"Morning glory seeds man!" Charlie whispered.
"What's that got to do with the price of eggs?" Bill shrugged.
"Far out cook guy, LSD man, those tiny little seeds have acid in them."
"Let's just get some chow Charlie," Bill sighed, wondering if this acid stuff was anything like pot.
"Right on!" Bongo gasped, "I'm like from Starvationville."
When they got to the Hilltop, Bill told Charlie to wait out back while he prepared their lunch. He brought Harry up to speed, and said that he would cook the cheeseburgers and fries. Bill got the meal together, grabbed two cokes from the cooler, and returned to where Charlie was waiting. He had stuffed the burgers into a paper bag, and wrapped the chips in newspaper.
"We can have our eats in the school bus that's parked behind the community center," Bill said, pointing across the street.
"Out there man," Charlie nodded, eyeing the bag of goodies like a hungry lion.
As they sat in the yellow canary devouring their lunch, Charlie mumbled, his mouth half-full, "You know man this is just like Christmas. I mean, it's infuckingcredible."
They ate the rest of their gourmet meal in silence. Charlie hoovered up the last of the fries, thanked Bill for the out of sight grub, then left for another adventure.
It was two o'clock when Bill returned to the café. He went up to the communal washroom to indulge in the three S's; a shit, shave and shower. He was a new man able to leap a tall building in a single bound, faster than a speeding bullet. At three he flew into the kitchen, and took over from Harry.
For the rest of the afternoon, and all of the evening, he was busier than a three-legged beagle running a snowshoe rabbit. After locking up, Billy said goodnight to Jen, then headed straight for the rack.

23
*

Billy wiped the yellow sleepy grubs from his eyes, before assuming the vertical at seven. He treated himself to a hearty breakfast of scrambled eggs, bacon, sausage, pancakes, brown toast, and an order of home fries. For some reason he had a case of the big hungers or, as his uncle Olie would say, "I could have eaten the arsehole out of a skunk."

Paul was there at seven, and moved over to the passengers seat, to give Bill free rein at the wheel. Halfway to Bracebridge, Paul unrolled his sleeping bag, laid it out on the floor of the van, and was softly snoring in no time flat. Bill figured that he must have had a rough night, or with a wife as good looking as Sally, maybe just a busy one. They made great time, travelling like a smoking sled-rocket along the connecting ribbons of asphalt, and pulled into Bill's driveway at ten-thirty. Paul came to in the back of the van, and was amazed to learn that they were already in Georgetown.

"Time flies when you're having fun," Bill grinned.

"Well as a matter of fact I was having a very interesting dream," Paul snickered, as he shook his head, trying to get the cobwebs out a sleep-soaked brain, "I'll pick you up sometime Monday afternoon Billy." He climbed into the drivers seat, started the engine, then headed for Toronto the good.

As Bill entered the house he noticed his grandmother sitting at the kitchen table, drinking a cup of tea, and smoking one of her roll-your-owns. She looked at Bill in total disbelief, then walked slowly towards him as if approaching a ghost. She placed her arms around his shoulders, and with a tear in her eye said, "Sonny, what a surprise."

"Sorry I couldn't call you Grandma, but this trip just sort of happened."

"Is everything all right?" she asked, thinking that he looked a little thin.

"Things are just fine," he smiled. "Any word from Mom and Dad?"

"No, and I don't expect any, unless there's a problem."

"I guess they're having a great time over there," Bill said, a touch of regret in his voice.

"Well you could have gone with them Sonny."

"Yeah I know, but I told Mom my reasons."

Summer of '61

"Just between you and me, when your father heard about what you had said to your mother, I think he was proud of you for honoring your agreement."
"That's great news, I knew Pop would understand."
"How long can you stay for Billy?"
"Only overnight, Paul said he'd pick me up Monday afternoon."
It was lunch time so Granny McNair got out her chrome plated waffle iron, and made him a stack of golden brown waffles. He slathered them with maple syrup, then washed down the ambrosial combination with a cup of fresh perked coffee. Stuffed to the ears, he pushed back from the table sighing contentedly.
"Now that your finished Sonny, could you go down to McQueen's Variety, and get me a can of tobacco?" his grandmother asked, handing him five dollars.
"Sure thing Gram," Bill responded sluggishly, as he moved slowly towards the front door.
He walked lazily along the sidewalk, enjoying the familiar sights, sounds, and smells of his home town. It was a sunny, warm, early August afternoon, and all was well in his part of the cosmos. Bill was just about to enter McQueen's, when he heard a delighted squeal that froze him in his tracks.
"Billy!" she cried, her voice gurgling musically like a cold stream in the forest.
"Holy shit, Doris! Whoops sorry, what are you doing here?"
"I live here, or had you forgotten?" she whispered, grabbing his hand.
They stood there for a moment just enjoying the sight of one another. There was pure electricity in the air.
"A-Are you still going out with Pete?" Bill stammered, crossing his fingers.
"He's gone up to his parents cottage for awhile, so I haven't seen him since the last week in July."
"Are you two going steady?" he asked anxiously.
"Well not exactly, we had a fight just before he left, so we're sort of unofficially broken up," Doris said, brushing a wind-blown strand of auburn hair from the corner of her eye. "Are you home to stay?"

"Jeez, I wish I were," he rasped, completely immobilized by her dancing hazel eyes. "I'm here overnight, but I've got to be back in Port Carter late Monday."

"My parents are away for the long weekend, so if you'd like to come over to my place this evening, we could talk," she said innocently.

Bill had an instant vision of Santa Claus. Perhaps a little early, but definitely a very cheery guy in a red suit.

"W-What time would you like me to drop over?" Bill sputtered, having a hard time keeping his voice steady.

"Bout seven," the most gorgeous creature on the planet said. "See you later Billy." Doris slowly walked away with a roll of the hips and bosom, that gave absolute promise to the continuation of the species.

Bill watched her till she disappeared around a corner, then went into McQueen's. The air in the store always teased his nostrils with a fragrant mixture of jaw-breakers, bubble gum, and cherry lifesavers.

"Is the tobacco for your grandmother laddie?" Mr. McQueen asked, in a thick Scottish accent.

"Yes sir, and could I please have an Eat-More candy bar?"

"Aye Billy, and my best to you're wee Granny."

He walked quickly back to his parent's place marveling at the wondrous events of the past twenty-four hours. Life was a bowl of cherries.

When he got home, Bill helped his grandmother with her cigarette machine. After the paper and tobacco had been rolled in into foot-long smokes, it was his job to chop them up into standard lengths using a razor blade. As soon as the coffin nails were cut, he placed them into an empty tobacco can.

The fag contract finished, he spent the rest of the afternoon watching baseball on television. The New York Yankees were playing the Boston Red Sox, and Roger Maris had just hit his thirty-ninth home run. Mel Allen was already predicting, that the young Yankee outfielder would break the Babe's record. No way Bill thought, Ruth was untouchable.

24

For supper his grandmother put together a beef and kidney stew, complete with dumplings. Shortly after dinner, Granny McNair got out a bottle of Hudson's Bay whiskey, and added a liberal shot to her tea.

"The doctor said I was to take care of me self," she sighed, leaning back in her easy chair, and lighting up a smoke.

Bill had to suppress a laugh because this is what his grandmother would always say when she wanted an early drink. He pitched in with the dishes, and when they were dried he said, "I'm going over to visit Doris, and I may be home a little late."

"I thought it was all over between you two."

"Yeah, me too Gram, but she's busted up with Pete, and maybe we can get back together."

"You're a big boy now Billy, and I won't wait up." She then kissed him on the cheek, and shooed him on his way.

Bill knocked softly on the door of the bungalow where Doris lived. As soon as he was inside, she placed her arms around him, and gave Bill a deep lingering kiss. Wow, he thought, this is the way it ought to be. She eagerly grabbed his hand, before leading him down to the recreation room, where they sat very close together on a cracked leather couch, and pretended to watch the "Ed Sullivan Show".

"It's sure great to be here again," Bill said, drinking in the spicy fragrance of her bath-soap."I've really missed you since I went up north."

Doris didn't want to open old wounds, so she never mentioned her letter.

Instead she stocked his inner thigh, and whispered that she was also very glad to see him. Bill figured this was as close to heaven as he'd ever get. They soon got down to some serious above and below the waist petting. Bill carefully removed Doris's panties, and demonstrated some of the skills he had learned from Sandra's patient tutelage. Doris moaned with pleasure, and experienced a monumental earthquake event that was probably felt on Vancouver Island.

"Where did you learn to do that?" she murmured, after the couch stopped shaking.

"Oh, one of the guys had this sex manual that a friend of his picked up from someone in Toronto," he improvised, trying to sound convincing.
Doris didn't believe him for a moment, but she was too content to pursue it any further.
"Well you sure have come a long way Billy Carlsen," she said, opening his fly, and gently fondling him. "Oh my God! I want you inside me right now, but we don't have any protection."
Bill had a silly grin on his face as he reached into the back pocket of his pants, and pulled out his wallet. He extracted the foil wrapped package, then handed it to Doris.
"Why Billy baby, you sly little man," Doris cooed. "I assume this is also the result of the manual handed on from someone at sometime."
"Something like that," he rasped.
"Let's see what we can do here," Doris said, as she opened the package, and removed the lubricated prophylactic. She then delicately rolled the condom down the shaft of his very erect penis. With the latex firmly in place, she started to slowly run her finger tips over the taut surface of his scorching scrotum.
He was too worked up to hold back any longer, and had one of the most magnificent premature ejaculations ever, into the cozy confines of the condom. "I guess we'd better wait awhile," Bill croaked lamely.
Before Doris could answer the phone rang. She got up quickly, and went up to the kitchen. When she returned, Bill was informed that her grandparents had called, and would be popping over for a visit in twenty minutes. Doris asked him if he wouldn't mind leaving, because she was after all, supposed to be home alone. The bubble had burst, and Bill was feeling as frustrated as a cock rooster trapped on the wrong side of the hen house fence. He quickly cleaned up in the washroom, then returned to the front door to kiss Doris good night . Before he knew it, he was out in the fresh air, and on his way home.
"Surprised to see you back so soon Sonny," his grandmother smiled, when Bill entered the living room.
"I thought I'd better not be too late," Bill said, attempting to sound upbeat. "Doris has to be on duty at the pool Monday morning, so I came home early."
It was the summer, and the only thing on TV were reruns. Before he sat down Granny McNair asked him to change the channel to NBC.

Summer of '61

"Jack Parr's on at ten, and he's still my favorite." she sighed contentedly.

Sure enough, several minutes later Hugh Downs came on the screen, and welcomed everyone to the "Tonight Show."

His grandmother was in the kitchen getting her bedtime drink when Bill called out, "Hey Gram, you don't want to miss Charley Weaver."

Cliff Arquette was in fine form, and they really enjoyed his performance. Bill Cosby a new stand-up comic was on the Parr show for the first time, and before he finished Grandma McNair had tears of laughter running down her cheeks.

At eleven o'clock Bill kissed his grandmother good night, and went upstairs to his bedroom. It was pure luxury to sleep in his own bed. Despite the frustrations of the early evening he drifted off into a land filled with willing maidens offering him, grapes, wine, and comfort, from his arduous peregrinations.

The next morning he got up at eight, and hurried down to the kitchen. After a month and a half of cooking for everyone else, it was a treat to have someone else prepare a meal for him. His grandmother served up a plate of scrambled eggs and bacon, that was like manna from heaven. After finishing the last morsel of toast he thanked Granny McNair for a great breakfast, then decided to take a walk around town.

It was the holiday Monday, all the stores were closed, and the town seemed to be contentedly half-asleep. Part way along Main Street was the entrance to the municipal parking.It was a drive-through tunnel that had been hacked out of one of the buildings. There was warehouse space above the opening, and storefronts attached to either side. The most prominent of these adjacent businesses was the LCBO. The towns people referred to this cave like gap as, the-hole-in-the-wall.

Bill wanted to go to Memorial Park, and the quickest way to get there was a shortcut through the hole. Emerging on the parking lot side he heard someone say, "Is it warm enough for ya Billy?"

He turned and saw Slim Brown holding onto a door frame, in order to maintain his balance. Slim was one of the town wino's, and was probably waiting for the liquor store to open on Tuesday.

"Sure is Mr. Brown, but we'll be glad for this heat come February."

"How's your Mother doin' there young feller?"

"She's just fine Mr. Brown. My mom, dad and Brenda are over in Europe right now."

"I got to go to Europe in 1943," Slim whistled slightly, revealing a pair of missing front teeth. "An all expenses paid visit, courtesy of the Canadian Army. The accommodations weren't much, and the locals kept on shooting at me. All in all though, I got to see Italy, France, Holland and Germany, but no one stamped my passport." Fully appreciating his own wit, Slim broke into a high pitched laugh.

The first time that Bill had met Mr. Brown, was one day last winter when he and his mother were passing through the poorly lit hole-in-the-wall, on their way to where the family chariot was parked. It was mid-January, and Slim opened up with his seasonal line, "Is it cold enough for ya lady?" He was feeling no pain and the words—fire hazard—could have been used to describe the whiskey fumes rolling forth on his steamy breath. Bill's Mother was acquainted with Mr. Brown because she issued the welfare cheques for the Town and, Slim's name was near the top of the list.

"Are you warm enough Slim?" Mrs. Carlsen asked, a note of concern in her voice.

"No problem lady, I've got lots of anti-freeze in me."

"Well you take care, and try to stay out of the wind," she said, pressing a two dollar bill into his hand.

Mrs. Carlsen with Bill in tow left Slim to his hazy world of dreams. Mother and son walked like a pair of penguins across the icy parking lot in order to get to the Biscayne. When they finally reached the Chevy, Bill spun around and said, "Jeez Mom! Why would you even talk to that old rummy?"

"Mr. Brown's still a man dear, and he's had some bad breaks. Folks say he was never the same after the war, but he was able to cope. His wife died of cancer last year, and he's gone downhill ever since."

She didn't have to say any more. From that day on Bill would usually stop to talk with Slim, and always addressed him as Mr. Brown.

Memorial Park was a two acre, maple-shaded sanctuary, decorated with park benches and sturdy cedar picnic tables. It was also the site of the local Cenotaph. There wasn't a soul to be seen, so Bill sat for a moment enjoying the peace and quite.

Summer of '61

Being a small town, he wasn't surprised when he heard someone behind him say, "How are you today Billy?" He turned in the direction of the inquiring voice and saw Bert Jones coming up one of the crushed stone pathways.

"Thought you were up north for the summer," Bert wheezed, stopping to chat.

"I was Mr. Jones, but my boss had to come south to pick up a quarter ton of spuds, and I tagged along to help with the loading and driving."

Bert was the grounds keeper at the cemetery, and was also responsible for Memorial Park.

"Just looking to see if the grass here needs cutting tomorrow," Bert said, staring misty eyed at the stone angel who cradled a fallen soldier in her eternal arms.

"Are you all right sir?" Bill asked, noticing a tear flowing down the side of Bert's face.

"Yeah, I'm okay," he answered gruffly. "I was just thinking back to Vimy. I lost a few friends that day, in April of seventeen when we took the Ridge."

Bert was born in eighteen ninety-eight, and was just about ready to retire. As Bert would tell anyone who would care to listen. "Just two more years to go, and I get the old age, that along with my veterans and town pension should set me up for life."

Bill had asked Mr. Jones before about his war experiences, but he had always clammed up. Today however, Bert seemed ready to talk.

"My Grandfather was wounded at Vimy Ridge," Bill offered, in an attempt to break the ice.

"Yes I remember you're Granny McNair telling me that. I wish I had met him, but he wasn't in my Company."

"What was it really like Mr. Jones?"

"Terrifying is the only word I can use to describe it. They were pretty liberal with the rum rations before we went over the top, but I was still plenty scared. We advanced behind a rolling barrage, and when we got to the German trenches the hand-to-hand fighting was brutal. I was hit in the back of the neck by a trench shovel, and that's the last thing I remembered until I came to in an aid station. I was told that a buddy of mine, Grant Williams dragged me there. I was just thinking of him.

After he made sure I was safe and cared for, he returned to the battle. Later on, I was told that he got blown to bits by a grenade. I never saw him again."

Bert shut down abruptly as if an internal switch has been thrown, and didn't say anymore. Bill wanted to continue asking questions, but figured that Mr. Jones needed to be alone with his thoughts. He politely excused himself, then headed back home.

*

Billy's grandmother made him his favorite for lunch—a toasted peanut butter and tomato sandwich with lots of mayo. After they had finished eating, Bill and Granny McNair sat by the window awaiting Paul's arrival. There was certainly a touch of deja vu about the whole thing, and for some reason a profound sense of pease.

"I talked to Bert Jones down at Memorial Park Grandma. I sure have a better idea now of what you must have gone through during the Great War."

"We weren't married till your grandfather got back, but I know the war affected him like nothing else ever had. He was only fifty-four when he passed away, and I think serving in the first war, then being with the Canadian Expeditionary Force in the second, was more than one man could stand in a lifetime."

"He must have been a wonderful person; I'm just sorry I was too young to get to know him, or really remember him."

"Don't worry Sonny he knew you as a baby and small child. He was very proud of his first grandson."

It was Billy's turn to have tears in his eye, and he was relieved to see the blue Volkswagen Van pull into the driveway. He gave his grandmother an affectionate kiss on the cheek, then walked out the door.

When they were ten miles east of Georgetown, Bill asked, "Is your sister going be all right?"

"She'll be fine," Paul replied uneasily. "Her arm was broken, but that's starting to heal. She still has nightmares about the drunk who came across the center-line and rammed her, but I think that will all go away in time." Paul didn't want to talk about it anymore, so Bill remained quite.

Summer of '61

When they got to the farm near Beeton, Paul told Bill to back up to the steel-sided storage shed. Shortly after the Volks was in position, a stooped, weather-tanned farmer emerged from his fortress-like limestone house, and shook Paul's hand.

"We'll need ten fifty pounders Doug."

"Okay Paul, I hope you don't mind if I can't give you a hand loading, but the old lumbago is killing me."

"Yeah Doug, my back has been acting up lately too."

Billy finally understood the real reason for his coming along on the trip.

"You two guys relax. I need the exercise to get in shape for football season, so let me at those spuds," Bill shouted, as he charged into the shed.

The two men thankfully leaned up against a grey, knurled, cedar rail fence, and watched Bill carry the heavy, earth-oily sacks, into the van.

25
*

They arrived back in Port Carter at four-thirty. Paul played foreman while Bill and Joey stacked the bags of potatoes inside the storeroom of his gilt-edged restaurant.

"We're running a little late Billy," Paul said, when they had finished. "I told Harry to stay till we got back, so you'd better get up there to cover the rest of your shift,"

No rest for the serfs Bill groused to himself, as he double-timed it up to the Hilltop. He entered the rear door of the kitchen, and found Harry standing by the grill shooting the breeze with Jennifer Rossini.

"Hey Slick you're back, how were things down south."

"Couldn't be better Harry."

"Okay, Billy the Kid, I'm on my way to the links. Have one for me eh?" Harry winked, before making like Jessie Owens, and sprinting for his car.

"So what's happening in your world Jen?" Bill asked, admiring the curvacious contents of Miss Rossini's uniform.

He was stunned when she suddenly burst into tears. Another romantic crisis he thought, while he held her in his arms until she cried it out.

"My boyfriend met a girl at Western, and he wants to let things cool off for awhile," she managed to choke out between snorts and snuffles.

"This bonehead must be out of his tree Jen! You're better than any bimbo babe from some ivory tower," Bill replied in a rush. "Hey, I've just had a full scale brain wave. The Glenn Miller Band is playing at Dunn's on Wednesday, and if I can get Harry's car, then we could double date with Virg and Gibby."

"Oh Slick, you're so neat, that would be out of sight," she said, squeezing his hand.

Bill felt better because Jen was feeling better. He wasn't exactly a knight in shining armour, but he did hate to see anyone who was unhappy. Especially someone as beautiful as Miss Rossini.

They worked their buns off till ten-fifteen, then as if someone had pulled the customers need not enter switch, the restaurant became silent. After everything was cleaned up, Bill walked Jen back to the Harb. Just before they arrived at the entrance to the girl's quarters, Jen told him to wait a minute while she talked to Virginia.

Summer of '61

She came back down the stairs two minutes later and bubbled, " Virg thinks that it would be great, and she's sure that Gib will want to go."

"Okay I'll work on Harry tomorrow. He still owes me a bit of time from a double shift I did for him earlier this summer, so I don't think it'll be a problem."

"Billy, you don't know how much better I feel," Jen sighed, pulling him towards her and rewarding him with a warm passionate kiss. He was completely surprised, but soon recovered, and returned her gesture of good will.

Bill was beginning to explore first base when Jen slowly disengaged and said, "Time for bed Slick, and you know what? That son-of-a-bitch can have his bit of sorority fluff."

"That's a good one Gracie," Bill grinned, leaping into a George Burns routine. "Now say good night Gracie."

"Good night Gracie," Jennifer responded, picking up the straight-line.

They started to giggle like children, laughter that came right from the belly, gurgling upwards, and escaping into the air on the wings of pure joyfulness.

After a slow, yawn filled saunter, back to the café, Billy climbed the stairs leading to the Hilltop Hilton's fashionable penthouse, slipped beneath the covers, and during that transition zone of half-a-sleep, he thought of one of his mother's favorite expressions. "You never know your luck."

He was finally going to do it with Doris. He entered her sweet love canal, and experienced several minutes of unimaginable bliss before letting loose his life savings of semen. He awoke slowly, fully expecting Doris to be there in bed with him. Instead he became suddenly aware of a wet, gooey, sticky feeling on his belly. He was laying on his back, and realized that he just had an encounter with Joe W. Dream. He was as quiet as a tree frog during a dry spell when he tip-toed towards the washroom to clean up.

"Boy, it was so real!" he whispered, "Well maybe one of these days, it won't be a dream."

"Oh great, now I'm talking to myself," Bill muttered, talking to himself. He quickly washed up, went back to his bunk, crawled in and enjoyed the sleep of a dreamland lover boy.

He placed his feet on the cold bedroom floor at six-thirty, and was in the kitchen by a quarter to seven, ready for the opening bell. Another day at the Mickey Mouse Club.

Half-way through the morning Bongo Charlie oozed into the kitchen. "Hey man, what's happening?" Charlie rasped, holding up his index finger and its buddy—indicating the sign for peace. Bill felt like he'd been thrust into a rerun of, "The Many Lives of Dobbie Gillis", and was face-to-face with Maynard G. Krebs. Charlie even looked like Bob Denver.

"Not a whole hell of a lot," Bill shrugged, flipping an egg, once over lightly.

"Yeah, this place is real Dullsville. Listen man, I got this cool letter from my friend in the Village," Charlie beamed, pulling a dirty, wrinkled piece of paper out of his shirt pocket.

"Is that a small town near here?" Bill asked, as he placed a slice of bread into the toaster.

"Total Squaresville cookie, like the real Village," Charlie sputtered, as if Bill were a visitor from Jupiter. "I mean like Greenwich Village, New York, where it's happening, man. This new cat Bob Dylan is singing in one of the coffee houses there, he's far out ."

"Why's he so great Charlie?"

"Protest man, it's starting to happen, the establishment is going to freak out. The times they're a changing. Civil rights is where it's at man."

Charlie was running out of steam, and sat down on a chair by the screen door. Bill figured that Bongo was finished with his dissertation and asked him if he wanted something to eat. "Yeah man, I'm like travelling on the fumes."

Billy had saved several stale doughnuts, and gave these to Charlie. "Some day I'm going to do you a big one man," Charlie promised. Carefully guarding his prize, he disappeared like a puff of aerosol, into the pure air beyond the rear door.

Bonnie Baker entered the kitchen to pick up the order that Bill had just prepared and said, "I hear that you and Jen are going to Dunn's Wednesday night."

No secrets in Dullsville, Bill thought, but the restaurant crew were almost like family now. "Yeah, if I can get Harry's car we're going to double with Virg and Gibby."

Summer of '61

"That's oh so cool, because the Doc and I are doubling with Danny and Donna," she burbled excitedly, before returning to the dinning room.

The afternoon went by like a movie shown in slow motion, but got back to normal speed when Harry arrived at three.

"I've got a huge favor to ask," Bill began tentatively, before Harry went out to the counter to get a coffee.

"Shoot Kid."

"I need to borrow your car tomorrow evening."

"No problem Billy. I owe you one anyway."

"Virg, Jen , Gibby and me are going to Dunn's, but we won't be back till well after midnight."

"I'll crash upstairs on the extra roll-away, so don't sweat it Slick."

"Harry you're a Prince among men."

"Now don't go getting all sentimental on me Billy boy," Harry grinned, looking around for his apron.

After cleaning up, Bill hustled down the hill to tell Jen about getting the car.

"Wow, that's terrific news Billy. I'll tell Virginia right away," Jen shouted, jumping up and down like a lovesick marsupial. "Do you mind going up to the A&P to let Gibby know what's happening?"

"Glad to fair maiden," Bill smiled, imaging himself as a knight on a noble mission.

Leaving the security of the castle, he crossed the drawbridge and found Sir Gilford Gibbons stacking a shelf with cans of tomato soup.

"I'll pick you up at seven tomorrow," Bill said, after telling Gibby about borrowing Harry's Bel Air.

"Hey that's swell Slick, it'll give me a chance to wear my white sports coat and my old pair of white bucks."

"Don't forget the pink carnation Gib," Bill joked.

"Gee wilikers, that's a good one Slick."

"Yeah, a laugh minute on the Billy Carlsen show."

"Well, I'd better get back to the salt mine, I don't want old man Parker chewing my ass," Gibby grumbled, looking nervously over his shoulder.

On the way back to the Hilltop Bill met Joey, and they got to talking about hockey.

"I think Tim Horton's the best blueliner the Leaf's have got," Joey said, swinging his arms sideways to slap at an imaginary puck.

"Yeah my dad says he's the strongest guy in the league," Bill replied solemnly.

"I guess that's why no one wants to fight him," Joey nodded respectfully.

"You know with Carl Brewer, Alan Stanley and Bobby Baun helping Horton at the blueline, they're going to be mighty tough," Bill predicted, doing a Ward Cornell type summary.

"How about Red Kelly eh? They convert him to a centre, and he wins the Lady Bying," Joey said, feeling the magic that comes with mentioning the name of one of your heros.

"That Imlach's a fucking genius," Billy concluded, great reverence in his voice.

"He shoots he scores,"Joey roared, into his fist microphone.

"Hey Foster Hewitt never sounded so good," Bill shouted, picturing the great man sitting in the Gondola.

Their trip to Hockeyland came to a crashing halt when Joey entered the kitchen, and began to attack the waiting mound of dishes. Leaving Joey to his labours, Bill walked down Bailer Street to the beach.

The area was deserted except for a solitary couple sitting at picnic table. He headed in the opposite direction, and soon had the far end of the beach all to himself. Billy picked up a half-dozen flat stones, and skipped them one-by-one across the water. He watched the repeated rings move out from where the stones nicked the calm surface of the river. Much like life Bill thought, you bounce along, leave a few ripples, then they disappear. A King Fisher smashed into the water off to his left. Smiling to himself, because he realized that just like people every once in awhile you get to make a big splash, then back to waiting.

Feeling peaceful yet tired, Bill returned to the penthouse, and went lights out. He woke up with a start an hour later, but was reassured when he noticed Danny comfortably slouched in a chair staring at a hotrod magazine.

"Welcome back from Snoozeville," Danny grinned.

"So what's up with you Danderoo?"

Summer of '61

"Just reading about a way to modify a Flathead eight."

"Boy, I sure wish we had a radio in here," Bill stretched, starting to come fully awake.

"Yeah, you'd think that Paul could give us a crystal set or something," Danny groused. "Hey do you remember sitting around the old walnut-stained Philco on a Sunday night listening to "The Shadow" or "Boston Blackie?"

"I remember that," Bill sighed, a touch of nostalgia in his voice. "Did your family ever listen to "Fibber McGee and Molly?"

"Sure did, and got a lot of laughs too," Danny chuckled. "I used to love that commercial on "Space Patrol", when the announcer would say that Quaker-Puff-Rice and Quaker-Puff-Wheat were shot from guns."

The two young men, one seventeen and the other eighteen, sighed contentedly thinking that yes, those were the good old days.

"The Doc's going into Bracebridge tomorrow to pick up a mickey of rye for the dance," Danny said, when they got around to discussing their plans for Bala.

"Could you ask him to get one up for me too?"

"No problem Slick, I know that you and the Doc are pals."

"Yeah he's a good shit," Bill nodded, as he handed Danny two dollars.

"Think I'll head down to the Harb, and see what Donna's doing," Danny yawned, getting up from the table.

"You've got it pretty bad for her eh?"

"Not really, just a summer fling," Danny said unconvincingly. "What are you about to do Slick?"

"Believe it or not Mr. Ripley, I'm going to read a book."

Danny picked up the paperback by Bill's bed. *"Peyton Place!* That's real mean Billy boy."

Bill heard Danny's fading footsteps on the back stairs, followed by the sound of the screened-door slamming shut. He tried his best to read, but his eyelids felt like lead lined window shades. The book dropped slowly from his hand on to his chest, and he went to sleep.

26
*

When Bill went home on the potato trip he snatched his navy blue blazer, and grey flannel slacks out of the top hall closet, figuring that this getup would be needed if he ever got to Dunn's, and lo and behold tonight was the night. In addition, he had thrown in a pair of black Oxfords, a white dress shirt, and a clip-on black bow tie. With this outfit Billy was not only set for the trip to Bala to see the Glenn Miller Band, but if the occasion should arise he was ready to meet Her Royal Majesty, Queen of England and Sovereign of the great Dominion. Should Liz drop by, he would offer her a free Black Label. William Francis knew how to treat a lady eh?

Virginia was working at the Hilltop that morning, so Bill was able to discuss their plans for the evening. After settling on times and locations Virginia hurried into the dinning room to take the first breakfast orders.

The day was like a rocket, it blasted off and kept on accelerating. Time shifted magically about the great markers of the universe, and before you could say holy mackerel, Harry appeared in a glittering shower of sparkles at three.

"Here's the key Kid," Harry said, removing his golf jacket. "My only advice is; don't have more than two drinks, I'd hate to see my beautiful Bel Air, and your head wrapped around a Hydro pole."

"I catch your drift Harry," Bill smiled, grabbing the brass ring. After saying good-bye to Sammy T., he high stepped it up the back stairway to indulge in the three S's.

Billy returned to the kitchen at six to make himself a club sandwich for supper, and was behind the wheel of the Chevy heading for the Harb by seven.

The girls looked like debutantes in their full length gowns. The biggest dance of the year at Georgetown High was called the Formal, and this sure as short strokes reminded Bill of the illustrious ball. It was a warm, gentle evening, and he took his time driving to Bala.

When they arrived at Dunn's, Bill and Gibby had to pay ten dollars each, before the fabulous foursome were allowed to make their grand entrance into the inner sanctum of the hallowed hall. The cavernous building consisted of a lower dance floor, an elevated seating area, a large stage, and a balcony level connected by a wide staircase to the spaces below. The girls wanted to sit at a ringside table for eight.

Summer of '61

This suited Bill just fine because he loved to dance. Jennifer was truly radiant, and he figured that a lot of rug cutting would likely be the order of the evening. The Doc, Bonnie, Danny and Donna joined them fifteen minutes later.

"Hey, Billy the Kid, Gibby, how are things," the Doc smiled, shaking hands all round.

"Just great Doc. Did you get that order I gave to Danny?" Bill asked expectantly.

"Yep," the Doc said, discreetly extracting a 12 ouncer of Canadian Club from the inside pocket of his sports coat.

"This is real good stuff Doc. Do I owe you anymore coin of the realm?"

"No problem Kid, any extra's on the house."

Bill was about to put the bottle of rye under the table when the Doc cleared his throat, "I'd have Jen stow that in her purse if I were you Billy. I talked to one of my buddies on the OPP the other day, and there's likely to be a close check here tonight."

Bill handed the mickey to Jen, and she transferred it to her handbag. He didn't want any hassles with the Ontario Provincial Police. Dunn's operated without a liquor license, but the jug under the table was an accepted tradition as long as things were kept under control.

"My cop pal says, there have been complaints from the locals about drunks rolling out of here after a dance," the Doc explained. "I was also informed that road checks were possible, so I'd watch the booze consumption." Danny and Bill were quick to agree on a two drink limit.

A waitress came to the table to take their order. After a brief conference they decided that two large bottles of ginger ale plus a bowl of ice would be enough. The young girl who was serving them returned two minutes later, and collected ten dollars for the rocks and mix. "I can sure see how they make their money here," Bonnie grouched.

Jen removed the whiskey bottle from her purse, then poured healthy shots into each of the eight glasses. When the ginger and ice were added the Doc proposed a toast.

"To good times, good friends, and to those who are absent from this table," the Doc said, raising his glass.

Bill remembered that the Doc's father had been killed in the war, and understood the significance of the simple words.

The Glenn Miller Band filed on to the elevated stage, then took their places behind the appropriate music stands. The drummer gave a perfunctory roll, and Ray McKinley came to the microphone accompanied by a burst of applause from the audience.

McKinley said three words into the mike, and the audience went wild—"String of Pearls".

Bill and Jen danced well together, and thoroughly enjoyed the multitude of Miller hits. They agreed that, "In the Mood", "Pennsylvania 6-5000", and "Little Brown Jug were their favorites. As the famous melodies drifted over the grey-blue blanket of the smoke filled hall, Bill slid into a fantasy mode. He pretended to be Jimmy Stewart as Glenn Miller, and his lovely wife was June Allyson, subtly disguised as Jennifer Rossini. The Glenn Miller story suddenly became as real to him as breathing. He stayed in this dreamlike state until Ray McKinley returned to the microphone, and announced that it was time for the intermission.

"They're oh so groovy," Bonnie gushed, when everyone was seated at the table.

"Yeah I like Elvis and all, but these guys are really good," Danny agreed.

"Boy, it's been a fantastic summer at Dunn's," the Doc said excitedly. "Woody Herman, Tommy Dorsey and now Glenn Miller. Wow! What a combination."

True to the Doc's prediction, two OPP officers appeared on the scene, each carrying a long handled flashlight. They looked carefully under every table, and confiscated any liquor bottles that were spotted.

"How's it goin' Ernie?" the Doc shouted, when the two policemen approached them. The young officer laughed, but still did his duty, meticulously scanning the numerous hiding spots guarded by eight pairs of shoes.

"Are you charging those people?" Danny asked, when they'd finished their inspection.

"No, just giving them a warning, but any booze we find is on a one-way down the sink," Ernie replied, in a friendly tone."

Summer of '61

"If you folks are heading back to Port Carter, just remember there will be a pair of cruisers at the edge of town."

"You gentlemen have a great night and thanks for keeping our great Province safe from bank robbers and murderers," Gibby smirked.

Virginia was pissed off, and gave Gil a swift, under the table kick. He just about spit out his pipe, but recovering quickly stammered, "S-Seriously we really appreciate the friendly warning that you guys just gave us."

"You folks enjoy yourselves, and we'll see you later Doc," Ernie said, riveting Gibby with a steely look, before leaving their table.

"Well in my opinion those jerks have uniformities, just like the Gestapo," Gibby fumed, as smoke ladened sparks erupted form his hardwood weed burner.

"You know Gilford, opinions are like assholes, everybody has one," Virginia growled, stiffening her spine.

Oh, oh, Bill thought, this could be the end of a not so beautiful relationship.

The band reappeared before further volleys could be exchanged, and began to play "Chattanooga Choo Choo". The dance floor was packed solid again, and the rest of the evening was filled with the incredible music of one the best Big Bands of the Forties.

Bill and Jen could have stayed there forever, but shortly before midnight Ray McKinley returned to the mike and said, "Thank you ladies and gentlemen, we've enjoyed playing for you this evening, and the last dance of course will be, "Moonlight Serenade".

All Bill could see was Doris's face—this was their song. He was dancing with Jen, but his mystic transport machine had dropped him into another world where only he and Doris were in the room. He was embarrassed when the band stopped playing, because he figured Jen might catch on and be offended.

"To be perfectly honest Billy that song reminds me of my boyfriend Don, and I was fantasizing about being with him. I know that's not fair to you, so please forgive me," Jen confessed, when the music ended.

"I don't mind," Bill sighed. "Be where you want to be, and with the one you miss the most."

Virginia and Gilford Gibbons were as quiet as a pair of church mice on the return trip to Port Carter.

Billy deposited Virg and Gibby at the Harb, and wasn't surprised to hear curt goodnights, then rapid departures in separate directions. When he arrived at the Hilltop with the ravishing Miss Rossini by his side, he was surprised to find Harry still wide awake, but soon agreed that Sammy T. would likely get a better nights sleep if he headed for his own soft pit.

Shortly after the tail lights of the Chevy faded into the blackness, Jen and Bill decided to take a stroll along the river pathway that led to Lake Raddison.

"I guess all matches aren't made in heaven," Jennifer frowned.

"Yeah, Virg was really ticked. I'll bet she and Gil are history now."

"Who were you thinking of during that last dance Billy?"

"You're pretty smart for a girl," he chuckled. "I was dreaming about my girlfriend Doris. Well she's not really mine anymore since we broke up, but when I went home her new boyfriend was away, and we had a great time together. Holy mackinaw! You know, I'm totally confused."

"I sure understand Billy. I'm still hurting from what my boyfriend told me."

They reached the end of the cement walkway and sat on a park bench. Jen had a sweater, and Bill was wearing his blazer—neither one of them were cold. It had become crystal clear to Bill that they were becoming a brother and sister act, so he was content to just sit and chat.

"You know today is, or was August sixth," Bill said seriously.

"Okay Slick, you've got a calender over your bed, and I'm really impressed."

It was obvious that the gorgeous Miss Rossini was not a keen student of things historical, so he tried to give her a few clues.

"If I said *Enola Gay* or *Manhattan Project* would that help."

"Are they Broadway musicals?" Jen asked, catching on, but leading him on.

Bill was about to explain further when she said, " It was necessary you know. My father was training on Vancouver Island for the invasion of Japan. He told me, if it weren't for the A-bomb he'd have been gonesville."

Summer of '61

Bill was astonished by Jen's reply and added, "Yeah and my dad says that millions of Japanese would have been killed defending their homeland."

"No matter how you cut it, a horrible thing happened, but it did end the war," Jen sighed.

They sat there in silence enjoying the moon beams reflecting off the lake. Only the occasional haunting cry of a solitary loon, shattered the stillness of the star spattered night.

"Do you think there will ever be a true period of peace on this planet?" Jen asked, in a bemusing tone.

"Sure as God made little green apples, "Bill replied, with the uncluttered optimism of youth. "Now that we've got the world in order, I think it's time for a little shut eye."

He walked Jennifer back to the girls side door at the Harb, and gave her a brotherly kiss on the forehead.

"Slick if you were only a few years older, I think I'd be madly in love."

"That seems to be the theme from this summer place," Bill grumbled. "Sleep tight and don't let the bed bugs bite." Looking a lot like Jackie Gleason's "Poor Soul", he made his way slowly up the hill.

Six-thirty caught up to him at jet speed. Billy had managed to get only four hours sleep, but was able to make it through the day. He was just about on the ropes when Harry arrived to take over. As tired as he was, Bill had been hatching a plan over the course of the afternoon.

"Remember a while back when I told you that I might have a big one to ask ?" Bill began, when Harry was halfway through his coffee.

"Sure do Kid, what's on your mind?"

"Tomorrow's my day off, so if you'd work for me Saturday, and if I could borrow your car, then I'd be able to take a run up to Bigwin to see my buddy Dave Graham," Bill said, holding his breath.

"No problem Slick, it's a deal," Harry answered with a fox-like grin.

Bill could not believe his ears, but noticing the cat-and-canary look on Harry's face he said," What's the catch?"

"Funny you should mention that Billy. Tuesday and Wednesday next week I'd like to play in a tournament at Woodbridge, so I was hoping you'd be able to cover for me."

Billy thought for a moment, because this would mean two sixteen hour days, but he desperately wanted to see Tex. Shaking Harry's outstretched hand, he agreed.

"That's great Kid, and we both got what we wanted."

"Yeah if countries could get along as well as we do, then the world would be a hell of lot more peaceful."

*

After supper Bill went over to the theatre to see Ken. He made his way backstage, and found him watching things from the wings. The current production was *A Streetcar Named Desire*. Ken only had a moment, but he seemed really excited.

"You won't believe this Billy-boo, but I got the job at the Stratford Shakespearean Festival."

"Hey that's terrific! How about Tim?" Bill asked, pleased for his friend.

"He's going to be a carpenter there. It'll be just like old home week," Ken whooped, dancing a little jig. "Well Billy, I've got to get back to work, so I'll see you later."

Bill hung around for the rest of the first act. He liked Tennessee Williams because, *Cat On A Hot Tin Roof* was one of his favorite flicks. In all honesty he thought that the star of the movie, Elizabeth Taylor, was the hottest pussy he'd ever seen.

27
*

He got to bed early, hoping to be on the road first thing the next morning, and was ready to go by seven. Harry was busily flipping eggs when Billy entered the kitchen.

"Have a good trip Kid," he said, his lips spreading into a toothy smile.

"Thanks a million Harry," Bill grinned, catching the keys to freedom.

It was a cool overcast day, but the roads were dry and the traffic light. He picked up highway eleven at Bracebridge, then headed north until he reached the Dorset turn off. He was at the Bigwin dock by eleven. Bill parked the Bel Air in the shade of a spreading red oak, before making his way to a small ferry boat that was lashed to the government wharf. As luck would have it; the barge-like craft was ready to leave for the island. It was a ten minute crossing, and he was pointed in the general direction of the Lodge to look for Dave, as soon as they hit the shore.

The staff cabins were located well out of sight of the main buildings. The island had been used as a prisoner of war camp during WW II, and German POW's had lived in these huts. Bill figured they were probably in much better shape during the forties. The tin roofs were badly rusted, and the old wooden bunks bolted to the rough-cut walls looked like they had seen one too many coats of yellow paint.The compound that Bill had come to was the boys area. Another group of cabins located on the other side of the island was the exclusive domain of the female staff.

A short, redheaded, blimp-shaped creature, resting his ample butt on the porch of one of the dilapidated structures, informed Bill that Dave was on shift at the kitchen.

"Could you tell me how to get there?" Billy asked, looking uncertainly in the direction of the castle-like spires that identified the location of the main lodge.

"I was just heading over that way. Follow me and I'll show you where Dave works," the pimple-faced-carrot-top wheezed, squinting at Bill through a pair of thick bifocals.

"Gee thanks! My name's Bill Carlsen."

"I'm Delbert Reed, but everyone calls me Fly," the Fly said, vigorously pumping Bill's hand.

When they finally reached the Inn's huge kitchen, Bill found Tex hard at work, up to his elbows in soap suds.

"Hey Dave how's it goin'?" Bill shouted gleefully.

"Billy, how the hell did you get here?"

"I borrowed Harrys wheels, and drove up to the Island this morning."

"How long can you stay?"

"I should be on my way back to the Port tomorrow afternoon."

"I'll be finished up here at three," Dave said, wiping his hands with a dry rag. "Fly, could you take Billy to the staff dining hall, and make sure he gets something to eat before you show him where my cabin is?"

"Sure thing Tex," the Fly smiled, starting towards the heavy steel exit door.

"I'll see you later Billy, we're kind of busy right now."

"Okay Tex, and thanks for the chow invite, I'm so hungry, I could eat a beaver for breakfast."

"Get this man some real food," Dave snorted, as he reached for another pot to scrub.

Del Reed led Bill to a large staff dinning room that had been tastefully decorated in early war surplus. They started along a cafeteria style serving counter where the Fly grabbed a dark brown plastic tray, then overloaded it with thick cut ham sandwiches, large slices of apple pie and several cartons of milk. While they were eating their lunch, a pair of knockdown gorgeous snuggies, one a redhead and the other a blonde, approached the counter. After picking up a selection of food and drinks, they headed straight for the table where Bill and the Fly were sitting, and placed their trays directly across from the two boys.

"Hi Fly, who's your friend?" the blonde asked, while flashing Bill an alluring smile.

"This is Billy Carlsen, and he's a buddy of Tex Grahams."

"Hello there Billy my name's Pam, and this is my roommate Julie," the blonde crooned seductively.

"Pleased to meet you two lovely ladies," Bill replied smoothly.

"Aren't you the proper gentleman," Julie smiled, her voice full of sugar and promise.

Summer of '61

"Where do you work Bill?" Pam asked, slowly stirring the ice in her cola with a straw.

"I've got a job as a short-order cook at a restaurant in Port Carter."

"How about that," Julie said incredulously. "I'm from Oakville, but my uncle has a cottage on Lake Raddison five miles out of town. Do you cook at the Harb?"

"No, I do work for Paul Evans, but at his new café, the Hilltop."

"I was there, after a play put on by the Port Town Players."

"That's the place," Bill grinned.

"There's a staff dance here tonight. Will you and Tex be coming?" Pam asked.

"Yep, or just breathing hard," Bill whispered innocently. "What time does it start?"

"Eight-thirty," Julie winked, a wicked grin forming on her bee stung lips.

The Fly had finished lunch, and wanted to get back to his cabin. Billy shot the girls a friendly good-bye smile, then followed him out the door.

"Nice chicks," Bill said, still marvelling at the splendor of Julie's perfect set of headlights.

"Yeah, they work as chamber maids, and that Julie's one hot piece of chicken pie," the Fly buzzed, reverently.

After escorting Bill to the place where he had left his duffel bag, the Fly guided him to a cabin at the edge of the bush.

"This is where Tex lives. He only has one roommie, so there are two empty top bunks," the Fly puffed, turning on the bare-bulbed overhead light.

Billy threw his bag on to one of the unused uppers, then followed Delbert out to the porch where they sat on metal folding chairs. The Fly and Bill kicked back enjoying the sun that had just emerged from behind a large dark cloud.

"What do you do around here Fly?" Bill asked, starting to unwind from his trip.

"I work in Room Service, and I'm on duty at three," the Fly said, glancing nervously at his watch. "Holy Toledo! I'd best be on my way. I've got to take care of a few things before I go on shift."

"Thanks for your help Fly, and maybe we'll see you at the dance."

"Sure thing Billy," the Fly grunted, as he oozed out his chair.

28

Bill had just woken up from an afternoon siesta, when Dave entered the cabin.

"Are you all settled in Billy?"

"Snug as a bug Tex."

"How's Kitty?" Dave asked, as he plopped noisily on to a bottom bunk.

"I didn't get a chance to see her before I left, but the last time we talked she said to say hello if I ever got up this way. I think you made quite an impression there Romeo."

"She's a real babe," Dave murmured, in a thickening voice.

"Well Tex, she is twenty-one. Isn't that a little long in the tooth for you?"

"Billy old buddy, like fine wine, women get better as they age. Besides think of all the experience you can get from someone who's experienced."

"Tex, I think you're becoming a great philosopher, or just developing into a dirty old man."

"Dirty, maybe Slick but not too soon old I hope."

"Hey Dave I was wondering, how did Delbert Reed come by his nickname?"

"My roommate, Al Crawford thinks that Del is a lot like Piggy from the book, *Lord of the Flies*," Dave said, looking around for a clean shirt. "Piggy was a little harsh, so we settled on Fly. Getting back to serious matters, William Francis my fine feathered friend, did you manage to pick up any booze?"

Bill smiled, then drew a twenty-sixer of rye whiskey from his duffel bag. Danny's ID had worked just fine at the Dorset liquor store.

"I propose that we toast the health of good Queen Bess before supper. What say you, Sir William of Carter?"

"Tex, cut the Robin Hood crap, and get us a couple of glasses."

Dave returned with two peanut butter jars and said, "Sorry but the fancy china got smashed at our last party, and we haven't had a chance to liberate anymore."

"These will do fine, but what about mix?" Bill chuckled.

"Here's a tip for you Billy. Learn to drink your rye with water, or if you want to get real sophisticated, water with a few ice cubes thrown in. You'll never be without mix, and it's a hell of a lot cheaper."

Summer of '61

"By golly Dave you're not just getting older, you're also getting smarter."

Tex the rookie genius and his sidekick Slick sat on the hard metal chairs, and lazily sipped whiskey with water, letting the afternoon slowly run out.

When they returned from supper at the staff dinning hall they found Al Crawford sitting on the porch reading a dog-eared copy of Stag magazine. He got up from his chair, and came over to meet Bill. After the introductions were complete, the three Kings of Bigwin decided to a have a little after dinner cocktail.

"Hey, this is good stuff Billy," Al declared, gulping down the amber contents of his jar.

"Sip it Crawfish you lush. It'll last a lot longer," Dave scolded, as he savoured the aromatic taste of the whiskey.

"You know at times like this he can be just like your mother," the Crawfish groaned.

"So are we going to this dance tonight, or what?" Bill shouted, beginning to feel the effects of the forty percent by volume.

"You're ruckin fight we are," Dave bellowed, as he leaned back in his chair.

It was half-past-nine when they walked into the staff dinning hall. Tables and chairs had been arranged around the perimeter of the large room, and a portable record player provided the music. Bill spotted Julie right away, and went over to ask her to dance.

"I was hoping you'd be here Billy," Julie sighed, as she snuggled in real close to the soft strains of a thirty-three and a third grooving out, "The Theme From a Summer Place".

"Boy, do you ever smell good Julie. That's real sexy perfume you're wearing."

"It's called Youth Dew, and I'm glad you like it."

"Do you think you might get down to your uncle's cottage before the summers over?" Bill asked hopefully.

"Probably not. I've got to be here till the middle of August, then it's back home to get ready for school."

The song ended, but hard on it's heels the penetrating beat of Elvis' "You Ain't Nothing But a Hound Dog" got the joint a rockin'. After jiving up a storm they went over to the table where Dave and Pam were sitting.

The two couples chatted away about music and movies, thoroughly enjoying each others company.

"You know the girls in Port Carter call old Carlsen here, Teddy," Dave grinned, giving Bill a playful tap on the shoulder.

"Thanks a lot Tex, sometimes you've got a big mouth," Bill growled angrily.

"Relax!" Julie said, "I think Teddy is real cute."

"Yeah, all girls love their Teddy bears," Pam whispered suggestively.

"Especially if they're cuddly, and don't mind being hugged in bed," Julie added, in a sultry voice.

When Jimmy Dean's record, "Big Bad John" was played they all sang along, and speculated as to why John was considered so big and so bad. Julie had downed a couple of stiff drinks before coming to the dance, and stated boldly that John was probably hung like a horse. After making her pronouncement, she carefully placed her hand under the table, and began to investigate Bill's hanging's.

"Maybe it should be big bad Teddy," Julie breathed into Bill's left ear. His world was definitely progressing from good to gooder.

"Boy it sure would be nice to have a real cold drink," Pam said, beginning to feel the heat from the crowded dance hall.

Tex walked over to a chest freezer located behind the serving counter, and returned with a large plastic bowl packed full of ice cubes.

"Let's go to my place, and have that really cool drink," Dave suggested, mopping his brow.

"You've got our vote," Pam purred luxuriously.

Five minutes later they were making their way along the moon lit path that led to the boy's compound.

"You'll really like Stalag Seventeen Pam," Dave joked.

"I'll bet the POW's probably named it the same thing," Bill shuddered, looking around apprehensively for wartime ghosts.

"Yeah, it kind of gives you the creeps," Julie whispered, a cold shiver running up her spine.

29
*

Shortly after arriving at Dave's den of delights, Bill poured hefty shots of rye into four clean jars, and by the second round things were starting to get very relaxed.

"This sure is good stuff," Julie thundered, slurring her words.

"Nothing but the best for a beautiful lady," Bill smiled, freshening her drink.

"You're a charmer Billy," Julie laughed loudly, as she peeled off her blouse. "Let's go skinny-dipping."

"I-I'm up for that!" Dave sputtered, unable to take his eyes off the contents of Julies lacy black bra.

"Moi aussi," Bill said, in his best high school French, Miss Marble would have been overjoyed.

When their jars were empty, Dave picked up a pair of towels, jumped off the porch, and guided the gaggle of giggling dippers to the staff beach. The girls removed their clothes behind a hobbleberry bush, then ran squealing and laughing into the cool refreshing water. The boys had already doffed their duds, and were standing chest deep, awaiting the bare naked ladies.There was a great deal of splashing and general horseplay, then all went quite as an unclad boy discovered an unclad girl.

Bill and Julie wound up at the waters edge, wrapped in each others arms, thoroughly aroused by the intimate contact of their highly sensitive bodies. Julie moaned deep in her throat as he guided her gently onto a large beach towel.

"Billy we need to take precautions," she pleaded breathlessly.

Bill wondered to himself—precautions? Oh, I get it, protection, thank you Sandra. He hurried over to the cedar driftlog where he'd left his pants, then took out his wallet. He removed a foil wrapped condom, and returned to the beautiful creature waiting patiently on the towel. Trying to learn from his past experience with Doris, he decided that the best thing to do, was think about liver and onions. Bill hated liver and onions, and figured if he could concentrate hard enough, then he wouldn't become a premature statistic. Julie was indeed ravishing. She had long red hair, and breasts that would have been rated grade A Citrus by any grapefruit company.

"Let me put that on for you," Julie murmured confidently.

Remember liver and onions, liver and onions—it was finally in place, and he was still okay. Julie lay back on the towel, then willingly spread her well toned legs. Bill eagerly began the timeless dance of man and a woman, and gradually reached a state of prolonged ecstasy—soaring like an eagle. His silver bullet became part of the passing parade, and all he could think of was—Holy smokers, I just got laid. Julie riding her own wave of passion exploded upward just about the time that Bill was having his encounter with history. The young lovers lay entangled in each others arms until they heard a collection of late night merrymakers coming down the trail. They got up reluctantly, and went to look for their scattered clothes.

"Call me Mr. Lucky Slick," Dave winked confidentially, when Billy approached the cedar log.

"Yeah me too," Bill whispered hoarsely, a mile wide grin etched on his face.

"No shit!" Dave whooped delightedly.

They were all fully clothed by the time the cacophonous gang of party animals arrived on the scene.

"Hey Tex, how's the water?" one of the revelers yelled.

"Cool, real cool man!" Dave quipped.

This brought the expected smiles and chuckles from the assembled multitudes. "See you later," Dave hollered over his shoulder, as they began the short route march back to the cabin.

The contented foursome sat quietly on the front porch enjoying a night cap. Shortly after finishing their drinks Pam and Dave disappeared into the cabin to play a game of bunk rugby.

Alone at last with Julie, Bill asked hesitantly, "Can I see you again this summer?"

"I doubt it Teddy. Things are slowing down here, and I'm heading home on August fifteenth. I start first year at Queen's in the fall, and I won't be around Oakville much," Julie said, trying to let him down gently.

"I'll always remember this night Julie. I guess you probably think that's a little bit corny, but it's the truth."

"Teddy you're a real sweetheart and don't ever change," Julie smiled warmly, reaching out for his hand. "I was honoured to be your first."

"H-How did you know that?" he gasped, completely taken off guard.

Summer of '61

"Just a suspicion till now," Julie teased. "Relax Billy you were marvelous."

Bill suddenly felt like he had just won the Irish Sweepstakes. Maybe he could start a whole new career as the most famous gigolo ever to emerge from the great Dominion, or perhaps a little more research had to be done on the subject.

While Billy immersed himself in the Hollywood version of: Numero Uno Lover Of The Great White North, Julie was getting ready to leave.

"I've really got to go Teddy. Be good, and think of me now and again," she said, stretching her subtle body, like a sleek rippling leopard.

"Julie right now you're in first place on my all time hit parade," he beamed.

She gave him a long gift-of-her-young-womanhood kiss good-bye, then slowly walked down the trail to the girl's compound. Bill could still feel the lingering warmth of Julie's lips when Pam and Dave drifted out to the porch.

"It was real nice meeting you Teddy," Pam whispered sleepily. She gave Tex a quick peck on the cheek, and was soon beyond the light sphere of the cabin.

"I'm on at six-thirty, so I guess we'd better turn in," Dave murmured.

"Well partner this has been one hell of a night," Bill sighed deeply.

Two tired, but happy passengers travelling on the third planet from the sun climbed into their tiny pits, and slept and slept and.....

Billy awoke with a start. It was broad daylight, and his head felt like a large fuzz ball. Was that a dream or was it real, he mused sluggishly, in his half-awake state. He was just starting to think clearly when Al Crawford walked into the cabin.

"Hi Al," Bill yawned, "I guess you never made it to the dance last night eh?"

"I was there, but you'd already gone when I arrived," the Crawfish smiled, as he sat down on his bunk. "Tex wants you to drop by the kitchen before you leave. If you're hungry, then go over to the dinning hall, and they'll take care of you."

Bill dressed quickly, picked up his duffel bag, said good-bye to Al, and was out the door in a flash.

He hurried to the kitchen, and found Dave up to his arm pits in dirty dishes.

"I can see you're real busy Tex, so I'll make it short. Thanks for the great time, and give my best to Julie the next time you see her."

"Sure will Billy, and you take care. I guess we won't see each other again until school starts," Dave said, a note of sadness in his voice. His boss was giving him the hairy eyeball, so he shook Bill's hand, and unwillingly got back to the waiting mound of pots and pans.

William Francis seriously considered putting on the feed bag, but feeling the pressure of the journey ahead, he decided to skip the dinning hall and headed straight for the ferry dock. He had to wait fifteen minutes, but was behind the wheel of the Bel Air at high noon. Just like Gary Cooper waiting for the train and the bad guys, he thought to himself. Billy was still in a state of euphoria, and took his time on the return trip to Port Carter. The convertible's top was down, it was a warm sunny day, the wind was playing in his hair, and oh, what a glorious night!

30
*

"Jeez Kid it's good to see ya! How was Bigwin?" Harry shouted, as Bill entered the kitchen.

"Out of sight Harry. Right off the scale."

"I'll take that as a very good," Harry grinned.

"Yeah, as Bongo Charlie would say, far out man!"

"How did the old bucket of bolts perform?" Harry asked, when Bill handed him the keys.

"She purred like a kitten all the way there and back."

"Yeah, that little six has been running like a Swiss watch," Harry nodded, holding the screened-door half open. "Catch you later buddy." Well, Bill thought, when he heard the car door slam, just like Gene Autry, I'm back in the saddle again.

Two minutes later Jennifer Rossini came into the kitchen, wrapped her arms around him and squealed delightedly, " Billy you're back!"

"Boy, do you ever look gorgeous," Bill smiled, giving her a loving squeeze on the left buttock.

"A little wandering hand trouble there Slick," she scolded, immediately pulling away from him.

It was back to brother, and sis, but he could always hope.

Jen took a yellow order pad from her apron pocket, and rattled orders like a machine gun, "Hamburg-works, fries, BLT, toasted on brown, hold the mayo." She then turned around, and headed quickly for the dinning area. The two days at Bigwin had passed into memory, but the dream lived on.

Later that evening Doc Livingstone wandered into the kitchen to say hello.

"Hey Kid, what's happenin'?" the Doc asked, as he watched Bill scoop a mound of coleslaw on to a clean plate. "How was the trip?"

"It was terrific Doc! I had a fantastic time with my best friend Tex, went to a swinging dance, and met a gangbusters snuggy."

"Sounds like pennies from heaven to me Billy."

"Hey Doc I need a real big favor."

"Anything Kid."

"Could you drive around the back? I've got a case of empties I'd like to get rid of."

"Sure thing partner, I'll meet you at the rear door in sixty seconds."

The Doc drove his fifty-six Meteor to the back entrance, while Bill hustled up to the bedroom, and picked up a two-four of dead soldiers hidden under his bunk. The Doc was standing next to the right taillight of his car by the time Bill hit the bottom step.

"Gee thanks Doc," Bill puffed, as he placed the box of bottles into the trunk of the Ford. "I've got a funny feeling, that it's just a matter of time before Paul finds out about my suds for sale operation. This is definitely, the last of the Mohicans."

"Smart move Billy. I thought you may have been pushing your luck," the Doc said, looking at his watch. "Jeez, it's just about nine, and I've got a date with Bonnie."

"Later Doc, and thanks a million," Bill waved.

The Doc leaped into his car, and laid a long black line of rubber, in his hurry to get to the Harb.

Billy returned to the kitchen just in time to pick up an order for onion rings. As he was deep frying the grease laden, golden brown taste treats, he did a little math, and calculated that his entrepreneurial venture was up by twenty-seven bucks. Not exactly a get-rich-quick-scheme, but it did amount to a weeks wages.

He was startled when Bongo Charlie magically appeared beside him at the grill. Somehow the unkempt beatnik was able to move around as silent as a shadow.

"Hey man, how's it goin'?" Charlie asked, sounding like he was trying to hold his breath.

"The universe is unfolding as it should Charlie," Bill grinned, playing his part.

"That's a beautiful concept man. You should write poetry cook guy."

"I'll leave that to you Charlie," Bill said genially.

"Some day I'm going to show you my stuff. I think you'll really dig it."

"Okay Charlie, but in the mean time would like an old beef sandwich I was about to throw out?"

"That would be sensational man," Charlie smiled, traces of saliva forming at the corners of his mouth.

Bill went to the fridge and took out a beef on white that a customer had returned because he thought the bread was stale.

Summer of '61

"Thanks man. You know, I'm from the lower forty-eight, but you Canucks are so hip, that I feel we're just like brothers. One of these days I'm going to pay you back big time," Charlie said, grabbing for the sandwich. Bill closed the fridge door, and by the time he turned around, Bongo had noiselessly drifted away into the gloaming.

At eleven o'clock that evening, he said good night to Jen, cleaned up quickly around the grill, locked all the doors, then went straight to bed.

The next morning before the restaurant opened, Bill stood quietly by the rear screen-door, and watched the swirls of golden mist slowly become the clear air of the day. It was a very peaceful moment, and helped to calm him down before the frantic feeding frenzy began. After the ravenous breakfast crowd had dispersed, he was able to come out to the counter for a short break.

"How was your date with the Doc last night Bonnie?" Bill asked, when she returned from cleaning one of the tables.

"We broke up and I don't care if I ever see that bastard again," she said caustically. "You know that Gibby who works at the A&P is real cute, and he told me if I ever stopped going with the Doc, then he'd love to take me out."

"I guess this is Gibby's lucky day," Bill chuckled.

"I think you're real nice too Slick," Bonnie whispered in her best Monroe-like little girls voice.

"Holy leapin' lizards Bonnie! That's a real compliment, but I"m only seventeen, and no match for someone like Gilford Gibbons," Bill blurted out, thinking that the Doc would be really pissed if he started dating Bonnie.

"Yeah, I guess you're right Billy; it'd be kind of like robbing the cradle," Bonnie replied haughtily, as a customer came into the café.

Bill took this opportunity to hustle back to the kitchen, and begin preparations for the lunch hour. His head was somewhere between Saturn and Pluto for the rest of the day, but he slowly returned to earth when Harry arrived at three-fifteen.

"You can still cover for me Tuesday and Wednesday, right Kid?" Harry asked, before the door was closed behind him.

"Sure thing Harry that's the deal," Bill said, awakening from an erotic reverie that included the pliable Miss Baker.

"You know, I think I've got a real chance at this tournament. During the past two weeks, I've played some of the best golf of my life," Harry bragged.

"Well, Stan Leonard and Al Balding had better take notice," Bill laughed, starting to share Harry's enthusiasm.

"Thanks for the vote of confidence Billy," Harry grinned.

"Enjoy the moment Harry, that's what it's all about."

When Bill entered the Hilltop's bunkhouse, Danny was stretched out on his bed reading Bill's smudgy, well worn copy of *Peyton Place*.

"Hey Slick how come these two pages are stuck together? I was just getting to a juicy part," Danny snickered.

"Must have spilled some jam on them, or something," Bill replied lamely.

" More than likely it was a pair of pecker tracks," Danny chortled devilishly.

"So how's Donna doing?" Bill asked, steering Danny away from further speculation.

"She's fine. We're taking in a movie at the Bracebridge Drive-In tonight," Danny said, closing the book.

"What's playing?" Bill yawned, trying to sound interested.

"I don't know, besides I never planned on watching much of the picture anyway, if you catch my drift," Danny grinned wickedly.

"Yeah, they're called passion pits for a good reason," Bill smirked.

"Hey Slick, when you were gone we found out a real interesting thing about Old Bob, and you'll never believe it."

"Are you going to tell me Danderoo, or is this Garry Moore and "I've Got A Secret?"

"Okay Billy, don't have a bird. The short version is: Bob's a sleep walker."

"Why hasn't anyone noticed that before?" Bill asked, starting to pay attention.

"That's because we've all been asleep when Bob was up about, you dummy!"

"There's some irrefutable logic in what you say, oh Dangerous One," Bill replied, tongue in cheek.

Summer of '61

"Well, when Joey was awake one night, he saw Bob get up, walk around the room a couple of times, then sit at the table. Joey said he was having a hard time sleeping, so he went over and tried to talk to him. He was amazed that Bob just sat there staring straight ahead."

"What happened next?" Bill inquired, his curiosity fully aroused.

"Joey figured that His Oldness was in a trance, or some kind of hypnotic state, so he tried a little experiment. In a very soft voice he told him to lie on the floor, and sure enough he did."

"Did Bob wake up then?" Bill asked, totally flabbergasted at what he was hearing.

"Nope, he was still asleep, or whatever. Joey then told Bob to get up, and stand on his right foot. He did that, and several other things that Joey suggested."

"S-Sounds awfully weird to me," Bill stuttered, feeling the hairs raise up on the back of his neck.

"It was real spooky story!" Danny shivered unconsciously.

"Well sometimes as they say, truth is stranger than fiction," Bill joked, trying to lighten things up.

"You know Slick, I've always wondered who they, really are?"

"Just the collective wisdom of mankind Danny, and with that settled, I'm going to clean up, grab a little chow, then go out for a breath of fresh air, as they say."

"There you go again Carlsen, I guess they'll never let us alone."

"You know Dan the Man, I think you may be turning into an intellectual."

"Yeah, and fuck you too Billy the Kid."

Bill hit the can, rolled on the Ban, then entered the realm of the great outdoors. He was halfway across the bridge when he met Kitty Carson. She was still in her nurses uniform, and obviously on her way home from work.

"Hi Teddy, it was such a nice day, I walked to office this morning. Once a month we run a Sunday drop-in Clinic for the cottagers."

"Gee whiz Kitty, am I ever glad I bumped into you. I was up at Bigwin, and Tex says hello."

"How's Dave?" Kitty asked, her eyes sparkling like sunlight on a cluster of uncut diamonds.

"He's having a great summer, and enjoying the Island."

"Did you have a good time up there Billy?"

"The best!" Bill said, picturing the beach, and Julie's lascivious smile.

"Well it must have been pretty terrific, because you're grinning like Alice's Cheshire cat," Kitty teased, giving him a playful poke in the ribs. "Say Teddy if you're not doing anything how would you like to come over to the cottage and have dinner with me?"

"And who'll do the cooking fair Princess?" Bill chuckled, bowing at the waist.

"You of course sweet Prince," Kitty smiled, doing a perfect curtsey.

Billy found a tin of sockeye salmon in the cupboard, and the fixings for a salad in the refrigerator. He discovered four fresh rolls in the bread box and placed these on the dinning room table along with butter, a plate of sliced dill pickles, and wedges of cheddar cheese. He served the salmon salad, lightly covered with an oil and vinegar dressing. Kitty produced a bottle of Burgundy and the table was set.

"I should start calling you King William, because this truly is a meal fit for one," Kitty said approvingly.

"Okay then you're Queen Elizabeth," Bill saluted, by raising his glass.

"You know that's my real name. I didn't really like it, or Betty or Libby or Liz. When I was a little girl I asked my mom to call me Kitty," she sighed, images from the past dancing strobe-like across the wide screen of her mind.

"Gosh, I like the name Liz," Bill said, a little glassy eyed. "Liz Taylor is one of my all time favorite actresses. She was fantastic in, *Cat On A Hot Tin Roof.*"

"That's just because you like women who parade around in smoky silk slips, giving you tantalizing glances of bare thigh, garter belt and nylons," Kitty said mischievously.

"Yeah that too," Bill gulped noisily.

"Cheers Teddy," she smiled, as they clinked their wine glasses together.

"Is it okay if I call you Liz?" Bill asked, after taking a swallow of the rich red wine.

"No problem, I call you Teddy, and all's fair in love and war."

Kitty was trying to be light and breezy, but Bill sensed she was worried about something.

Summer of '61

"How are things in the world of Doctors and Nurses?" he inquired, discreetly probing.

Kitty was about to answer, but she broke down completely. Her shoulders began to shake, and all he could make out between sobs was; "Lousy, just friggin lousy."

He got up from his chair, and went over to where she was sitting. He crouched down beside her, gently took her hand and whispered, "Do you want to talk about it, or would you just like me to leave?"

"Lets go sit on the couch, I've got to tell someone," she snuffled, managing to pull herself together. Bill poured her a glass of wine, and waited for the story to unfold.

"On and off for most of the summer I've been having an affair with one of the doctors at the Clinic. He's married, and it's been a real strain on the both of us. He told me today that it's all over, because he wasn't willing to take the chance any longer of his wife finding out. I've been dropped like a hot potato and it really hurts."

"I don't know quite what to say Liz, but if the guy's married, then it's a no win situation for you in the long run."

"That's what my head tells me too, but my heart's still sore," Kitty sniffed, her melancholy beginning to subside.

"Hell, you're a gorgeous chick, bright and personable, so you'll have to buy a baseball bat to fend off all the men who'll be after you for the rest of the summer."

Kitty thought this over for a while, then she brightened, allowing her full lips to curve into a smile. "You're right Teddy! I have to have confidence in myself. He would never leave his precious wife to be with me, and I'm better off without him. You've really helped me to feel a whole lot better."

"Well, in that case Miss, my work here is done , and it's time to move on. Tonto and I have other people to rescue and towns to clean up," Billy grinned, looking around for Jay Silverheels.

"You sure lead a rich fantasy life," Kitty chuckled, after blowing her nose.

"Yes ma'am, but when you're the Lone Ranger, it's all in a days work."

"Okay, you and Silver had better ride off into the sunset. Seriously Billy, you've perked me up, and I think I'll be all right now."

He got up from the couch, and moved slowly towards the door. Kitty gave her cowboy hero a quick kiss on the lips, and wished him pleasant dreams.
   Bill made his way back to the Hilltop, and struggled through two chapters of *Peyton Place*. It was nine-thirty, and the fallout from the Bigwin trip was starting to catch up with him. Before drifting off to sleep, he suddenly became aware of the date. Holy cow! Today is August the 10th, and it's my birthday! Jeez, I'm eighteen! Whoopee shit, now I can legally drink beer in Buffalo.

31

"Up and at em Slick," Joey bugled, after giving Bill's shoulder a hearty shake. "You've been moaning away about some broad named Julie, for the last five minutes."

"Thanks Joey, I didn't mean to sleep in, but I was having this nifty dream," Bill yawned, still savouring the sensual images slowly being washed from the back of his eyelids.

"By the look of that tent poll under your sheet, this Julie must be some babe."

"Just an illusion Joey," Bill mumbled.

He got up quickly, pulled on his clothes, scrubbed up in the bathroom, then hurried down to the grease pit. Bill was already thinking about the two double shifts looming darkly on the horizon, but without agreeing to these sixteen hour marathons Bigwin would never have happened. All in all, it was a fair deal. He was pleasantly surprised when Ken wandered into the kitchen at ten-thirty.

"How was your trip Billy-boo?" Ken asked, leaning casually against the door frame.

"It was a terrific two days away from the fry shack," Bill said brightly. "So how are things with the grease paint gang?"

"Party time! There's a big bash Tuesday for the cast, crew, and any friends they want to invite. If you'd like to come we'll pick you up at eight o'clock. There won't be a performance that day, so everyone has the evening free."

"Humph," Bill grunted. "Everyone but me Mc-boo, I'm covering for Harry both Tuesday and Wednesday. It's S.O.L. for this kid."

"If that's the way it's gotta be, we'll have a few pints for you, but if things change let me know right away," Ken said, as he left the kitchen.

The remainder of the day went by without incident, and Bill was free and clear when Harry arrived at three. He felt as low as the worn scales on a pythons belly, and decided that some sack time would be the cure-all.

When he woke up at six, he was hungrier than a chipmunk in April, and set a new land speed record on his mad dash to the kitchen. He gave Harry a break by preparing fish and chips for himself and several hot beef dinners for customers out front. When Harry returned Bill took his plate of food up to the penthouse.

It was actually quite a relief to be alone. He ate his meal slowly, savouring the tartar sauce, and the taste of fresh squeezed lemon juice on the battered fish. Just as he was finishing the last morsel of halibut Danny came into the room.

"Remember the other night when I told you all that strange stuff about Old Bob?" Danny began, as he sat down at the table.

"You mean the sleep walking and all?"

"Exactly! Joey and me were talking it over this afternoon, and here's the plan. Tonight when Bob's fast asleep, we're going to have a little fun."

"I'm almost afraid to ask," Bill muttered, holding his breath.

"Don't go getting your ass in a ringer Billy, all we're going to do is make a suggestion or two, then see what happens."

"Okay, but nothing weird eh?"

"Mom's apple pie Slick. Well I've got to make tracks, me and Donna are driving into Bracebridge to get a chocolate sundae at the Tasty Freeze."

The Danderoo wasted no time at all, whistling out of the room faster than a prairie twister.

Bill was feeling restless and decided to take a walk uptown. He was past the bridge and almost at the A&P when he spotted Sandra King walking in front of Dingleberry's Drugstore.

He crossed the street quickly and stammered, "G-Golly, is it ever neat to see you."

"Billy you look wonderful," she said haltingly.

"Yeah, and I feel pretty great too. How are things going with you and Brian?"

"Oh, all right I guess, but I still think of you," she replied shyly.

"You've been on my mind a lot too Sandi, but I figure that the way things have turned out, will be for the greater good of all mankind."

"My God Billy you're such a scream. You know I really miss that," she sighed, gently brushing his hand.

"Hell, we had a fantastic time together, and I'll always remember that," he rasped, as his heart threatened to leap into his throat. Sandra was going to say something else but couldn't. She gave him an affectionate squeeze on the shoulder, then walked away slowly without looking back.

Summer of '61

    He wandered aimlessly around town for a while, then decided to make an early night of it. He got to bed at ten, and had been sleeping for an hour when he felt someone wiggling the toes on his right foot. Bill woke up with a start. His heart was going a mile a minute until he finally recognized Joey standing at the end of the bed—index finger against his lips indicating the sign for silence. He recalled the conversation he had with Danny earlier that day, and got up immediately. He dressed quickly and quietly, like a thief in the night.
    Joey went over to where Bob was sleeping, and said in a soft but firm voice, "Get up and stand over there."
    Bob got out of bed dressed only in his jockey shorts, went over to the bright yellow arborite table, and stood at attention like a soldier on parade.
    Joey assumed the role of a regimental sergeant major and said, "Take off your underwear."
    Bob complied with alacrity, and faster than a winters sunset in Yellowknife, he was completely naked.
    "Bob, go down to the Harb and borrow a roll of toilet paper from the girls," Joey ordered, in an authoritative tone.
    Old Bob walked through the open bedroom door, proceeded down the hall, and was at the bottom of the stairs before anyone could react. Slowly getting their wits about them, the three boys arrived at the upper landing just in time to see Rapid Robert disappearing through the outside door.
    "Jeez, we'd better follow him," Bill piped up, starting to panic.
    "No way!" Danny interjected. "Or they'll know we put him up to this stunt."
    Twenty-five minutes later Joey was looking out the front window when he hollered, "Holy shit, Pistol Pete just pulled up in his police car!"
    Pete Martin was the Port Carter town cop. He was the law in Dodge. The three conspirators dived into their beds, and assumed instant postures of peaceful repose. A few minutes later, Pete burst into their room, turned on the light, and gave the table three pistol-like raps with his nightstick, fully intending to arouse the dead, or those faking sleep. The boys pretended to awaken from the depths of slummer by yawning, then rubbing their eyes. By golly Billy thought, we could win the Academy Award with this performance.

When Pete saw that the three sleepy heads were safely in the land of the living, he whispered, "Is that bottom bunk over there Bob's?"

"Yeah," Danny mumbled drowsily. What's going on?"

"I just got a call from Elmira Snodgrass. She was all in a flap about a naked man walking around the streets of Port Carter. I was fast asleep when the phone rang, so I dressed quickly, then jumped into the cruiser. Halfway up Bridge street, I see Bob here, strolling along in his birthday suit, carrying a roll of toilet paper."

Bill slowly turned his head to where Pete was pointing, and spied Old Bob standing by the door, periodically squeezing the Charmin.

"I figured from the blank look on his face that he might be sleepwalking, so I suggested that he get in the car, and here we are."

"Boy that's quite a story Officer Martin," Joey said respectfully.

Pete the cop seeming to be in a friendly mood said, "Now lets put Bob right to bed, because waking somebody from a sleepwalk could be dangerous."

When Robert Tucker was safely tucked in, Pete indicated to the boys that he wanted to have a word with them out in the hallway.

"I may be wrong, but I think that you three sleeping beauties may have had something to do with this. If Bob had of stepped in front of a car or fallen off the bridge, then maybe things wouldn't be quite as humorous as you might have planned. If you were in anyway responsible for tonights shenanigans, then a word to the wise. NO MORE SCREWING AROUND ON MY BEAT!"

Pete's loud, hissing whisper was still ringing in their ears, when they looked out the window, and watched the flashing lights of the town's bubble gum machine, fade into the distance.

"I guess we'd better not fuck around with that one again eh?" Danny said lightly.

The tension broken, all three shook with spasms of suppressed laughter. They almost started to laugh out loud when Bob began to snore. As it turned out, Old Bob was the only one to get a decent nights sleep.

32
*

    The next morning Bill started the first of his two long haul shifts. He was just about to think over the part in the Bible that dealt with the wages of sin, when Virginia walked into the kitchen with the first order of the day.
    "Hi Slick, you're not going to believe me when I tell you this."
    "What's that?" Bill asked, assuming his best babe-in-the-woods expression.
    "About one o'clock this morning I heard someone knocking on our bedroom door, so I stumbled out of bed to see who it was. The rest of the girls didn't wake up, which left me all by my lonesome when I answered the door."
    "What happened then?" Bill asked, digging his fingernails into the palms of his hands.
    "Old Bob was standing there stark naked, and calmly asked me if he could borrow a roll of toilet paper. I was about to give him a swift kick in the cookies when I noticed the blank look on his face, and guess what?"
    "Not in a million years," Bill shrugged.
    "He was sleep walking!"
    "Amazing!" he said, trying very hard to sound amazed.
    "I didn't know what to do, but I decided to play along. I went into our bathroom, grabbed a roll of toilet paper from the vanity, then handed it to Bob. He stood there just like Jacob Marley, so I told him to return to the Hilltop. The last I saw of him, was his bare ass disappearing through the door at the bottom of the stairs."
    "Boy that sure is a strange one," Billy said, biting the inside of his lip.
    "Did you guys know that Bob's a sleepwalker?"
    Fingers crossed behind his back, he smiled innocently, "That's news to us Virg. At least no one has mentioned it to me."
    "Well anyway Slick I need two specials."
    "Coming up," he muttered, as Virginia returned to the dining area.
    I guess we've learned a valuable lesson, Bill thought. As Pistol Pete suggested, we're damned lucky this didn't turn into something real serious.
    It was a tough go until eleven that evening. He was very aware of the extended day, and the insomniac activities of the night before.

At eleven-fifteen he cleaned the kitchen and locked up. He then dragged his sorry ass up the stairs, and was asleep before the sheets got wrinkled.

Billy was just about to score the winning touchdown in the last minute of the Grey Cup game, when he head someone saying, "Hey Carlsen get the lead out." This was terribly unfair because the goal line was only five yards away. Unexpectedly a burly middle linebacker was shaking his shoulder, but he looked an awful lot like Old Bob. Reality gradually set in, and he realized it was time for work. He begrudgingly thanked Robert T. for waking him, then headed directly to the shower. He was on deck, and ready for another sixteen hours of fun filled culinary escapades by the time the clock struck seven.

Things started to slacken of about ten, and he was delighted to see Kitty Carson walk into the kitchen.

"Hi Teddy, a real nice girl named Jen, said that I'd find you back here."

"Is everything okay?" he asked, remembering the story about Dr. Heartbreak.

"Oh I'm fine, I just dropped by to thank you for helping me the other night."

"Gee that's great, no more gushers from the old tear ducts eh?"

"Nope," she smiled. "It's just like you said; I'm better off without him."

"Have you got the day off Liz?" Bill grinned, relieved to see her happy again.

"I wish I did. The office doesn't open till noon, but I've got a free morning. I"m on duty tomorrow evening though, from six to nine-thirty. I have some lab. work to do."

"What does that involve?" Bill asked, as he placed several eggs into a saucepan.

"I draw blood, collect urine samples, and administer allergy shots."

"Sounds like pretty serious stuff to me," Bill said impressed.

"It's usually not too busy, so I was wondering, if you'd like to come over and keep me company?"

"I'd love to Liz! Calling you Liz is still okay isn't it ?"

"It's my real name and considering the things you said about Liz Taylor, I find it sort of flattering," Kitty chuckled.

Summer of '61

Jen barged into the kitchen with an order for a cheeseburger, and it was salt mine time in the valley once again.

Nice ass Bill thought, as he watched Kitty walk slowly away. He started into a very exotic fantasy, but experienced an instant reality check. It suddenly occurred to him that he was only eighteen, whereas she was twenty-one. Yeah, and the Russians will give up communism someday—ho! fucking ho!

He placed a hamburg pattie on the grill, and when the fat began to sizzle, he pressed the wide metal flipper onto the circular mass of beef in order to squeeze out some of the grease. He turned the pattie over, then slapped a slice of processed cheese on top, one minute before the meat was ready to serve. When the burger was done he placed it on a toasted buttered bun, and topped it off with lettuce, tomato, mustard, ketchup, dill pickle, onion, and a little mayo—the works—a grade A, number one, first class, state of the art cheeseburger. A scoop of fries fresh from the super heated vegetable oil capped off a meal that would be fit for Vincent Massey the Governor General of the great Dominion. After all, this is Canada eh! The sun was directly over the yardarm, and he had eleven hours to go. What the hell Bill thought, it's better than writing a French exam.

Sometime after the lunch rush, he was sitting at the counter sipping on a root beer float when Ken strolled into the restaurant.

"Hey Mc-boo how was the party?"

"It was quite a night Billy. Ari Gant and his best friend Bruce got into one hell of a fight, and Bruce had to be taken to the Bracebridge Emergency with a broken nose," Ken said, as he sat down beside Bill.

"I guess all matches aren't made in heaven," Bill frowned, feigning sympathy.

Ken let out a loud snort, then continued with his tale. "As you know, Tim's latest snuggy is Laura Collins, and they were having a great time doing it in the boat house, until Martha told the assembled throng to quietly follow her outside. To make a long story short, when everyone had gathered and were looking through the windows, she suddenly opened the door, and turned on the lights."

"So what happened then?" Bill asked impatiently.

"Well, lets just say the American judge gave Tim and Laura a five-point-nine for their participation in the pairs contest."

"Was there anything else?" Bill murmured, feeling like a castaway on a desert island.

"It was pretty calm after that, except for the part when everyone decided to go skinny- dipping, and the ensuing orgy."

His eyes popping, Billy shouted. "Holy cow! That's the wildest party I've ever heard of."

"Yeah, the theatre crowd are a bunch of free spirits," Ken concluded. "Sorry you missed it Billy-boo."

"Tell me about it," William Francis replied, totally dejected.

"I need a half-dozen cokes, so here's sixty cents," Ken said, as he walked over to the cooler

Bill sighed mournfully, like an old hound dog that had lost his way in the bush, as he watched Ken carry the six bottles of pop over to the theatre.

*

By the time the clock chimed eleven, Billy was the most worn out collection of cells on this great green earth. Jen was working with him, so he felt honour bound to walk her back to the Harb. He was still playing at being the universal big brother. This was a kind, loving sibling, not the intrusive, totalitarian creature of *Brave New World*. Holy shit, we're getting all artsy fartsy here, back to the trees and the forest.

After saying good night to Jen, he slowly made his way to the Hilltop, enjoying the cool air of the mid-August evening. He went straight up to the bunkhouse, and at long last Teddy the short-order cook tumbled into bed.

Just eight hours to go, then back to normal—the finishing line was is sight. He was half-asleep cooking an order of bacon and poached eggs when Bonnie came into the kitchen with four more yellow slips.

"Gibby and I had a great time when we went to the staff dance at Judd House last night," Bonnie gushed.

"I'm sincerely pleased for the both of you," he smirked.

"Your former girl friend Sandra was there with a real good looking guy, and they had a marvelous time," Bonnie snapped back, turning the knife.

"That's her steady boyfriend Brian, they've been going together since kindergarten," Bill grouched, in a get-off-my-case tone.

"What's the matter Billy? A little jealous are we?"

Summer of '61

"Hell no Bonnie if I can't have you, then life isn't worth living anyway."

"You know Slick sometimes you're a real sweetheart," Bonnie vamped, fluttering her mascara ladened eyelashes.

"Yeah Bonnie, me and Tommy Sands eh?" Bill snickered, rapidly raising his eyebrows like Grocho Marx.

"Oh, he's so cute!" she squealed, like a frenzied teenie-bopper.

The day passed by slower than a snail oozing about in a tomato patch, and Billy was greatly relieved when Harry arrived at two-forty-five This was the first time he'd been early all summer, and Sammy T. was sporting a grin that stretched from coast to coast.

"I won Kid! The golf Gods opened up their big book in the sky, and decided it was time old Harry Thompson had his moment in the sun."

"Wow! That's terrific," Bill whooped, shaking Harry's hand.

"The real great news is; I've got a job as Assistant Pro at the Barrie course next summer, and they've hired me on as the cook at the Royal Simcoe Curling Club for the winter."

"Congratulations Harry, you've got it made in the shade."

"It's too bad that you're out of the bootlegging business Slick, or we could have a few beers to celebrate."

Bill slapped him on the back before saying, "We'll get together for a victory drink real soon, but right now I'm as tired as a one armed gorilla living in the hold of a banana boat. It's off to the festering pit for me."

He staggered up the stairs to the Penthouse, and was asleep before you could say Jackie Robinson.

33
*

    Billy awoke at six-fifteen, feeling well rested, but suddenly remembered that Kitty wanted him to keep her company at the Clinic. He figured she needed reassurance after her big bust up, and his was the perfect shoulder. He went down to the kitchen, and made himself a hot turkey sandwich. After gobbling down the sumptuous meal, he scooted up to the washroom to brush his teeth. Bill was out the door, and on his way to see Kitty by seven. He entered the Port Carter Health Clinic ten minutes later.
    The place seemed to be completely deserted, so he sat quietly on a chair in the reception area. He was beginning to think that he had gotten things mixed up when Kitty and an elderly women came out of one of the examination rooms.
    "Your blood pressure's just fine Mrs. Snodgrass," Kitty soothed reassuringly.
    "I'm so glad to hear that dearie, because I've been having the flutters lately."
    "The results of your electrocardiogram will be back in a week, and Doctor North will discuss things with you then," Kitty replied kindly.
    "You've been so wonderful Miss Carson. I'll drop by tomorrow with some of my homemade Chelsea Buns."
    "That would be very nice," Kitty smiled, as she escorted Elmira Snodgrass to the door.
    "Hi Liz, you really are a nurse," Bill said, as he got to his feet. "What I mean is; someone tells you what they do, but when you see them in action it's much more than you expected."
    "Thanks Teddy! It's a good job, because you get to help some real nice people."
    Kitty was dressed in her nurses uniform, complete with cap. She looked very efficient and professional.
    "Boy this is a really neat doctor's office," Bill enthused, rubbernecking in all directions.
    "It was built in nineteen-fifty-nine, so everything's just about brand new. I'll show you around if you want Billy."
    "Sure thing Liz, let's have the grand tour," he said, mouth agape.
    Kitty showed him the three doctor's offices, each with an adjoining examining room. She then guided him to the small laboratory where Mrs. Snodgrass had just been tested.

Summer of '61

He knew all about the waiting area, so the tour was complete.

"Since that night when you told me about your involvement with one of the doctors and all," Bill began hesitantly. "I guess what I'm trying to ask is; why Tex?"

"That weekend when your friend Dave was here, I'd just had a big fight with Norm. Doctor North to be specific. My God if he knew I was telling you this, he'd have a bird."

"Don't worry Liz I'm not a blabbermouth."

"I know that Teddy," she sighed, reaching for his hand. "Anyway, when I saw you and Tex trying to sneak into Johnnies, I was really in the mood for company, and as they say, the rest is history."

"How are you feeling now?" he inquired gently, giving her hand a reassuring squeeze.

"A hell of a lot better since I talked to you that day," she said, her incandescent smile lighting the room like a sunbeam.

"Jeez that's terrific Liz," he grinned, while admiring her bedazzling blue eyes.

"Billy, if you don't mind, I want you to go into Dr. North's office, and wait there. It's nearly seven-thirty, and Mr. Bumgardner's going to be here in a few minutes to have his blood tested."

"Okay Liz, I'll see you when you're finished."

He entered the empty doctors office, and sat on the solid oak desk. He heard a distant male voice coming from the reception area, and figured that it had to be Mr. Bumfarter, or whatever his name was. It seemed like a long wait until he heard voices again, followed by the faint click of the entrance door. When Kitty walked into the office she seemed to be thinking something over, then her face brightened, as she reached a decision.

"You know Teddy, you really are awfully cute," she said, taking off her nurses cap.

"Gee thanks Liz, because from where I'm sitting, you look like a living doll."

"Teddy, sit in that straight backed chair in front of the desk," she purred, authoritatively.

This was where the patients sat when they were talking to the doctor. Bill complied with Kitty's request wondering what was going to happen next.

He didn't have to wait very long, because she settled herself astride his thighs, placed her arms around his neck, and proceeded to give him a thorough demonstration of the art of French kissing. On an excitement scale of one to ten Billy was registering a thirteen.

"Teddy, take your pants and underpants down, so they'll puddle around your ankles," Kitty ordered, sounding very much like a head nurse.

Bill, ever the gentleman figured in this case the lady knew best. As he was dropping his drawers, she went over to a white metal wall cabinet, and returned with a small box containing three condoms. Oh shit he thought, liver and onions, liver and onions. It worked again, because Kitty had installed the condom, and he was still, ready Teddy to rock 'n' roll. She stood in front of him, and slowly pulled up her white nurses uniform. This presented Billy with the most erotic sight that he ever seen in his brief, but spectacular encounters with the opposite sex. Kitty was wearing a garter belt to hold up her smokey white nylons, but she was definitely not wearing panties. She slowly lowered herself on to his very erect latex coated penis, and they began to play bucking bronco. The little bucker was having a ball, and despite his attempts to prolong things he bucked off shortly after the chute was opened.

"Billy you're a tiger, not a teddy bear, boy did I get things wrong," Kitty gasped.

"Did you come too?" Bill asked politely, his heart still going a mile a minute.

"Not this time Tiger, but who knows, we don't close till nine-thirty," she chuckled, reluctantly disengaging . "I've got a patient scheduled at eight for an electrocardiogram."

Holding his pants and jockey shorts at half-mast , Bill managed to waddle into the washroom. After performing a multitude of delicate scrubbings and washings, he returned to desk-sitting. He was just starting to swing his legs when nice nurse Carson waltzed through the door.

There were two prophylactics left, and as Bill's Uncle Olie would say, "Condoms should be used on every conceivable occasion."

"Well Tiger are you ready to assist a lady in distress?" Kitty cooed, in a sultry Mae West-like voice.

Summer of '61

With a little encouragement he was again in a state of preparedness. This time she sat on the big mustang backwards. He had a great view of the back of Kitty's head, and noticed that during the festivities the middle finger of her right hand was very busy between her thighs. This time explosive sounds like, yahoo, and whoopee, accompanied by a series of earth shaking shudders, indicated to Bill that Nurse Carson was indeed amused. In the after glow of all things beautiful, he held Kitty in his arms, and gently stocked her sweet smelling red hair. They were both at peace, and content to spend the rest of their lives in the doctors office.

Their bubble burst when they heard a female voice yodel, "Yoo! Hoo! Is there anybody here?"

"Well there's Mrs. Cardwell right on time," Kitty sighed. "Don't go away Teddy, like General McArthur once said, I shall return."

Bill was alone again. He was a little tired, but—WOW!—what an evening so far. There was one condom remaining, and who knows. It was nine-thirty when Kitty returned to the office.

"Time to close the Clinic down Tiger," Kitty said decisively.

"Okay Liz, I'll walk you home."

"Better still my car's out front, and you can drive me there."

"Sold American," Bill sang out like a Lucky Strike Auctioneer, as they headed for her Ford Falcon.

*

After Kitty opened the front door of the cottage she asked, "Would you like some coffee, or would you rather have a drink?"

"A drink would be just fine," Bill said, licking his lips.

"There's some rum on the dry sink by the kitchen door and a bottle of Coke in the fridge," Kitty shouted over her shoulder, as she hurried into her bedroom to change.

She reappeared two minutes later wearing jeans and a white blouse. Bill handed her a rolly-polly glass all tinkling with ice, mix, and a shot of Captain Morgan's finest.

"Here's to the wild west," Kitty smiled.

"Happy trails to you Miss," Bill said, not feeling much like Roy Rogers.

"Well I sure as hell ain't Dale Evans, and this isn't a Saturday morning TV program, so off with your clothes Tiger," Kitty barked, as she reached for the zipper on Bill's slacks.

Boy! Billy thought, this rum sure beats the stuffings out of lemon gin. Kitty led him into her bedroom where they played an advanced game of hide the salami. I guess three goes and you're out was Bill's prognostication when all was said and come. He was as accurate as Dizzy Dean calling balls and strikes for a Mickey Mantle at bat.

"Time to call it a night Teddy, we both have to work tomorrow," Kitty yawned, stretching out on the bed like a contented lioness.

"Yeah I know, but sometimes you wish that things could last forever," he murmured, in a soft sleepy whisper.

34
*

    Billy was riding a pink fluffy cloud, when he slowly emerged from the rack early the next morning. Lascivious images sharper than wasp bites, punctured his sleep-fogged brain, while he splashed cold water over his face. Several minutes later he was ready for the breakfast traffic at seven.
    "Eggs over easy, sausage, brown toast, pancakes, bacon, and cream of wheat with brown sugar," Virginia rumbled, as she burst into the kitchen.
    "I love you too Virg," Bill shot back, as he watched her scurry away to collect additional orders.
    Young Master Carlsen was still in loveland awash with the afterglow of the most amazing night of his tender years. "Two scrambled, two sunny side up, bacon, white toast no butter," Virginia roared, bringing him back to earth with a thud.
    The morning continued at a hectic pace, but just before ten things began to settle down, and he was finally able to relax. Doc Livingstone came in to grab a quick coffee shortly after Billy emerged from the kitchen.
    "Howdy Kid," the Doc said, giving Bill's hair a playful brush. "If you're not doing anything Monday, Wayne and I are going into Gravenhurst to shoot a round of golf at the Royal Muskoka, and you're welcome to come along."
    "Jeez I'd love to Doc, but I don't have a set of clubs," Bill replied ruefully.
    "Not to worry Billy, Wayne says you can borrow his father's set."
    "That would be swell, because that's my day off," Billy grinned, picturing himself hitting a perfect drive straight down a tunnel-like fairway.
    "Fuckin A Kid, I'll pick you up at one-thirty," the Doc waved, as he got up quickly and hurried towards the door.
    Just before the lunch rush Bill was totally amazed to see Kitty walk into the kitchen. She looked terribly sad, and seemed to be in a state of panic.
    "Teddy, I've got to go home. My father just had a heart attack, and he's in the Intensive Care Unit at Toledo General," Kitty snuffled, as she wiped a tear from her eye.

"Golly, I'm real sorry to hear that," Bill said, his voice a little shaky. "Look, I want you to take it easy on your drive down south, and don't speed. Your mom and dad will need you big time when you get there."

"Thanks Teddy, I'll remember that," she whispered hoarsely. "If I don't return to Port Carter by the end of the summer, I'll give you a call."

"You're the best Liz, and think about what I said when you're on the road," Bill replied soothingly, as he placed his arms around her. She gave him a quick kiss on the lips, held his hand for a moment, then left the café to begin her long journey home.

He found it hard to concentrate, but managed to get through the afternoon. Harry sauntered in at three all full of smiles, he seemed to be at peace with the world.

"Just turned fifty thousand on the old Chevy, and you know, she's running like a top," he crowed proudly.

"Yeah, that's a great car, and I'll bet you get a hundred thousand out of her," Bill predicted, tossing Harry a clean apron.

"See ya later Kid, and yeah, the fifty-seven Chevy is the best car the General ever built," Harry nodded wisely.

Bill was still worried about Kitty, and needed to get some fresh air. Deep in thought he made his way to the beach. It was a cool afternoon and the swimming area was deserted. He sat for a while at a picnic table, and watched a pair of terns circling overhead in their never ending search for food. He was startled when a pileated woodpecker started hacking away on a birch tree behind him. The industrious bird sounded like a lumber jack using a double bladed axe. The timeless dance of the natural world quieted Bill's jangled soul, and he felt much better. Leaving the tranquility of the shoreline, he decided to check out the Port Town theatre.

Ken and Tim were hard at work putting the finishing touches on the sets for the evening performance.

"What's happening Billy-boo?" Ken shouted, when he saw his friend enter the hall.

"Just hanging around Mc-boo," Bill replied cheerfully.

"This weeks play has kept us all busy, but It's been a lot of fun," Ken said, wiping the sweat away from his eyes.

"I've sort of lost track, what's the current production." Bill asked conversationally.

Summer of '61

"Oscar bleedin' Wilde mate, *The Importance of Being Earnest*," Tim responded, as he handed Ken a screwdriver.

"Never heard of it," Bill said, shrugging his shoulders. "Is it about some guy named Ernie?"

"You may be a little more clever than you look," Ken snorted. "I'll leave you a ticket at the box office. It's going to be pretty hectic backstage during the play, and Martha has issued a crew only edict."

"Thanks Ken, I'll be over just before curtain time. See you guys later," Bill said, as he leaped off the stage.

He picked up his complimentary pass at seven, and was nicely settled in when the curtain went up ten minutes later. The story centered around two priggish Englishmen who wanted to be called Ernest. Bill found the tale rather trivial, and was relieved when the cast took their final curtain call. He waited for the crowds to clear, then went backstage. He was able to help Ken put things away for the night, and was surprised to find that if was past eleven when they finished.

"Do you want to have a beer Billy? Ken asked, as he pushed the last of the wardrobe racks into the wings.

"Yeah, that sounds great but only one, I'm on the dawn patrol tomorrow as usual."

"Doesn't Harry ever work the early shift?"

"He's a golf nut Ken, and loves to play in the morning. I really don't mind and besides I'm used to it."

Ken went to the basement, and retrieved two bottles of Molson Export that were hidden behind a piece of plywood.

They left the theatre and walked towards the old school bus. It was a cool night, and Bill began to shiver.

His teeth chattering, Bill stuttered like a bren gun, "B-Boy's it ever chilly. Let's make a fast sally to the restaurant, and sit at the counter. It's closed, and nobody's ever there this late."

He found a church key behind a coffee pot, and used it to snap the caps on the two bottles of ale. Bill told Ken about Kitty having to go home, and was half way through his beer when the door unexpectedly banged open.

"What in the hell are you doing here?" Paul bellowed, as he turned on the lights.

"Taboo eh, Paul?" Bill rasped.

"You're damn right it's taboo!" Paul snarled, as he grabbed the green bottles, and poured their contents down the sink. "That's going to cost you twenty-five bucks Carlsen, and If I wasn't so desperate for a cook between now and Labour Day, I'd fire you right here on the spot."

"Gosh, I'm sorry Paul, I should have known better."

"Look!" Paul roared, his face red with anger. "You and your friend get the fuck out of here. I've got some accounts that I want to bring up to date."

"Yes sir," Bill mumbled apologetically.

When they were safely beyond the range of the dragon's flaming breath Bill said, "Sorry Kenny-boo I should have known that he works a lot at night."

"Hey, it's my fault Billy. I was the one who suggested that we have a beer, and you're the guy who's out the money."

"What the heck! You win some and screw the rest," Bill replied unconvincingly.

"Well, if you're sure you're okay, then it's time for this old stagehand to assume the horizontal," Ken said glumly, seeing the worried look on his friends face.

"Yeah, I'm whipped too," Bill groaned. "I'll try and hook up with you tomorrow." A dark, heavy load had settled upon his weary, slumping shoulders.

35
*

Bill pounded his pillow, tossed and turned. The events of the evening kept rattling around in his head like a stone in a rusty tin can. He finally concluded, that he must have horseshoes up the old wazoo, because even though the bootleg operation was a thing of the past, he never got busted. The arithmetic worked out just about even—what he lost on the apples, he gained on the oranges. The life long lesson? Crime doesn't pay—especially if you get caught. Al Capone relax!

Billy made certain that he was on the job extra early the next morning. He was afraid that Paul might be there pink slip in hand. Jen kept him busy for the first three hours with what seemed like an endless stream of hurry up orders. Just as things were starting to slack off, the spirit-like form of Bongo Charlie silently materialized beside the grill.

"I'm out of here man," Charlie burbled, his voice full of excitement.

"Y-You're leaving the Port?" Bill stammered, taken aback by Bongo's sudden appearance.

"Right on, fry-guy," Charlie beamed.

Jen came in from the counter with a late order for a ham omelette, brown toast.

"Okay Jen I'll get cracking," Bill quipped, going all bug-eyed like Eddie Cantor.

"My God Slick, sometimes you're such a corn ball." She gave Charlie a speedy once-over, then returned to the dinning room.

"So where are you heading Charlie?" Bill asked sleepily.

"To the center of the universe man, the Village," Charlie smiled, lighting up like ground zero. "There's this new cat, Timothy Learey who says, turn on , tune in and drop out. He's really hip."

"Well good luck," Bill said, not fully understanding what Charlie was trying to say. "If you need a lunch for your trip, then I've got a bag of goodies for you."

"Thanks man! You know, I might have starved up here if it weren't for you."

"No sweat, this food would have gone to waste anyway," Bill grinned, handing over a sac full of leftovers, he had just liberated from the fridge.

"That's why you're so cool Billy, it didn't," Charlie whispered.

"How are you going to get there?" Bill asked, realizing that Bongo had just called him by name for the first time.

"Hitch man, I haven't got enough bread for the bus," Charlie wheezed, as he clasped Bill's hand.

Billy was distracted by the jarring sound of the pop-up toaster. He extracted two pieces of brown, and quickly buttered them. When he turned around Charlie had mysteriously vaporized like dry ice on a wet day.

"That Bongo Charlie sure looks like he needs a bath. I'll bet his hair's full of cooties," Jen grimaced, as she entered the kitchen.

"Yeah, you may not want to borrow Charlies comb, but he's okay. Have you ever had cooties Jen?"

"Of course not, that's just for dirty beatniks like Charlie," she snapped back testily.

"I can sure tell that you're a city girl," Bill said, sticking out his chin. "When I was a kid we lived on a farm near Toronto, and one hot summer my sister and I picked up head lice."

"That's so gross," Jen shuddered, a look of total disgust on her face.

"The worst part was having your head shaved, then coated with coal oil. Boy did it ever sting, but it got rid of the cooties."

"Do you have anymore life experiences that you wish to share with me?" Jen asked, as she stood in the doorway unconsciously scratching her head in apparent sympathy.

"No, that'll do for now," Bill smiled, handing her the omelette and toast each on separate plates. "Jeez, watch out for the cooties on top of the toast."

Jen dropped the toast plate, and jumped back as if she had seen a snake.

"Gotcha!" Bill crowed triumphantly.

"You little rat-fink," Jen exploded, looking like she wanted to brain him with a fry pan.

They instantly saw the humor in what had just happened, and were bent over double laughing uncontrollably, their eyes running like icy streams in the springtime.

"Take the omelette to the table, and say the cook had to go to the storeroom for another loaf of brown bread," Bill gasped, as he damped a flood of salty tears from around his eyes.

Summer of '61

"Billy I'll bet if you were the devil you could talk your way into heaven," she chuckled.

"Yeah, but I couldn't talk my way out of a twenty-five dollar fine," he muttered angrily under his breath.

The rest of the day shot by like an express train, and Harry was there to take over right on time. When Bill got up to the penthouse, he noticed Joey sitting at the table reading the *Star Weekly*.

"Hey Slick, there's an article in here about the Ex," Joey said, referring to Toronto's Canadian National Exhibition.

"Holy doodle! It starts next week eh?"

"Yeah, but being up here we're S.O.L. for going this year," Joey grumbled.

"When I was a kid, we used to go almost every year," Bill smiled, taking a hop, skip and a jump down memory lane.

"I loved the midway the best," Joey sighed, conjuring up all the great rides.

"We never had much money when we lived on the farm, so me and my buddy Bobby Henricks got our lunch by trying all the free samples at the Foods Building," Bill licked his lips, imaging tasty bits of smokey salami impaled on tiny toothpicks.

"I remember my mom wouldn't let us go to the Ex for several years in the early fifties because of the polio scare," Joey frowned.

"Gosh I'd almost forgotten that; those were tense times," Bill murmured, a cold tremor in his voice. "I can still see those poor kids in the iron lungs, that they used to show on TV."

"Thank God for Jonas Salk. He sure turned things around," Joey said gratefully.

"Did you get to many of the Grandstand Shows?" Bill asked abruptly, wanting to escape the chilling recollections of polio.

"No way!" Joey grouched. "Our family just couldn't afford it."

"Yeah, we were in the same boat, but I did get into the Grandstand once," Bill boasted.

"How did that happen?" Joey asked amazed.

"Well me and my pal Bobby got separated from our mothers one year, and wound up at the side entrance to the Grandstand track. We were standing there like two kids trying to peek through a pair of knot holes to watch a baseball game, when this Shriner who was guarding the gate says; You two young fellas got enough money for tickets?

"No sir I said. He handed us two passes, motioned for us to go around him and said. Enjoy the show."

"What did you see?"

"The the Hell Drivers," Bill declared proudly. "They jumped cars, crashed cars, and even drove a car on two wheels half way around the track."

"Yeah, I saw them once up at the Pinecrest Speedway, they were real good," Joey agreed.

"It seems funny now, but both our mothers were really worried, and had been looking for us all afternoon," Bill sighed. "At the end of the show an announcement came over the PA saying; If Billy Carlsen and Bobby Hendricks are in the Grandstand, then report immediately to the box office. Jeez whiz, we were celebrities."

"I'll bet your mother was pissed off?" Joey gave a rumbling laugh.

"I thought she would be furious, but the first thing she did was give me a big hug," Bill recalled fondly.

"How about Bobby's mother?"

"She was just as relieved, but I think from the look I saw in her eyes, it was going to be the wooden spoon for poor old Bobby when he got home."

"Yeah, I still hate rulers and wooden spoons," Joey said, feeling his backside warm slightly.

They chatted away for several minutes, then Joey left for the second half of his split shift. Bill leaned back in his chair enjoying a quiet moment of reflection. It had been a great summer to date. Considering all that had happened, getting caught red-handed with a couple of beers was really small potatoes. He smiled, remembering that the Doc and Wayne would be there tomorrow to take him golfing. Life was good!

36

A new week dawned like a fresh born babe, sniffing pure clean air for the first time. This glorious beginning was grade A large, extra special aged, because it was Billy Carlsen's day off. He kicked around town in the morning enjoying the absolute luxury of nothing to do, and being on his own twenty-four hour schedule. True to their word, the Doc and Wayne arrived at one-thirty sharp to pick him up. Wayne was driving his Edsel, and as promised, had a spare set of clubs stored in the trunk of the Ford.

"Ready to have a little fun on the links Kid?" the Doc asked cheerfully.

"Yeah, but I haven't been golfing for a year, so this ought to be interesting," Bill replied uneasily.

"Don't worry Billy, it's like riding a bicycle or a woman. You never forget how to do it eh?" Wayne pontificated, grinning like a pimp at a hooker's convention.

Wayne had the pedal to the metal all the way to Gravenhurst, and they were ready to tee off at three. The Doc hired a caddy, and gave him what appeared to be a spare set of clubs. Wayne and the Doc made par on the first hole, but Bill came up short with a bogey. The reason for the extra set of golf sticks became apparent halfway to the second tee. The Doc grabbed the golf bag from the young caddy, and like a magician pulled three cold beers from the counterfeit silk hat. Bill could see water starting to drip from the bottom of the bag, and realized it was bulging with ice and ales.

"Don't worry," the Doc snickered, slipping the kid a fifty-cent-piece. "This heavy load you're entrusted with, will get lighter at every green."

By the time they were ready to tee off at the fourth, the threesome had begun to enjoy themselves immensely. The Doc was impatient with the foursome ahead, and decided to try a motivational tactic. Just as one of the players was about to hit a second shot the Doc let go a monster drive, and yelled fore at the precise moment that his ball nailed the unsuspecting golfer in the ass.

"Gosh I'm real sorry," the Doc hollered at the top of his lungs. " Do you's guys want us to play through?" The four heads in front of them conferred for a moment, then waved a white towel to indicate their surrender.

One of the basic principles of the universe is; that beer has a very short life span in the human body. "My back teeth are floating so bad, I think I'll have to throw them a life preserver," Wayne moaned, when they arrived at the sixth tee.

"Yeah me too!" the Doc grimaced, shuffling his feet from side to side.

"Let's step in there and take a piss," Wayne pointed, eyeing the bushes beside them.

This seemed like the right thing to do, but after stepping into and through the narrow strip of shrubs they emerged onto the eleventh tee. Wayne and the Doc were feeling no pain, and seemed completely oblivious to their surroundings. They were contentedly in midstream when a group of ladies came up the walkway from the tenth. Wayne ever respectful of the fairer sex turned to the women, and saluted them with his free hand. The Doc not to be out done did the same.

The startled females let out a collective scream, then retreated in disarray as if they were being chased by a pack of wolves.

"I guess something must have scared them," Wayne said bewildered.

"Beats me what that could have been ," the Doc replied serenely.

Bill asked them about all the commotion on the other side of the bushes when they returned.

"It was just a nervous female foursome who spied a rattlesnake or something," Wayne chortled, after emitting a blue ribbon belch.

"Time for another beer," the Doc said, signaling the caddy to hand over the golf bag cooler.

When they strolled up to the seventh tee the late afternoon sun was baking them like bread in an oven. Wayne and the Doc stripped off their shirts in order to cool down. Bill was worried, because he knew that at the Georgetown Club going shirtless was a major no! no! After carding three more holes, and consuming several more beers the Doc and Wayne were pleasantly hammered. Bill a little gun shy had limited himself to one bottle of suds, and still had his shirt on. Walking up to the tenth tee Wayne let go a thunderous fart that was probably heard in Halifax. This seemed to have the same response that a bull mouse might get in the mating season because four snorting angry rivals came running along the walkway to the tee.

Summer of '61

These challengers however, had their drivers slung over their shoulders like baseball bats, and were ready for combat.

"Are you the guys who have been causing all the problems?" the first and largest of the group snarled.

"Hell, no shirts is enough to ban them from the course," the second member of the hostile band bellowed loudly.

"Yeah, and that one there getting ready to tee off, is the numb nuts who hit me in the rear with his golf ball," the third hissed, accusingly.

"Judging by what my wife told me, these are the Neanderthals who were exposing themselves on the eleventh," the fourth whined, sniffing self-righteously.

Wayne and the Doc stood there patiently, silly grins plastered on their faces. Wayne played Senior A hockey in the winters for the Orillia Tigers. He was the enforcer on his team, and liked that term better than goon. He was in no mood, to take no carp, from no one.

"If you fuckers are going to do anything with those clubs, then you'd better start, but I sure hope that your life insurance policies are paid up," Wayne growled belligerently.

The first one of the not so fearsome foursome to speak was the club pro. He saw that Rocket Richard look in Wayne's eyes and said in a placatory tone, "We don't want any trouble here, we just want you guys to leave."

"No problem," the Doc replied amicably. "We're out of ice and beer anyway."

"Yeah, and we really don't like this course either," Wayne shot back defiantly.

The Doc reached into his wallet and gave the caddy a two dollar bill. "Gee thanks mister," the kid gasped. The usual fee for eighteen holes was a buck.

"Now if you gentlemen will excuse us; we're going to make like Canada Geese in the fall, and get the flock out of here," the Doc grinned, drawing himself up to his full height.

The four sanctimonious men didn't say a thing as the three wise guys headed for the parking lot.

"You drive Billy the Kid. I've had one too many for the road," Wayne murmured, slurring his words. He handed over the keys, then followed the Doc into the security of the Edsel's back seat.

By the time they were halfway to Bracebridge, the two sleeping beauties occupying the rear bench were just about finished their first bush cord. The trip back to Port Carter took the best part of an hour as Bill was reluctant to exceed the speed limit.

When they arrived at the Hilltop, Wayne awoke from the dead and mumbled, "Are we there yet?"

Bill had to laugh, because he sounded just like a young kid on a long trip, and not very much like the mean old bear who was ready to take on the world with his number one wood.

"We're in the Port," Bill said, flashing a grin.

"Beauty," Wayne snorted softly.

The Doc was still in a deep sleep, so Wayne quietly slid out of the back seat, and came around to the drivers side.

"I'm okay now Kid, so you go on in, and get some grub. I'll drive the Doc home."

"Have a good one Wayne, and thanks for taking me golfing," Bill said, as he climbed out of the car.

"Pretty cool huh? We done good eh?" Wayne grunted drowsily. He settled in behind the wheel, put the big Edsel into D for drive, then pointed the hood ornament in the general direction of the Livingstone's residence.

After washing up, Billy went down to the kitchen to check things out. Paul was there doing the evening shift, so William Francis in an attempt to score brownie points offered to take over if Chef Evans wanted a break.

"I've got to go down to the Harb for a minute, so thanks," Paul smiled appreciatively.

It wasn't very busy, so Cook Carlsen was able to grab a bite to eat between orders. Paul returned an hour later, and took over at the grill.

"There's a call for you," Virginia shouted excitedly, just as Bill was about to head up the stairs.

"Hello?" Bill squeaked apprehensively, when he reached the telephone.

"It's Kitty, how are you?"

Thank God, was his first reaction, no plane crashes. He was really worried about his parents return from Europe.

"Hi Liz, just great, how's your dad?" Bill asked relieved.

Summer of '61

"He's doing fine. They have him out of the ICU, and he'll probably be home in a day or two," Kitty said, a note of calmness evident in her voice.

"Golly whiz, that's wonderful news," Bill sighed, sinking into a chair next to the phone.

"We're real lucky it was only a mild heart attack, and no serious damage was done," she said confidently.

"Will you be coming back up to the Port?" he asked, holding his breath.

"No, my mom wants me to stick around while my father's recovering."

"I can sure understand that, you being a nurse and all," Bill said, trying not to sound disappointed.

"The Toledo General is in desperate need of nurses, and I've got a job waiting for me in September," she bubbled happily.

"It sounds like you're all set," Bill smiled, riding along on the crest of her sunny wave.

"Listen Teddy, I can't stay on the phone much longer, so thanks for being my guardian angel this summer."

"I'm the lucky one just to have known you," Bill murmured, a lump forming in his throat.

"Be good Billy, and if you think of it, drop me a line now and again."

"So long Liz, and remember the Good Ship Lollipop," he whispered.

"You too Teddy!" It seemed like the world had come to a grinding halt, as the humming monotony of the dial-tone, droned lonely in his ear.

Two hours later Billy flopped onto his bottom bunk. Life can be strange with all it's twists and turns he thought, but it's the only life we've got. You have no choice of how you come into this world, and can do very little about how you'll eventually leave it, so in between you just have to do the best you can.

The haze of sleep came peacefully upon him, and he had a soothing dream about being back on the farm when he was eight years old. He was about to scoop up a handful of fat juicy blackberries from a bush growing tight against the weathered barn wall, when his built in alarm clock went off like a gun fired over open water. It was six-thirty; another day in Shangri-La.

37
*

The summer was winding down. The dog days had passed, and it wouldn't be long before Bill was back in school. He was smack-dab in the middle of a football daydream when Virginia burst into the kitchen.

"I've got an order for bacon and eggs, over easy, white toast," Virginia said, treating him to a rare, sunny golden smile.

"Coming right up Virg. Is it my imagination, or are we less busy this morning?" Bill mused openly.

"Things are beginning to taper off Slick," Virginia sighed, staring out the back window. "The Ex is on, and the parents up here in cottage country are starting to hear the distant ringing of school bells."

"Yeah, I guess they're getting ready to whistle the kids down south; like a bunch of ducks eh?" he joked. "What will you be doing this fall?"

"I just got word from St. Michael's Hospital, and I've been accepted into their Medical Technologist course," Virginia replied proudly

"I know you'll be a good one Virg!"

"Yeah and there is a Santa Claus," Virgin for short chuckled, recalling the first time they met.

"You're a keeper Virginia! Don't ever change," Billy whispered, his voice thickening.

Miss Hudson gave him one of her best Ava Gardner poses, then hurried back to the dinning room.

The next two weeks whizzed on by like a red squirrel being chased by a brush wolf. Before you could say banana-fanna, Labour Day weekend arrived, and it was time for farewells. On Friday, Ken came into the restaurant to say good-bye.

"Well Billy-boo it's been a real trip, and don't forget you promised to come up to Stratford this fall."

"You can count on that one Mc-Boo, so I'll just say see you later." He reached out to shake Ken's hand, but received a king-sized bear hug instead. Ken broke away quickly, then headed for the door.

Bill's last day in the kitchen was Sunday. He and Danny were going to drive home together on holiday Monday, in the souped-up Ford. After finishing his shift, he shook Harry's hand, thanked him for the use of the Bel Air, and wished him good luck with his new job.

Summer of '61

He then went down to the Harb, and received a sister-like peck on the cheek from Bonnie, Donna and Jennifer. All three girls were going on to their first year at university. He dropped by the kitchen to bid Leo and Joan farewell, then went to Paul's office to pick up his cheque. Paul wasn't overly friendly, but the fine had been waived. When he finally emerged on to River Road, Virginia was standing beside the door. She placed her arms around Bill and gave him a very un-sister-like kiss.

"There!" she said archly. "I've been waiting all summer to do that."

"Holy smoke Virg, if I'd known that, I would have let you start a lot earlier," Bill grinned, enjoying the candy flavor of her lipstick.

"You take care Billy Carlsen," she whispered affectionately.

*

The next morning he wished lean, cadaverous Old Bob, good luck with his first year at the University of Toronto, then duffel bag slung casually over his shoulder, he descended the penthouse steps for the last time. Joey was waiting for him at the bottom of the stairs.

"Gee whiz, you were a real pal this summer," Bill smiled, as he pumped Joey's hand.

"Take it easy Slick, and read a little more Hemingway eh?"

"Sure thing good buddy," Bill said, slapping him on the back.

He walked slowly towards Danny's car, climbed in, and the summer gradually began its transition towards all things past. He was happy, though a little sad, when they left the Hilltop parking lot. Just as they were approaching Bailer street, Bill noticed the Doc running up to the intersection signaling for them to stop. Danny pulled over immediately, then Bill jumped out of the car.

"I'm glad I caught you Kid before you left for good," the Doc puffed, short of breath.

"Doc it's been great, and we had a lot of good times," Bill rasped, his voice breaking slightly. "Give Wayne my best the next time you see him eh?"

"Sure thing Kid, and I'll say a big hello from you, to Gloria and Debbie," the Doc grinned wickedly.

"Yeah, that was quite a day for me Doc, and God bless the working girl," Bill said solemnly, his hand over his heart.

The Doc laughed heartily before saying, "If you're ever in this neck of the woods again partner, then look me up."

They shook hands awkwardly, before Billy got back into the car.

"Keep both eyes on the road there Dangerous Dan," the Doc shouted cheerfully.

Danny smiled, gave the Doc a friendly salute, put the car in gear, then slowly pulled away.

They were homeward bound at last. He had the letter from Doris safely tucked into the breast pocket of his shirt. She had busted up with Pete for good, and would be wearing Bill's class pin again when he got home. The entropy of his personnel universe had drastically decreased, and he was content.

As the miles sped on by Billy realized that he was definitely not the same person who had arrived in Port Carter to begin his summer of '61. He was different in many ways. William Francis Carlsen had learned the first law of life. The only constant in this world is change. Considering that during July and August planet earth completed sixty two rotations, it was hardly surprising that one of it's passengers *had* changed. That was just plain common sense, or as Bill's Uncle Olie would say,"If there's only have one piece of toilet paper left, and you've got to wipe your arse and blow your nose with it, then blow your nose first."

Epilogue

Two young men, singing at the top of their lungs, while driving back to the big smoke in a customized 1950 Ford.

    Away, away with fife and drum
    Here we come full of rum
    Looking for women who peddle their bum
    In the North Atlantic Squadron.

ISBN 1-41205411-7